BATTLE OF HEARTS

TANIA ROBERTS

BATTLE OF HEARTS
First published in New Zealand in September 2023 by
Red Rose Publishing, New Plymouth

A catalogue record for the book is available from the National Library of New Zealand.

Format: Print on Demand
ISBN   978-1-99-117465-9
Format: Print on Demand
ISBN   978-1-99-117466-6
Format: EPUB
ISBN   978-1-99-117467-3

Cover Design: Kura Carpenter Design,
thebookcarpenter.co.nz
Cover Image: Arcangel Images Limited,
Back Cover Image: Alamy

BATTLE OF HEARTS

CHAPTER 1

Wartime came with the expectation that everyone made do with what they had.

For Betsy, a typist from the city, that meant passing on her newly acquired farming skills to the next intake of land girls at *Whipsnade Farm*. Rosey, Peggy, and Jean seemed nice enough, a tight-knit group who had all known each other in Christchurch. They now occupied Captain Boyle's homestead and Betsy was settling into a small, single bedroom in the farm manager's house.

She'd only been farming for three months so was apprehensive for her first day with the new girls. The nerves that had churned her insides from dawn till dusk, finally settled as she leaned back against the closed door of her bedroom. She found solace in the quietness, away from the excited chatter of the land girls. Betsy sighed. She was on the outer but she was comfortable; she didn't want to have to make new friends and share her story.

Her new room had previously been used by Duncan's farm worker, John, but he'd enlisted and been gone a good six months. Duncan's wife Nel had been kind enough to air the room, replace the blue quilt with a patchwork lemon and white one and leave a folded crochet throw at the foot of the bed for the cool winter nights.

Beneath the bed, Betsy stowed her shoebox of letters. Inside the box were two bundles, each held together by a piece of string in which she had tied a bow. Roland's bundle sat on top, as it should rightfully do so. As her fiancé, his letters took priority. Betsy told herself this each night when she pored through the contents of both his and William's letters. Her emotions roller-coasted with all the uncertainties that came with being in a world at war. What ifs played like movie trailers in her mind. What if Roland, her childhood sweetheart, was no longer missing in action but on his way home? Would that end with them living happily ever after? What if Roland was already dead? Shouldn't she reply to William's letters with more than just news? He was the man whose mere presence set her insides alight. If she let her mind wander, Betsy could see her own children occupying the bed she sat on, William and her running the farm, Duncan and Nel retired to town. Guilt ensured this train of thought never continued for too long.

Betsy insisted she be the one to check the letterbox each day. It had become a ritual before breakfast, and sometimes again after breakfast, when there had been nothing on the first look and she hoped it was because the mailman was late. The receipt of mail, or the absence thereof, dictated her mood for the remainder of the day.

As was often the case, Nel kept an eye on the comings and goings from the kitchen sink. When Betsy returned from the letterbox, head downcast and feet dragging lethargically, she would find Nel waiting in the washhouse with open arms. Their comforting embrace lasted as long as was necessary to convince them both that all would be right in the world again one day.

"Tomorrow," Nel would say. "I'm sure there will be a letter tomorrow."

This morning, ice crunched under Betsy's feet as she made her way down the driveway, blowing steam into the crisp morning air. It was her favourite time of the day, when the Orari countryside was peaceful and serene, even the birds still roosting sleepily in the trees. The white blanket of frost made everything appear clean and untarnished and that's how Betsy liked it.

She trod lightly on the ice, trying not to shatter the brittle frost and imagined how she would describe it in a letter. A letter she would write in response to the one that was surely in the letterbox. There hadn't been any news from either Roland or William for some weeks now, but Betsy felt certain today was the day.

"Please let there be mail." Looking up to the heavens she whispered to whomever might be listening. She blew warm air onto her bare fingers, both to warm them before she touched the cold steel door of the letterbox and to add a touch of good luck.

"Yes," she squealed when the open door revealed a single envelope. Betsy eagerly grabbed the envelope, crumpling it in both hands. She inhaled sharply, daring herself to be brave and look at the envelope. It was a telegram addressed to Mr D. McKnight. Red capital letters ran across the top, evenly spaced with gaps either side to emphasise their importance. Her heartbeat quickened as a multitude of possibilities raced through her mind. Only important messages and bad news came by telegram.

Betsy needed to get back inside and quick, so Duncan could share the news – good or bad. One foot slid on the ice as she turned, slipping out to the side, and forcing her to grab hold of the letterbox for balance. She took a deep breath, put the telegram safely into her overalls pocket so she had both hands free and then carefully retraced her footsteps, one step at a time.

A tightness ached in her chest by the time she reached the back door. Duncan's boots were absent from their usual spot in the washhouse, his hat was missing from the hook, and neither was Nel there to give her the hug she would surely need. Frustrated, Betsy slammed the wooden door. It crashed into the door frame and its small window rattled as if it was being battered in a storm.

"Duncan! Don't slam the door!" Nel growled as she turned toward the disturbance. "Oh, it's you Betsy. Sorry."

"Is Duncan here?"

"No, not yet. I thought you were him." Nel looked askance at Betsy. "What's up? It's not like you to slam the door."

Betsy pulled the telegram from her pocket. With trembling hands, she held it out in front of Nel.

"Oh! A telegram." Their eyes met; all their fears conveyed.

"Yes, a telegram."

"Come in by the range." Nel regained her composure first. "No point standing in the washhouse. Duncan won't be far away. The kettle is hot, I'll make us a cup of tea."

As Nel poured the tea, Betsy rested the envelope against the milk jug in the middle of the table. The women stared unseeing at its ominous presence, swallowing each mouthful of tea with a loud gulp. They both jumped when another slam of the back door signalled Duncan's return.

"Are you there, Betsy?" Duncan yelled from the washhouse before opening the door. "Good. Quick. Get your boots on. I need a hand. There's a heifer slipping. We may have lost the calf, but we don't want to lose the cow and we will if she goes down in this frost."

"There's a …." Nel lifted the telegram to show Duncan.

"No time for that now. Got to hurry. Come on, Betsy." Duncan turned and was back out the door before Nel could say any more.

She shrugged; resignation written all over her face as she put the envelope back on the table. "He won't be waylaid. His precious animals always come first. The sooner you go, the sooner you'll be back."

How could animals be more important than humans? How could Duncan think a heifer more important than his own son? Betsy wanted to scream at him to stop but he was already striding purposefully to the truck. She had no choice but to put her boots and jacket back on. Retrieving a woollen hat from her jacket pocket, she put it on and pulled it down over her ears as she followed her employer to the truck.

"It happens every year," Duncan groaned as he started the truck and eased it into gear.

"Pardon?" Betsy could think of many things that happened every year; she had no idea which one Duncan was referring to.

"One of the heifers, always seems to slip, right when there's a frost."

"Well, the ice is very slippery, I almost fell on the way back with the telegram."

Duncan shook his head and laughed. "When a heifer slips," he explained, "It means she loses her calf, aborts prematurely."

"Oh, but you said she goes down. I just assumed the heifer ended up on the ground."

"Yes, they usually end up on the ground, because they're unwell, not because they fall over."

"Oh." Betsy imagined Duncan rolling his eyes and decided she'd best not make any more assumptions. "What will we do if she is on the ground?"

"Before this blasted war, we would have had a tractor with a hoist to lift her up. Now, we'll just have to make her comfortable with some hay and a bucket of water, keep her hydrated and fed until she regains her strength, but hopefully it hasn't come to that yet."

There were only five heifers in the paddock, four were happily chewing their cud, the other paced awkwardly in the far corner, a bloody mucous trail hanging from her rear.

"Great, she's still standing. Grab the gate will you, Betsy?"

Four inquisitive heifers scampered over to the gate as Duncan drove through. They sniffed the air, bellowed a greeting, and waited expectantly. Duncan drove across to the calving animal, leaving Betsy to close the gate. When she turned to go and help, the heifers had lined up, effectively trapping her in the corner. Their large black eyes stared inquisitively and their saliva covered tongues extended within reach.

"Nothing for you today, girls," she said trying to sound calmer than she felt.

Betsy hadn't had much to do with the heifers in the short time she'd been at *Whipsnade Farm*. She'd milked the cows with Grace, Moira and Alice and the only incident was a kick to the shins the cow nicknamed Stroppy gave Moira. Whether the cow had sensed Moira's inattention, or the redhead had provoked the animal hoping for the three days off the doctor had ordered for her recovery, Betsy couldn't be sure.

Either way, she didn't think the heifers were dangerous. She edged her way around them and headed off across the paddock. She'd only taken a dozen or so steps when the thumping of hooves thundered like a stampede behind her. Betsy turned to find only the four heifers prancing, kicking their hind legs into the air like ballerinas. They may have just been playing but she decided to walk the perimeter of the paddock, hugging the fence in case she had to jump it in a hurry.

"What the hell have you been doing?" Duncan growled when she finally arrived at his side. "Quick, give me a hand. The bull must have got to her early. She's not aborting. She's trying to calve."

Betsy, mouth agape, was unable to move. Duncan's overalls were covered in blood, as was the hand he had pressed against the heifer's pelvic bone, but it was the location of Duncan's other hand that had Betsy stunned. His sleeve was rolled up to his armpit. It was all she could see, the rest of Duncan's arm was inside the heifer.

"The calf is still in here. We've got to get it out. It might still be alive, but I don't think so. Either way, it must come out. We don't want it rotting inside her."

Betsy's stomach churned at the thought, she shook her head, trying to regain focus. "What do you need?"

"Get two lengths of baling twine off the back of the truck. And a bucket of water out of the trough."

Getting the twine was easy but she had to smash the frozen crust on the trough to fill the bucket. Icy water splashed down the legs of her overalls.

"Wash the twine in the water," Duncan ordered, his arm remaining inside the heifer. "Fold each one in half and make a loop we can pull tight. Right. When I pull the foot out, put the loop over the foot and pull it firm, just enough to hold it, not too tight or you might rip it off."

The freezing water bit into Betsy's hands and her fingers became uncooperative robots, she had to re-programme them to follow Duncan's instructions.

His arm emerged, a small perfectly formed hoof in his hand. Gingerly, Betsy slipped the loop of twine over the limb and pulled it firm, not too tight, the thought of a hoof ripping off was abhorrent. The cow bellowed; Betsy jumped with fright, slackened her hold on the twine allowing the hoof to slide away.

"Bugger!" Duncan cursed. He reached back inside, wrenched the hoof out again and pulled the twine tight. "Right, stand out to the side a bit and don't let it go while I find the other one. I think it is bent under which is why it's not coming out by itself."

They repeated the process and soon had two tiny hooves protruding from the animal.

"I'll brace the cow. You pull down on the ropes. Gravity will help us."

Betsy was now directly behind the heifer. The baling twine was slippery in her hands, so she wrapped it around her fingers and pulled. Nothing happened.

"Kneel down," Duncan commanded. "Now, pull hard."

The heifer's prolonged bellow echoed Betsy's groan as she strained to pull down on the ropes. The twine bit into her cold hands, but she imagined her pain was nothing compared to the heifer which spread its legs and arched its back.

Eventually a tiny pink nose emerged. Duncan wiped the mucus from its nostrils, allowing the animal to breathe if its heart was still capable. With the next contraction the head was expelled into the world, big brown eyes stared lifelessly at Betsy and a long tongue hung limply from the calf's mouth. Sadness engulfed Betsy. The calf appeared dead; all she could think of was the telegram and silently prayed it wouldn't bring the same news.

"Don't stop! Move back! Pull again!" Duncan's order jolted Betsy back into action and she dragged her hands down towards the ground.

Another bellow from the cow and the calf's shoulders came out allowing the rest of its skinny torso to slide free.

"One more, come on, girl," Duncan encouraged.

Betsy was unsure if the coaxing was meant for her or the heifer, but she gave the ropes one more pull, and slumped to the ground as the calf landed with a thud on the earth. Duncan immediately released the heifer and focused his attention on the newborn. His finger in its mouth ensured its throat was clear, a thump on its chest encouraged its heart to kick into action. Betsy's heart pounded; willing the calf to do the same.

She blinked rapidly, seeking reassurance the movement she saw in the calf's chest was real. She raised her hand to cover her squeal of delight. It was a miracle. The calf took its first breath, steam rising from its mucus-covered torso.

Ignoring the afterbirth trailing from her uterus, the heifer's mothering instincts kicked in. It turned and reached down to lick the calf, cleaning her offspring, and providing herself with nutrients to aid her recovery from the ordeal.

"A success. Thank God for that." Duncan removed the baling twine from the calf's hooves. "We'll leave them to it then. We'll come back after breakfast and make sure they're still okay."

By the time they had rinsed their hands in the bucket of water, the calf had already made several attempts to stand on its gangling legs as natural instincts urged it to seek the sustenance of its mother's milk. Duncan and Betsy climbed into the truck and left them to it.

The drive back to the house seemed to take forever. Betsy pictured the telegram propped against the milk jug; its menacing presence had her heart beating rapidly. She willed it to contain good news. The best scenario was William had been promoted, that he was already heading up the army ranks and would soon be leading the troops from the safety of an office not the front lines. The worst scenario didn't bear thinking about; Betsy was certain it was impossible for the innocent looking envelope to contain news that William had been killed. Surely God would know Nel and Duncan only had one child, that it would be too cruel to take their son from them, when they had already lost so many to miscarriage and stillbirths.

The third scenario was one Betsy knew to be possible, for it had already happened to Roland. William could be missing in action. What kind of chaos were these soldiers being sent into, where it was possible for grown men to go missing? For no one to know where they were, when they were last seen alive, it made no sense to Betsy.

Nel met them at the kitchen door, the envelope held up in front of her so Duncan would have no choice but to reveal its contents.

"Duncan, please open the mail." She thrust the envelope at her husband.

"What? What is it?" Duncan took the envelope and turned it over in his hands. "We saved the calf, and the heifer looks like she'll be okay."

"Duncan! Now! Open the envelope! I can't wait any longer."

"Alright, alright dear, calm down. Let a man at least sit down, will you. I can't see why an envelope has got you in such a tither."

"Duncan, it's from the army. It will be about William."

Duncan looked from the envelope to his wife and back at the envelope. "Today's not going how I had planned." He sat down at the table and tucked his thumb under the envelope's flap to tear it open. Removing the single folded sheet of paper, Duncan's eyes scanned the telegram.

Betsy tried to read his face. Did she imagine the furrow in his forehead deepened as he swallowed loudly and scrunched his eyes shut? Did his skin take on a greyer shade of pale that aged him ten years in one second? His eyes were glassy when he finally looked their way. Betsy and Nel stood side by side, hands clasped together.

Duncan swallowed. Betsy watched his Adam's apple bob as if it was a light switch being flicked on. A switch that brought a brightness to Duncan's face, real or faked for their benefit, Betsy couldn't decide.

"He's coming home," Duncan announced.

"He's coming home?" Nel held a hand to her heart.

"Yes."

"When?"

Duncan glanced back at the piece of paper clasped tightly in his hands. "It doesn't say."

Betsy looked from Duncan to Nel. She sensed there was something missing. "Why is he coming home?" she asked.

"Umm … umm." Duncan stalled.

"Duncan! Why is William coming home?" Nel repeated.

"He's been injured."

Audible gasps filled the room. Afraid her legs would no longer support her, Betsy sat at the table.

"How? When? How bad?"

"It doesn't say. It just says he's been injured, and he's being shipped home."

"Oh no!" Nel bawled. She cradled her head in her hands and shook it from side to side.

"It'll be okay, love." Duncan tried to comfort his wife. "You'll see. We'll get him home and with your home cooking and the fresh country air, he'll be right as rain in no time. Mark my words."

"When will he get here?" Nel asked.

"It doesn't say."

"I'd better get moving, bake all of his favourite things." Nel fidgeted, wringing the corner of her apron.

"I don't think you need to hurry; it will take quite a while to arrive by ship."

Ignoring Duncan, Nel opened her flour bin to check its contents. "But they might have already left. The letter might have taken forever to get here. I'd best make a list of ingredients. You can get them when you next go to town."

"It's a telegram, Nel," Duncan replied.

Nel didn't hear, she was too busy in the cupboards, distracting herself. Betsy wished for her own distraction. Imagining the injuries that may have been inflicted on William, injuries so severe that he was being shipped home churned her stomach.

CHAPTER

2

The comforting sound of female voices broke the silence. William couldn't make out the words, but it had been a long time since he'd heard a woman's voice. A long time since he'd left home.

Mum? Was he back home? What would she say when she heard about the mess, he'd got himself into? She'd growl; that fake growl she had for Dad's benefit. She'd want to hug him, to wrap her arms around him like he was the most precious thing in the world, like she had when he was a boy and he needed somewhere safe to cry.

But I'm not a boy now.

He was a man, a soldier. He couldn't cry now. Never again. If he gave into crying, the floodgates would open, and he would never stop.

There were other women at home too, land girls. What were their names? He couldn't remember. A pretty one, whose name started with 'b'. Why couldn't he remember? What was wrong with him?

There were other noises too, unfamiliar sounds left William unsure where he was. He should open his eyes and look. If only it was that easy. Everything appeared black, his eyes unwilling to see. His head pounded, his entire body ached, and an incessant throbbing radiated from his right hand. Female voices continued a conversation he couldn't join.

"Welcome aboard, or should I say below. Your first shift, isn't it?"

"It's strange being thirty feet underground. At least the Germans won't find us here."

"Ermm. Don't be deluded by the muted sounds of the bombs. They're still close enough to get us, but we've been lucky so far."

'Lucky.' William made that word out, but he didn't feel at all lucky. It seemed as if he was pinned to the ground, it was more comfortable than what he'd been sleeping on for the last few nights but still his body ached. He thought he could relieve the pain if he rolled over. William willed his body to do as his mind wanted. A spasm tore through his abdomen, and he howled in agony but remained lying exactly where he'd been placed.

"Sounds like he's coming around now."

"Well, you never can tell, some of them scream the whole way through. Fearful nightmares they must be having after what they've seen. We only see the results. Imagine what it is like, to actually be in the midst of it."

Dust. Grit. Rats. Blood. Death.

William had been in the midst of it. He could still smell it. War had a stench all its own. It had seeped its way into his pores and there didn't seem to be any escape. There was another odour now, added to the mix, barely discernible but comforting, clean and offering a glimmer of hope. Perhaps he'd been lucky.

The thunder of bombs seemed muted, the screams of his mates no longer a constant. There were no commands being yelled at him. He didn't have to get out of the dugouts, scramble on his belly across the sand, squirm under coils of barbed wire into no-man's land, fearing with every breath the bullet of a sniper.

He didn't have to look at the big brown, pleading eyes of his mate, hold his hand and lie to him. Tell him he was okay, as life ebbed from him, his lower limbs blown to pieces.

William groaned. Which was worse? The pain of his memories or the pain of his physical injuries? He didn't know.

A warm hand touched his arm. "I'll sit with him a while."

Yes, please he wanted to say but he couldn't move his mouth to form anything more than a grunt.

"You won't have time to do that, we're full up. There are thirty soldiers in here, each one needing dressings changed, pain relief and feeding if they can't feed themselves, before they get shipped out and the next lot arrive."

The hand was gone and William, unable to protest was left to drift back into a fitful sleep.

He stirred again late in the night when a nurse placed her hand on his arm in a comforting gesture. The same nurse or a different one, he couldn't tell.

"Hello, soldier, welcome back," she said.

"Back … back where?" William croaked, his voice little more than a raspy mutter.

"Welcome back to the land of the living."

"My eyes …. my eyes … I can't see." William said with rising panic. He felt the bandage covering his eyes. "Where are my eyes?"

"They're still there." The nurse pulled William's hand away. "Calm down and I'll remove the bandage so we can have a look."

William hoped she was right, that he could have a look. If he couldn't see, life wouldn't be worth living. His frustration grew as the nurse carefully unwrapped the bandage and no brightness edged its way through the gauze.

"It's dark!" Anguish gripped at William's insides. He see-sawed between anger and despair. He needed to leap out of bed and kill the Huns that had put him there but if he never saw another battle, he would be eternally grateful.

"It's okay, soldier. It's night-time, it should be dark. The gas lamps have been extinguished so you can sleep. Gas is a precious resource out here, not to be wasted." The nurse had hung her dimly-lit lantern from a hook at the head of the cot so she could see. "There, bandage removed, how does that feel?"

William blinked his eyes several times, hoping the action would clear the blurry images that confronted him.

"I can't see!"

"Nothing?" The nurse held her finger out from William's face and moved it from left to right.

"Blurry. It's all blurry." He sensed a movement in front of him. Instinct told him to dodge.

Don't let the bullet hit you, he yelled to himself as he tried to move.

"Calm down, soldier. Be patient. It might take a while to refocus. I'll reapply the bandage to your right eye and the doctor can have a look in the morning."

Another soldier howled in agony on the opposite side of the ward.

"Here, have a sip of water before I go and see to the other fellow." The nurse helped William lift his head up enough to take a drink from the glass she held to his lips. "That's it. Now rest up. It's the best means of recovery."

Recovery. The word bounced around William's head like the shrapnel that had put him here. Of course, he wanted to recover. Being blind and with a hand he couldn't seem to make work wasn't an option that sat well with him. But what did recovery mean for a soldier? Did they turn around and send you back to the front, back to the heat that parched your skin and throat, the flies that landed on every bare surface devouring whatever open flesh or food that lay in their way, and the sand and grit that ground into every bodily orifice. All that to deal with before even imagining the fearful scream of the Sukas dive bombing at speed, the rattle of the Messerschmitts machine gunning the convoys or worst of all the sight of a fellow soldier less fortunate than you.

Or did recovery mean he would be sent home? What would be there for him? Who would have use for a man with no sight and a useless hand? No woman, not even the pretty land girl, would want to look at him, marred with battle scars. The prospect of recovery was grim either way he considered it.

"Get out, get off." The yells came from the cot next to William's. "Bloody Huns," cursed the soldier. "I'll kill the bloody lot of them."

Huns. William was instantly alert. His unbandaged eye scanned the room, searching out the threat, the swastika of his enemy.

"Nurse, hold his arms down. Calm down, Private. You're in hospital, you're safe here."

Hospital? Surely there can't be any Germans in hospital. The nurses were speaking English. William knew then he wasn't captured, a prisoner of war to face uncertainty.

"He's reopened the wound. I'll hold his arms; you apply pressure to stem the bleeding."

William watched, even with blurred vision he saw the moment when the man gave up his battle, his arms went limp under the nurse's. She let his arms go and felt for a pulse at his wrist. Her sigh was audible.

"It's a dull beat," she said. "But he's alive."

Angels. White. Clean. Pure. William knew in that moment that he was safe. That these delicately-built women, veils billowing as they rushed to help, wouldn't allow anything to happen to him.

"Nurse Mellow." An older stern-looking woman strode up to the cot. "I thought I told you to get some food."

"Yes, Sister." The nurse nodded to her superior and turned to leave. "Sorry, Sister, I lost track of time. It's difficult to tell underground, whether its day or night."

Following the sister was the doctor. The pair stopped in front of William's cot and the doctor picked up the clipboard that held William's details.

"Private McKnight." The doctor nodded in greeting as he reached over to remove William's head bandage. "The head wound should heal well. We can't do much when we're this close to the front."

William swallowed. *Can't do much.* What did he look like? What had they done?

"As yet unknown, is the extent of the damage to eyesight," the doctor continued as if William wasn't there.

Was that how the soldiers became just another patient in a long list of patients?

"We had bandaged both eyes as a precaution, but the injury is mainly to the right."

"Blindness is a possibility then."

"No," William protested. "No, I can see. It's just a little blurry. The nurse said …"

Where was that angel of a nurse that said his sight would be better by morning?

The doctor shone a tiny light into William's pupils. He felt them react. He was certain.

"Mmm." The doctor stood back; his arms folded across his chest. "Time, not nurses, will tell. And as for the hand, we did what we could."

If this doctor was trying to make William feel better, he was failing dismally.

"There is nerve damage in the right hand, most of the bones shattered." The doctor unwrapped the bandage covering William's hand. "I removed all the shrapnel and bone fragments I could and rearranged what was left. You're lucky to still have your hand, Private."

There was that word again.

Lucky.

Possible blindness, possibly a hand that would no longer do what was needed, William didn't feel lucky, but he guessed there were degrees of good fortune. He wasn't dead, so that was lucky. He wasn't still out on the frontline, so that was lucky.

He tried to move his fingers. Nothing but a throbbing in his forehead; he groaned with the pain.

"Shall I give him some more pain relief, doctor?"

"No." The reply was so short and sharp; William didn't think the doctor had even considered the option. "We don't know when the next delivery of chloroform will get through so we're only giving them the bare minimum to get them through the surgery and not much more."

"Shall I get a nurse to rewrap the bandage then?" the sister asked.

"Best disinfect again and change it for a clean dressing. There's a hint of infection we don't want to progress. I cleaned the wound as best I could, but in these conditions …. you never know."

They moved away to the next soldier and William was left alone with his thoughts. Thoughts no one would want to spend too much time with.

When he next woke Nurse Mellow was back on duty.

"Good morning, Private McKnight." Her greeting was cheerful. "How are you feeling today?"

William blinked and blinked again. He could make out the young, uniformed woman in front of him. Not every precise detail but more than he had been able to before. She was a beautiful vision to behold, her smile bright, cheerful, innocent, or possibly naïve. How could anyone smile like that if they knew what war did to people? But to realise he hadn't lost his sight totally was such a relief he grinned from ear to ear.

"I'm guessing that grin means you're feeling better," she observed. "That's good because you've got a journey ahead."

"A journey?"

"Yes, you're leaving here in a couple of hours." Nurse Mellow placed a bundle of clothes on the end of the cot. William's uniform had been torn and bloodied, beyond repair and infested with lice so it had been burnt on his arrival. "We need to get you dressed."

William felt all the blood drain from his face and the hairs on his arms stand to attention. He scanned the ward for an escape route and clung to the cot with his good hand, his knuckles white.

"Where to?" he asked, his voice shrill and his lips trembling uncontrollably.

"Away from here. The No 1 General Hospital in Helwan. They're way better equipped than us for your recovery. We're just a patch-up centre. They'll decide whether its home on the hospital ship anchored off Crete or not," she replied, going about her duties unperturbed by William's reaction. "Now, don't be bashful, Private, I've seen it all before. Swing your legs out and I'll help you into your trousers."

The realisation he was naked beneath the thin blanket sent heat running up into William's cheeks and all the way to the tips of his ears. It was one thing to live in close quarters in the dugouts with the blokes and be party to all their bodily functions but another altogether to be at the mercy of a young female nurse.

He had no choice. With one useless hand, it was going to be a battle for William to dress himself. He cleared his throat, sat up and swung his legs out over the edge of the cot. He looked at the floor, at the soldiers in the other cots, anywhere but at the nurse.

"Go, Billy. Nurse has got your willy." A whistle and a cheer came from down the ward until silenced by the glare of the sister.

His platoon had called him Billy, not just as a common shortening of William but after his hankering for a billy of tea, real tea, not the dirty water they'd been drinking in the camps and dugouts. It was nice to hear his nickname, it made him feel like he was back with his mates, enjoying a smoke or playing cards, revelling in the good times before the bad.

William was weak and needed the nurse to help him stand. As she bent and pulled his underpants and trousers on, he stared at the roof of the cavern, willing his cock not to betray him. It had been a long time since a female had been that close. He almost laughed when he felt relieved he remained flaccid.

He sat back down on the cot and rested while Nurse Mellow made a sling for his injured arm. She held out a clean shirt for him to thread his good arm through the sleeve and buttoned the shirt up adding another layer of protection to the injury cradled against his chest.

"Right, I'll fetch you a tray of food and you'll be ready to go."

William wasn't sure he was ready to go anywhere but the thought of food did make him smile. He inhaled, savoured the smell of cleanliness, unable to remember the last time he'd had a change of clothes. The uniform hung limply from his bony frame. It was probably the same size as he had always worn but his time in the desert heat with limited rations and even less water, marching for miles on end, ensured any excess fat he may have carried back in New Zealand was long gone.

"Here you are, soldier." A porter William didn't recall, handed him a bundle tied loosely with string.

"Thank you," he said, remembering the good manners his mother would want him to use.

He'd wondered what had happened to his kit, and here it was. He recognised his greatcoat and eagerly pulled at the string to see what else the bundle held. The treasures he'd collected on visits into Cairo, sat like happy memories in a photo album, wrapped safely in the greatcoat. They were reminders of the adventure they'd been expecting and had enjoyed until reality set in. William fished into the pockets of his coat and found his paybook and the last of his unspent pay. The top pocket held his remaining ration of cigarettes, a little crumpled but hopefully still smokeable. William salivated with the thought of food and a fag. It was easier to keep his mind in the present, not remember the horrors of the past nor anticipate the trials of the future.

CHAPTER

3

Three weeks went by without any news from abroad; no letters no reports on whether Roland was dead or alive, no update on William's condition or when he could be expected home. Betsy was grateful the cows had started calving again and there was a herd to be milked, morning and night.

It was an effort to pull herself from the warmth of her bed on the dark and cold winter's morning, but Betsy wanted to be alert and focused in the shed, determined not to be the target for a cow's ablutions as she had been when she'd first arrived at *Whipsnade Farm.*

"Ah, here she is." Duncan's face lit up as Rosey, one of the new land girl trainees, entered the cow shed. It didn't seem to matter she was late, and Betsy had already milked half of the mob of cows.

Betsy followed the path of Duncan's eyes. They settled on the part of Rosey that seemed to precede everything she did, her breasts. Physically, they entered the room first, the shoulder straps of her overalls extended to their limits, the buckles sitting proudly at the tips of the mounds like sentry guards protecting the nipples beneath. Rosey's buxomness changed the dynamics of the space and everyone in it.

Duncan's reaction confirmed Betsy's perception; Rosey's breasts turned men to mush. It appeared she could do no wrong, her faults were cushioned, overlooked in the shadow of her breasts.

"Betsy." Duncan spoke without looking at her. "Now I know you've remembered what to do, I'll leave you to teach Rosey how to milk the cows."

A sarcastic response sat on the tip of Betsy's tongue. She'd always tried to be non-judgemental; someone's physical appearance shouldn't be a source of scorn, but with Rosey it was difficult. It was like she knew the power of her appendages and used them to her advantage at every opportunity.

Betsy inhaled long and slow. It wouldn't pay to lose her temper, not while Duncan was still here.

"Right, we'd better get to it then." She released the cow she'd been milking and came out to round another into the bale. "Chase that cow up, will you."

Rosey stomped her way into the mob, waving her arms and yelling "yah, yah". The cows bellowed and scattered to the edges of the yard, waddling around their swollen udders, their hooves splattering the effluent.

"Don't do it like that!" Betsy snapped. She questioned her tone, was she tired and taking it out on the new land girl or was she jealous? Betsy had certainly never aspired to have breasts that big, but she did feel inadequate standing next to her.

"You'll get kicked," she added. At least it sounded like she was concerned for Rosey's welfare.

They encouraged a cow into the bale, attached the chain behind her rump and Betsy explained the process of cleaning the teats and attaching the cups. If it had been jealousy that had riled Betsy, it soon dissipated as she watched Rosey struggle to follow the simple procedure around the burden of her breasts.

"I hear there's a soldier coming home soon?" Rosey called the question over the noise of the milking machines.

"Yes, Duncan and Nel's son William," Betsy replied.

"Do you know him?"

Betsy paused, considering how well she knew William. "I met him when we first arrived, before his regiment shipped out."

"Is he handsome?"

"Mmm," Betsy said dreamily. "Yes." She realised how she sounded, and guilt silenced her. She pictured William's face, the way his dimple appeared when he smiled and his broad shoulders which made her feel like he could carry the weight of the world for them both. But he was injured now, the war had damaged him enough to send him home. Would he still look the same? Would he still have the same strength?

"Were you and he courting before he left?"

"No!" The crackle in Betsy's voice echoed the tightening in her chest. She'd always been faithful to Roland; how could anyone suggest otherwise? "Why would you ask that?"

"I just heard—"

"You heard what?" Betsy bit her lip. She had to stay quiet. If this land girl who'd only been at *Whipsnade* a few weeks had heard about her feelings for William, then such news could also travel via a letter to the other side of the world. What if this news found Roland even though the authorities couldn't?

"I just heard he liked one of the land girls and I assumed because you'd stayed here, it might be you."

"Well, you assumed wrong." Betsy huffed. "I stayed because I'm good with the animals, and I'm good at milking cows."

That was true, but it wasn't the whole truth. Betsy was glad there was a cow and a wooden fence between her and Rosey. Her cheeks had become beacons, signalling her guilt; luckily, they were out of Rosey's sight.

"That's good to know," Rosey replied. "I wouldn't like to step on anyone's toes."

Betsy wanted to protest, to yell 'don't you dare' but she couldn't. She had to stay true to the commitment she'd made to Roland. She couldn't follow her feelings for William while Roland was missing in action. She needed him to be found, dead or alive so her life could move ahead with certainty.

In the meantime, she had to trust William would look beyond what his father and every other man saw in Rosey. She hoped William was different.

In between the daily milkings, there was hay to be fed out, colostrum milk to be given to the calves, pig pens to be cleaned, sheep to be moved and all the other jobs that needed doing to keep the farm running smoothly and Betsy exhausted. She liked it that way, too busy to think about the what ifs, and too tired to dream about the maybes.

Despite Nel's numerous attempts to pile more food on Betsy's plate, she'd lost her appetite. Dark circles formed under her eyes, accentuating the slight hollow in her cheeks.

"Betsy needs a day off," Nel told Duncan as she delivered his plate of porridge to the table. "This month's Country Women's Institute meeting is today. I think Betsy should practise her driving skills and take me to the meeting. It's just in the Orari Hall. I would bike but the wind is coming straight off those Alps."

"Very well then," Duncan replied. "I can see you've already made your mind up."

"I'll just get a basket for the scones, love." Nel had taken to using the term of endearment with Betsy. "If you could put the cream I've whipped into a small bowl, and we'll need another jar of my blackberry jam. It's in the cupboard above the plates. Actually, two jars, one for the scones and one to put into the jam competition, that's being judged today."

Betsy did as she was asked, quietly contemplating what could be in a Country Women's Institute meeting for her.

It was the first time Betsy had driven on the road and she was grateful the hall was only a short distance from *Whipsnade Farm*. It would have been less worrisome if the bridge over the Orari River had been constructed a little wider. Betsy slowed her approach to a snail's pace to centre the truck between the wooden rails on either side, fearful the tray would scrape the railings, if not take them out altogether. She was oblivious to the car waiting its turn on the other side of the bridge until they tooted. Betsy didn't know if it was to say hello or hurry up and didn't dare to take her hands off the steering wheel to toot back.

From the passenger seat, Nel, seemingly unaware of Betsy's nervousness, chatted away.

"CWI is more important than ever in these times with all the women managing on their own. If I know a good thing, I've got to pass it on. It's the CWI injunction, did you know? Our monthly meetings always cheer me up with the programme of something to see, something to hear and something to do. I hope they do the same for you."

Betsy nodded an acknowledgement, only half-aware of what she was agreeing to.

"Well, if you were my real daughter, we might have been going to a League of Mothers meeting instead. I used to take William to play with the other children in the creche. But when I miscarried, it became unbearable to watch the other women with their bulging bellies and newborn babies." Nel went silent and gazed out the window.

The hall was a hive of activity when they arrived. A medley of women's voices reverberated off the high ceiling as preserves were placed on one table, contributions to morning tea on another and chairs assembled in the middle so the meeting could begin.

Memories of the last time Betsy had been in the hall, brought a mixture of emotions. It was the dance where she'd enjoyed the closeness of William spinning her around the dancefloor, his hand encouraging her body closer to his, but thanks to Moira the night hadn't ended well.

Betsy was putting Nel's blackberry jam on the assigned table when she overheard some of the women chatting.

"Did you hear the news?" a dark-haired woman asked excitedly.

"What gossip do you have now, Elinore?"

"Not gossip, Joan, the truth straight from the horse's mouth, so to speak."

"Well, what is it? Let us all in on the secret."

"Soldiers," Elinore said as if she needed to say no more.

Joan sighed. "Elinore! If you're going to tell us, just say it. Stop dilly-dallying about."

Betsy lingered. If there was news about soldiers, she wanted to hear it.

"I am not dilly-dallying," Elinore replied indignantly. "I just wanted to make sure I had your full attention for this very important news."

"Well, you do."

"Some of the injured ones," Elinore leaned in towards the small circle of women, "are coming home."

"That's what injured soldiers do, Elinore."

"Yes, but we know these ones and …" Elinore paused for effect, raising her eyebrows before she continued. "Apparently they arrive next week."

"Have you introduced yourself to these lovely ladies, Betsy?" Nel asked as she sidled up beside her. "Elinore, Joan, Margaret, this is Betsy. She's staying with Duncan and I, helping to train the land girls while William is away fighting."

The group of women parted awkwardly.

Elinore gave a genteel cough behind her hand. "Nel. Betsy. So nice to see you both."

"Elinore was just about to tell us some news about the soldiers," Joan said. "But I guess you hear all about that with William and all."

Elinore nudged Joan with her elbow, as if to silence her. It didn't have the desired effect.

"What did you hear?" Nel asked.

"Oh, nothing much." Elinore shrugged her shoulders, a gesture to reiterate her words. "Have you made some more of your prize-winning blackberry jam? Betsy, have you tried Nel's blackberry jam? It really is delicious. She must have a secret recipe. She gets prizes every year."

"Elinore! Really!" Joan scolded. "Just tell us what you know."

Elinore's eyes went wide, she inhaled deeply. "Well … it might not be true."

"You just assured us it wasn't gossip."

"Yes, but surely if it were true, it wouldn't be news to Nel. She'd already know."

"Already know what?" Nel asked.

"Umm … that William is coming home …"

"Yes, we know that," Nel replied. "Unfortunately, he's been injured, and he is being sent home but we're not sure when he's arriving."

"Next week." Betsy interjected with the news she'd overheard.

"Betsy?" Nel frowned at her, her expression hurt "You already knew, and didn't tell me. I thought we always shared William's letters."

"I didn't know," Betsy defended herself. "Not until I overheard these ladies talking."

"It was Elinore," Joan stated, absolving herself of any blame.

"How do you know, Elinore?" There was an accusatory tone to Nel's voice.

"Umm, my husband's brother-in-law's cousin works at the army headquarters in Christchurch and has seen the passenger list for the ship arriving next week," she sheepishly admitted.

"Right then." Nel lifted her chin a smidgeon, turned towards Betsy. "Betsy, we'd best take our seats before the meeting begins. I believe they are going to discuss this year's play and I think you would be perfect for one of the parts."

Nel was shaking by the time they took a seat at the other side of the hall, as far away from Elinore and Joan as they could manage, so they couldn't see the effect their news was having.

"Oh, Betsy," Nel said clutching the young woman's hand. "William. He's coming home next week. My boy, he's coming home. It'll be wonderful to see him again, won't it?"

Betsy took it as a rhetorical question and didn't proffer an answer. She didn't know what her response would be. Would she be happy to see William or angry, that he, and not Roland, was returning from the war?

"And while we are talking about gossip." Nel smoothed the folds of her dress over her knees, while she leaned over to whisper in Betsy's ear. "Apparently, there has been a regular visitor at Elinore's house while her husband is away on war duties. Heaven knows what will happen if he returns and finds another man has taken his place."

Betsy smiled. It was most unlike Nel to gossip.

The rest of the meeting proceeded without incident. It was decided, under the circumstances, this year's drama production would be a series of one-woman plays, songs, and poetry recitals instead of one play with a large cast. Betsy was glad as that meant she didn't have to commit to rehearsals and with a bit of luck, could avoid any involvement at all.

The weather was foul for the next week. Rain pelted for hours on end, saturating everything in its path. Freezing southerlies blew, often turning the rain to sleet and hail. Intermittent gale-force gusts whorled noisily through, threatening to uproot young saplings in their path. It was decided the calves were best left on their mothers until the storm had passed. Partly because it would be better for the calves and partly because it meant nobody had to brave the weather any more than necessary.

Instead, Duncan, Nel and Betsy sat listening to the news reports on the wireless and the land girls did the same from the comfort of Captain Boyle's home. Daily updates of news from abroad. It had always been on the other side of the world and seemed so far away but now, German raiders were circling off the coast of New Zealand. War was coming much closer to home.

"Mark my words, Nel," Duncan said. "It'll be *when* the Germans come, not *if*."

Nel gasped. "It's bad enough the war injuring William, we don't need or want it any closer to home. I hope you're wrong."

"I think we'd better do what they're suggesting," Duncan continued.

"Who is suggesting what?" The click-clacks of Nel's knitting needles paused.

"A lot of farmers are packing supplies into forty-four-gallon drums, stashing them at the back of their farms in case of invasion."

"Really?" Nel swallowed, put down the sock she'd been knitting and raised her hand to her heart. "Do you really think that is necessary?"

"Better to be prepared," Duncan replied. "I've got some drums at the back of the implement shed. I'll get the land girls onto it as soon as the weather breaks. You and Betsy can organise some supplies, blankets, canned food, preserves. Anything we can spare from here that might be needed, if we have to camp out for a few weeks."

That was how the letter sat in the letterbox for several days. Everyone had been so busy sorting out the supplies for the drums, no one had ventured down the driveway to check the box. At Nel's insistence she needed more flour, Duncan and Betsy had been to town to get some supplies. They stopped by the letterbox on their way back up the driveway. Duncan unwound his window, reached in and retrieved the newspaper and mail, all from the comfort of the driver's seat of the truck.

They were back inside enjoying a cup of tea before he unfolded the newspaper and read from the headlines.

"Ten thousand U.S. marines and army have arrived. Ten thousand. That's a hell of a lot."

"Where are they going to accommodate them?" Nel asked. "Not here, I hope."

"Auckland, Wellington, and Masterton. It's good that they've come to help fight the Japs, but it would have been better if they hadn't brought their war to the South Pacific at all." Duncan grunted and continued reading. "Blast, now tea is to be rationed too. If I have to go without a cup of tea just so Americans can have it, I won't be happy."

An envelope fell from the folds of the paper into Duncan's lap. From the quick glimpse Betsy got of the handwriting, she thought it was William's, but messy as if written in a rush. She saw Duncan glance down at it and frown, but he continued reading the paper and sipping at his tea as if nothing was amiss. William usually wrote to Betsy or Nel. Why was Duncan not handing it over?

"Was that a letter?" she dared to ask.

Duncan cleared his throat. "Umm, yes."

Betsy had been waiting for news for so long, she persisted despite Duncan's obvious reluctance. "Is it from William?"

The envelope had the words *HS Manganui* stamped in blue on the front.

"*HS Manganui*," he read as he glanced from Betsy to Nel and back again. "That's the hospital ship transferring injured soldiers back home."

"You've got a letter from William and you're reading the paper and not opening it?" Nel looked livid.

"Well." Duncan put the newspaper down to pick up the letter. "It is addressed to me, but …"

"But what?" Nel stood, her hands on her hips.

Duncan looked out from under his bushy eyebrows as if dubious he should continue. "It's not William's handwriting, at least not that I recognise."

"Duncan McKnight. You read that letter now! Or hand it over."

He pulled the single page letter from the envelope and read his son's message. Duncan rubbed the back of his neck before speaking.

"He'll be here soon. He wants me to collect him."

He folded the page, stuffed it back in the envelope, stowed the envelope in his pocket and resumed reading the newspaper as if the conversation were over.

"Duncan!" Nel's cheeks went scarlet as if she was ready to explode. "What does the letter say?"

"Dear." Duncan patted Nel's hand. "Calm down. I told you what it says, he's coming home, will be here soon and wants me to collect him."

Why couldn't he write himself? The answer filled Betsy with dread. It was so terrible she dared not voice it aloud. William's injuries were so horrific he was incapable of writing his own letter.

CHAPTER

4

A stretcher holding a patient was the first to be loaded; it took up one side of the rear of the truck. Six injured soldiers sat on a wooden slat bench seat on the opposite side, William included. He looked across at the man on the stretcher and noted there were two bandaged stumps where the soldier's knees should have been. William turned away, relief jostled with guilt; relief he had fared better than his comrade, and guilt he was happy his injuries were minor in comparison.

William thought he recognised the private huddled into the corner as Brian McPherson, one of the lads from back home but there was no acknowledgement from the man who stared vacantly ahead. He had no obvious injuries and William wondered if a bomb had rendered him blind or deaf. He'd heard of soldiers who suffered from shell shock, maybe he was one of them.

By the time they left the treatment station, the sun was high in the sky and the heat in the back of the truck stifling, despite the canvas flap that served as a door at the back, having been rolled up. The heat was the least of William's worries, every bump in the journey was like a judder bar. He had to support his injured arm with his good arm to limit the pain from each shudder. He clenched his jaw to brace himself.

Until they reached the road, the truck wove in and out of the camel thorn. At least it was daylight, and their driver could see the bushy shrubs which catch the drifting sand in their tangled branches and become dangerous solid lumps. They passed a burnt-out truck chassis. William assumed it had fallen victim to a camel thorn in the darkness of night and left exposed as a bomb target by day. Eventually they reached a road of sorts, hard rock where the veneer of sand had been blown away.

Then it came. The screaming siren signalled the Stuka's arrival pierced the day. Instinct told the soldiers to hide, to dive to the bottom of the trenches but they weren't in the trenches. How did they protect themselves in the back of the truck? William swore. He'd be gutted if he'd survived a battle only to be wiped out now. He could see the whites of the other men's eyes, wide with fear and imagined his would be the same. The soldier in the corner was trembling uncontrollably. He couldn't be deaf; he must have heard the war cry.

The truck swerved sharply to the side of the road. William heard the driver yell and slam the door as he escaped for cover. Should William? Could he do the same? If only it were possible for the patients in the back. Together they waited, held their collective breath, and counted the seconds until their fate was determined. Dead or alive? Would the bombs dropped by the planes connect with the truck or would they be spared?

Rrrrrrrrrrrr boom! Rrrrrrrrrrrr boom! Each time a bomb missed; the soldiers cried out in release. Relief flooded through the soldier in the corner, figuratively and literally as a wet stain coloured his crotch and dripped to the floor of the truck.

From the back of the truck William could see the tails of the planes as they soared skyward. It was an all too familiar sight that sent shivers of fear down his spine. He knew what would follow. The Messerschmitts. The Jerries always followed their bombers with a parade of machine gun. He could hear them. The threatening drone of engines. So much worse when you couldn't see the enemy's approach.

Rattattattat, rattattattat! William hunched, covered his head with his hand and hoped for the best, his heart pounding in his chest.

"Betsy, I'll see you in heaven," he whispered, then held his breath as if he expected it to be his last. At least he had remembered her name. It might be the final memory he had.

Ping! Ping! Ping! They'd been hit, a bullet hitting metal only made one sound. Time stood still while William waited for the explosion, none happened, the bullets must have missed the fuel tank. He dared to glimpse out the back of the truck as machine gun bullets ploughed a jagged line up the road.

When the planes were no more than a speck in the distance, the driver scurried back from wherever he'd taken cover.

"All right in the back?" he asked. Seeing all were still alive, he didn't wait for an answer and rushed back to his seat, inspecting the bullet holes on the way. The truck was a little worse for wear but still drivable.

Helwan Hospital was a welcome sight—a three-storey brick building south of Cairo and close to the military airport—that felt solid amongst the uncertainty of war. But it was only an overnight stay for William who was assessed as being unable to return to active duty. Early the next morning, he and the other soldiers like him were rallied onto another truck for the next part of their journey, a short drive to the Suez Canal where the Hospital Ship *Manganui* was anchored.

The relief of the soldiers who were one step closer to returning home was visible in grins, which despite injuries, were unable to be contained. The large red cross painted on the ship's white hull a blessing in more ways than one. William's truck was the last to arrive, the patients the last to board the ship to make up its full contingent of three hundred and forty patients.

Those able to walk were taken to a canteen where the YMCA provided a welcome meal and a cup of tea while they waited to board. William smiled at the volunteer who poured his cup of tea. He inhaled the comforting aroma, a bittersweet farewell to this land that was supposed to be an adventure. He listened to the cheerful hum as soldiers reunited with others from their regiments. The twang of an Australian accent gave away the presence of the Aussie soldiers amongst their midst. The war had killed and injured men from all walks of life, from all countries. Perhaps William was among the lucky ones. At least he was going home.

Having finished his meal, William stood and watched as orderlies came and escorted the soldier, he was certain was Brian McPherson, along with the others with the same distant face mask, to the stern of the ship, an area barred off from the rest of the vessel. The stretchered men were carried aboard next. One was on a makeshift stretcher, a greatcoat buttoned over two rifles. William smiled; Kiwi ingenuity had survived the battle.

Eventually, those who were able to walk of their own accord, were led down to C deck where all the wards were located. The ship's dining room had been converted along with eight other rooms all running off a central area. Rows of cots lined either side of the wards, each with a pillow at the head and a neatly folded woollen blanket. When William reached the cot, he'd been assigned, the lower of two, his knees buckled underneath him, he stumbled on wobbly legs and lay down as relief washed through him. A clean pillow and a blanket, simple items of comfort that signalled he'd made it. He sighed loudly and pressed his palm to his heart. His throat thickened and tears pricked at his closed eyelids.

He drifted off as the cots around him filled and the rumble of the ship's engine grew in intensity, readying itself for the voyage home. It was going to be a long journey in every sense of the word, the time it took to sail through the Suez Canal into the Red Sea, traverse the Indian Ocean to Australia and then into the Tasman Sea to Wellington. Would it be long enough for William to heal from his wounds? To become a man with a purpose and a life again.

The need to urinate brought him back to reality. He was on a ship, there would be toilets, real toilets. He got up and went in search of them. He also found a mirror, hung over the basin in which he washed his hands. He saw a face he barely recognised, tanned to a deep brown by the desert sun, his left eye was bloodshot, and he wondered if he'd ever be rid of the grit that felt like sandpaper under his eyelid. Worse though, was his right eye, still concealed beneath a bandage, only the stitches which ran a jagged line down the side of his face a visible sign of the ugliness that would be a constant reminder of this war.

William thought of Betsy, would she even want to look at him now? As for his hand, the throbbing was abating but he couldn't move his fingers beneath the thick bandages, and he had been trying. A man scarred in so many ways would be of no use to a young, beautiful woman like Betsy. She deserved better.

Then William remembered, Betsy was engaged to Roland. He'd met Roland one weekend he had gone to Cairo on leave. There was a whole group of blokes making merry hell in a local bar after a few too many beers had been imbibed as the Kiwis were renowned for doing. They'd talked of Betsy but for obvious reasons, William didn't reveal his feelings for Roland's fiancé. Roland was assigned to a different platoon, and they never saw each other again. William had heard Roland's platoon had suffered huge casualties, and some had been taken prisoner. His platoon had been too busy fighting their own battles for William to have the time to inquire further. He suspected Betsy would know more than him, of Roland's fate.

"Gidday cobber." A shaved head leaned over the top bunk's railing and greeted William.

The Australian's accent grated at William's throbbing forehead where tiny balls of perspiration beaded. He squinted. The light shining on him seemed to drill through to the back of his head.

"Turn the bloody light off."

"No light on, cobber. Just the sunlight through the porthole. We're in the Suez Canal. You're missing the view."

The soldier chuckled. "Well, it's not much of a view, just more desert. You're probably sick of desert by now but it's good to see it from the comfort of a bed."

William groaned; it was all he could manage. His mother would growl at him for being so rude. He should shake the man's hand, return the friendly gesture but William couldn't move. He felt like he was back in the underground hospital, pinned to his bed.

"You alright? Looks like you're burning up there. I'll get the nurse for you, cobber."

Yes, a nurse, a veiled angel that would make everything all right. That was what William needed. It had worked before; it could work again. He'd made it this far, there was no going back.

He sensed the nurse's presence as her hand brushed across his forehead.

"Looks like he's got a temperature," she said as she held his wrist, a finger on his pulse and glanced at the watch pinned to her chest. "Errm. And that's beating too fast as well."

"Remove those bandages, Nurse." The sister approached and issued the commands that her seniority allowed her to. "Inspect the wounds for infection."

The head bandage was the first to go, his right eye was revealed but itself revealed nothing.

"This appears to be healing well."

"Yes, I don't think that is the source of any infection. Best we inspect his hand."

The buttons of William's shirt were quickly undone, the knot of his sling untied, and his bandaged hand released from the binds. He willed his fingers to move. The red and swollen digits refused to respond to his commands. He couldn't even raise his head to look at them. It was no longer just the light that caused a pain behind his eyes, it was the dread, fear for whatever lay ahead. The fate of his fingers.

"I'll fetch the doctor," were the last words William heard.

Everything happened quickly after that, as if time was of the essence. He felt himself manhandled onto a gurney, sensed the eyes watching as he was whisked from the ward and bundled into a lift. He smelled the sterility of the operating theatre. He saw through his closed eyelids the bright lights above the operating table or was that heaven showing him the way? There were murmured voices in serious tones. He wanted to join them in discussing his fate but a mask over his face, a whisper in his ear instructing him to breathe, took him faraway. He hoped he'd make it back.

The lights were gone when William next came to. He struggled through the mess of his muddled head, trying to remember where he was. He looked skyward for the stars that had painted his ceiling over the past few months and gave him his bearings in a vast desert. There were none.

A constant humming felt reassuring. It was randomly interrupted by the rumbles of men snoring. At least William was still with his mates. He reached out with his good arm, felt the coolness of the metal bars each side of him, the softness of a pillow under his head. Memories returned; he was on a hospital ship bound for home. He'd been injured. A beautiful nurse had told him he was going to be alright. Despite her innocent voice, he sensed she was merely trying to placate him. Gingerly he touched his face, the stubble on his chin and a warm breath on his palm. He followed his nose, traced his left cheekbone, and felt his eyelashes flickering against the tips of his fingers. This side of him was whole but this side hadn't been damaged before. He summoned the courage and dared his fingers to touch the right side of his face. It was as his memory had told him. This side still lay hidden beneath a bandage. William hoped that meant it was still healing, the bandage was to ensure a full recovery. His right side would be whole again too.

The realisation that he, a right-handed man, was using his left hand brought a sense of panic. His lips trembled; his chin quivered. He remembered his fingers bandaged, the first doctor saying he did the best he could. Dread that his best wasn't good enough, filled William with a knot of trepidation bulging in his throat, threatening to suffocate him before he discovered the truth.

You're a soldier, he yelled silently to himself. *You've faced worse. Hell, your mates lost their lives, what have you got to worry about?*

William reached over to touch his fingers. He had no feeling. The bandage was not where he imagined it should be, just the blanket across his abdomen. His heartbeat quickened. Panicked he patted himself down. He crossed his left arm over his body and felt his shoulder. He traced his hand down his right arm and felt his elbow. But just below his elbow the bandage stopped. A stump. A useless stump.

His howl escaped like a torpedo propelled from his throat.

There was a loud thump, and the familiar Australian twang was beside William's ear. "It's alright there, cobber. You're just having a nightmare."

Was he right? Was it all just a bad nightmare? William wrapped his hand around the end of the stump. The tips of his fingers reached his elbow. This wasn't a nightmare; this was William's new living hell.

"That's it. That's the man. You just need to sleep. You'll feel much better in the morning."

William wanted to laugh at the irony of those words. Did hands grow back if you slept? No, of course not. If he was a man, he wouldn't be so stupid as to believe that. This wasn't a fairy tale with magic spells, this was real life, a life he was going to have to face as half a man.

He faked a snore. He wanted the Australian gone. He wanted to be alone, as alone as he could be in the darkness of his cot. He didn't want anyone to see the silent tear that seeped from the corner of his eye, painted a line down his cheek and dripped silently off his chin. It landed on his chest like a full stop, punctuating the time between life before and existence hereafter.

Cheerful banter and daylight brought William into the beginning of his new existence. He saw nurses doing their rounds, veils billowing behind them as they rushed down the aisle between the cots. Men who were able to sit, had doubled up on bunks and were playing cards. Others, confined to their beds were enjoying a cup of tea.

"How are you feeling today, soldier?" A nurse arrived at William's bedside and placed a thermometer under his tongue while she checked his heart rate.

"He had a rough night," the Australian replied on William's behalf.

"I'm fine, thank you," William mumbled around the thermometer. It was a lie, one he imagined he would repeat often from now on. He didn't want anyone's pity.

The nurse removed the thermometer and read the mercury level. "Your temperature is good. It looks like the infection is gone."

"Did you have to take my whole bloody hand to do it?" William spat the words out.

"You'll be fine, cobber."

William was sick and tired of hearing that voice. "And what the bloody hell would you know?"

He saw pyjama legs swing over the side of the cot above him. One leg with a foot hanging out the end and one without, the pyjama leg rolled up and secured with a safety pin.

William gulped. The Australian had lost a leg. He *did* know. He was worse off than William.

"I know you'll be fine, cobber, because we've got no choice. The alternative doesn't bear thinking about."

CHAPTER

5

The Australian's name was Jack. He was broad-shouldered and well-muscled. He needed to be, lifting, and lowering his body from the top cot took strength. Jack became William's daily reminder not to wallow in self-pity. There were plenty of reminders in the ward, soldiers William had fared better than. Some were wrapped up like mummies, facial skin, and hair, distant memories. A small hole where a nose should have been to breathe and another to carefully inch a straw in for sustenance. Others had no need for long pants at all.

When William finally reached a point where he no longer sought to blame someone else for his predicament, Jack took the opportunity to introduce himself. He reached out his left hand to shake William's. Unconsciously, William's right arm twitched, readying itself with the customary response. There was an awkward silence until his brain registered the absence of his right hand. He coughed in embarrassment and edged his left hand forward.

"Want to head up top for a fag, cobber?" Jack stood to the side of William's cot; a crutch hooked under his armpit.

"What I'd give for some nicotine." William could almost taste the tobacco. It wasn't just the calming effect of the drug, even the tiny glow of embers in the trenches at night was a welcome reminder he was never alone. He was one of the lads and they had memories no one at home could ever imagine.

"Well, you can't give your right hand for it, can you?" Jack's raucous laugh rang around the ward. "You ain't got one."

Jack's sense of humour demanded the smile that curved William's mouth and showed his dimple as he swung his legs over the cot railing and pulled himself up with his good hand. He grabbed his crumpled cigarette packet from his folded greatcoat and stuffed it into his shirt pocket.

"You got some matches?" he asked.

"Sure have, cobber." Jack led the way, a thump and a shuffle as his crutch and good leg headed towards the lift.

While William had been in recovery mode the *HS Manganui* had sailed out of the Suez Canal and into the Arabian Sea, making good speed towards the equator, its chimney stack billowing black smoke into an azure sky otherwise bereft of clouds. He and Jack headed towards the ship's bow where an open deck, partially covered by a canvas sail, provided a recreation area for the soldiers. The sun was directly overhead, its heat beating down, welcome but stifling at the same time.

Jack and William avoided the groups whose storytelling antics were at a volume louder than William could bear, and those who were maintaining their poker faces in a game of cards. They sidestepped others whose stretchers and wheelchairs had been wheeled outside on the basis that fresh air and sunshine was as good a medicine as any. These patients lay with their eyes closed or stared unseeingly into the distance as if urging their homeland to appear.

Eventually they found a seat close to the railing. There was no land in sight, the horizon a smudging of sky into sea in all directions. That didn't seem to worry the albatrosses gliding endlessly overhead on expansive wings. William wished he had their strength and freedom. One-handed, he managed to retrieve the cigarette packet from his pocket and remove a cigarette with his mouth but lighting it was another story. Jack must have anticipated the dilemma and leaned over with his hand cupped around a lit match.

"I might have to give up smoking." William touched the end of his cigarette to the flame and inhaled. "Or you'll have to come home to Orari with me."

"O-rare-rye? Where the hell is that?" When both cigarettes were lit, Jack blew out the match.

"O-rah-ree. South of Christchurch. South Island of New Zealand."

"Never heard of it. What's it famous for?"

William thought about his hometown, the tiny settlement where he'd lived his entire life, it wasn't famous for anything. No wonder he and his mates had wanted to sign up, go in search of adventure on the other side of the world. His eyes glazed over as movies of his 'adventure' played over in his mind. He wanted them to be black and white as if it was all being witnessed on a big screen at the cinema, but the images were smeared with blood and body parts and they surrounded him, threatened to drown him every way he turned. He shook his head and took another long drag on the cigarette.

"Beautiful women then?" Jack pulled a photograph from his pocket. A crinkled print of his wife that he kissed and rested against his chest. "You're not coming home with me. My Mrs might think you're better than me with your two legs."

William's thoughts drifted to Betsy. Would she even look at him, with his injuries? He pictured her dark brown eyes; remembered how they revealed her emotions, the anger, the jealousy. He'd be devastated if all he saw was pity. He could welcome her kindness and her caring but pity, never pity. None of the soldiers wanted that.

"So, you do have a lady waiting for you?" Jack interrupted William's thought with an elbow nudge and a wink.

"No. No, I don't. She's not mine, never was and probably never will be now. She deserves better."

"I think you'd best let her be the judge of that, cobber."

The *HS Manganui* was well-stocked with medical supplies and William's bandages were due to be changed. The moment had arrived. Confirmation there was no longer a hand where his brain kept telling him there was. He turned away while the nurse removed the bandage and took a deep breath, bracing himself for the ugliness of his new reality.

When he dared to look, there were no scars or bruising on his upper arm, his shoulder and elbow moved as they were supposed to. Everything appeared normal until it didn't. Four inches from his elbow, it all stopped, ceased to exist. There was irony in his predicament. They'd saved his skin, moulded it to form a smooth curve, stitched it to the other side. Aside from the redness and the stitches, it was almost graceful. If they could save his skin, why the hell couldn't they have saved his hand?

"That's coming along good," the doctor observed. "Clean it, nurse, and rebandage please. We should be able to take the stitches out in a day or two."

Self-pity threatened to drown William; like a tidal wave thundering towards the shore. Taking the stitches out wasn't going to improve its usefulness. *His usefulness.* He couldn't write. He couldn't even light a cigarette. He wouldn't be able to milk cows. He wouldn't be able to drive a tractor. The list was growing, like a tower threatening to topple him. Perhaps he should end it all now. Take himself topside, go beyond the safety railing and throw himself to the mercy of the ocean.

"I don't think we need to redress the head wound, nurse." The bright light the doctor shone into William's right eye was like a lighthouse drawing him away from a death at sea. "Perhaps get Private McKnight an eyepatch. We'll protect the eye from any irritants, but I think we may have seen all the improvement we are going to."

What? Was he trying to be funny? William wasn't worried about what they could see. It was his sight that needed to return. They should be concerned about what he could or couldn't see. His mouth went dry, holding the lump of denial forming in his throat, from being voiced out loud. What did this doctor know? He was just a doctor on a ship. William would make an appointment with a real doctor back in Christchurch. He didn't want to look like or be thought of as a pirate for the rest of his life.

"I'll check it out for myself," William mumbled as he made his way to the toilets after the medical team moved over to the next soldier needing their attention.

But the same mirror, he'd looked into on his first day aboard, had no more good news for him now than it did then. He welcomed the white of his left eye clear of burst blood vessels, but his right eye had too much whiteness, a film clouded his pupil. It was as if it was the eye of a storm, a swirling eddy where nothing was visible. A jagged scar ran down his forehead, dissecting his eyebrow and crossing his cheek like a flash of lightning. William stared into the mirror as if widening his eyes would make a difference. To his despair, it didn't.

His hair no longer sat in the short spikes of the requisite army cut. Perhaps he should let it grow, hide his injuries under a fringe, conceal the ugliness. If his right eye couldn't see, then it didn't need to be seen. Dejected, William returned to his cot.

"They'll be stopping in port soon to refuel." Jack was lying on his stomach, pen in hand. "Have you got any letters you want posting?"

"You think you're a bloody comedian, don't you?" William scowled at Jack.

"What?" Jack shook his head. "What's your problem, cobber?"

"How the hell am I supposed to write a letter home?" William waved his stump. "I'm bloody right-handed. Or I was."

Jack sat up. "Sorry, cobber. I wasn't thinking. Would you like me to pen something for you?"

"Sure," William scoffed. "Tell them their hero is coming home. Well, most of him."

"I'm certain you'll still be a hero in their eyes. They won't know what we've been through. You think on it. I'll just finish my letter to my wife and then I'll write yours."

The letters were written, the envelopes sealed and dropped to the ship's office on the way up for a cigarette. A cigarette that William drew long and hard on.

The hot temperatures continued and several days later meshed with the rough seas of a tropical storm. Rain lashed the ship, and everyone was confined to their cots. It was stifling inside; sleep was impossible, and perspiration ran off William almost as much as the rain ran down the porthole windows.

He soon discovered the reason for the steel railings around each cot; they were essential to ensure you weren't tossed onto the floor. Angry the ordeal was worsened by his missing hand, William struggled to brace himself. The rolling motion of the ship churned his stomach and he battled to hold down what little food he'd been able to eat.

It wasn't safe for the nurses to make their rounds. Everyone hunkered down. The soldier adjacent to William vomited through his bed and was left to lie in the stench. Determined not to do the same, William turned away and covered his face with his sleeve, filtering the air. He almost wished he was back in the trenches.

Tempers frayed; the acrid smell of vomit ran the length of the ward. Throughout the night men cried out in agony, fear, or rage. They swore and cursed; their howls echoed the winds whipping about the ship's hull. The ward was plunged into darkness until lightning flashed across the sky.

William must have drifted off at some point. He awoke with a start to hear Jack screaming a woman's name. "Maria! Maria!"

It must be his wife. Did Jack think we were going to sink? Drown in the middle of the ocean, never to be found again?

"Jack." It was William's turn to comfort his new friend. "It's alright, Jack. It's only a storm. We'll be through it soon."

William silently prayed for this to be true.

Jack had his hair slicked back, his teeth cleaned, and his kit bag packed long before the lighthouse at Fort Queenscliff signalled the entrance to Port Phillip Bay. It would be the first-time soldiers were allowed to disembark since they'd left Egypt and the excitement was palpable. Every able-bodied man wanted to be topside to witness the crowds greeting them. It didn't matter it wasn't their family. It didn't matter the New Zealanders still had another leg of the journey to go.

"Here you are, cobber." Jack handed William a folded piece of paper.

"What's that?"

"It's my address. Either you'll find a lovely lady who'll write your letters for you, or you'll learn to write left-handed but either way I'd like to hear from you."

William nodded. He was going to miss this annoying Australian who was right more times than William wanted to admit. He leaned in, wrapped his good arm around Jack and slapped him on the back.

"Thanks, cobber, thanks for everything." William mimicked Jack. "I should give you my address too."

Jack laughed. "I've already got it. I wrote it down when I addressed your letter home."

They made their way to the railing and scanned the crowd assembled on the docks. Streamers flew, hankies were waved in the air, squeals of joy and so many names called out that they all blended into one. A military band, its brass instruments glinting in the sunshine, played war tunes to add to the occasion.

"There she is." Jack pointed and yelled excitedly. "There's my Maria."

William couldn't tell which one of the thousands of faces belonged to Maria, but he could see Jack's emotion, relief, joy, and happiness formed the widest of grins. He wanted to share in that joy. He wanted to believe someone would be as excited to see him, but he knew that wasn't true. Partly because he'd requested only his father collect him and partly because he was painfully aware Betsy was still Roland's fiancé.

William was determined to make the most of the last leg of the journey. There weren't many fine days and he spent most of his time sitting on his cot with a pencil and paper a nurse had found for him. He gritted his teeth with concentration as he attempted to form legible letters with his left hand. The awkward shapes were like sloppy new soldiers unable to stand in a line. Lines refused to flow into graceful circles, instead diverging at angles or disappearing off the page altogether.

The *HS Manganui* made good time from Australia back to New Zealand and arrived in Wellington on a cold wintry day. Despite the pelting rain and a typical cold southerly that bent the trees to forty-five degrees, the enthusiasm of the crowd gathered on the wharf to meet the ship could not be dampened.

Standing topside, kitted out in his greatcoat, William waved, not because he knew someone would be waving to him but because he was caught up in the moment. Tears pricked at the corners of his eyes. His chest tightened and his throat ached as he tried to stifle his feelings but no-one could be immune to the emotion of those on the ship and those ashore. Finally, they were home.

The gangplank was lowered, a bridge between the past and the future. It shook as William walked its length and stepped back onto New Zealand soil.

How long had it been? He couldn't say exactly. It felt like a lifetime, but it was only a matter of months. He made his way through the crowd. His instructions were to head to the awaiting bus which would transport those not leaving the docks with loved ones to the Wellington hospital. He sucked his breath in through clenched teeth, he yearned to be one of the many men being embraced by a tearful woman, to be kissed with passion, love, and desperation, to have a taste, if only for a split second, that nothing had changed. Others were met by parents, tears of relief and joy pouring down their faces; he imagined his mother's reaction would be the same but hoped his father would come alone to collect him, as he'd requested. He was relying on his father to be staunch. He knew he would have the strength to conceal any pity. Dad's eyes would never reveal what he really thought. It was a trait William was going to have to master.

On the bus William stowed his kitbag on the overhead rack and slumped down into an aisle seat. He'd seen the soldier next to him on the ship but not had the opportunity to talk. Before the war, he would have reached out to shake his hand. Not now.

He soon discovered they were like a matching pair; salt and pepper shakers, useless one without the other. Roger was his name and he still had to make it to Dunedin before he could say he was home. It was his left arm that was missing, amputated below the elbow and that might have been mildly better than William's predicament, had Roger not been left-handed. They laughed at this revelation, deep belly laughs that echoed around the bus.

CHAPTER

6

News of a ship being sunk by German laid mines had Nel beside herself.

"What if it is William's ship? What if he gets all the way back to New Zealand only to be killed in our own waters? We should be safe here, Duncan. We should be safe."

Duncan rustled the newspaper and read on in search of details that might placate his wife. What else could he or anyone do?

"William is sailing to Wellington, not Auckland," he replied. "This ship has sunk in the Hauraki Gulf."

"They might have stopped off in Auckland for supplies." Nel's knitting needles were flying at a faster pace than usual, their click-clacking like a runaway train.

"This ship is called the *RMS Niagara*. It's a cruise liner."

Betsy let go the breath she'd been holding. She wasn't as panicked as Nel. She thought the *HS Manganui's* voyage from Crete to New Zealand waters would take longer but …

"What's a cruise liner doing here?" Nel continued her quest for information. "Don't they know there's a war on?"

"Carrying gold bars apparently, eight and a half tons of them." Duncan sounded intrigued by the gold cargo, now a sunken treasure. "I think that's how the Germans have managed to get so close; they just look like normal ships, freighters and cruise liners."

Staring at the back of the newspaper, Betsy's vision blurred. There was so much information in the *Temuka Leader*, yet the answer to the only question that plagued her thoughts remained aloof.

"I've got some things to do." She swallowed the last of her tea and left the kitchen.

In the privacy of her room, Betsy decided she had her own letters to write. She needed answers. It wasn't good enough Roland was simply 'missing in action', someone must know where he went missing and she intended to find out.

She tucked an errant strand of hair behind her ear and sat on the bed with pen and paper. Both quivered in her trembling hand. Did she really want to know where Roland was? What if knowledge only brought more grief? She owed it to her childhood friend, to ensure his memory, if that was all it was, could be preserved with all the detail. A laugh, etched with sarcasm, escaped when she wrote the date: the fourth of July, Independence Day. Independence. Freedom. If only Roland and all the other soldiers could be independent and free, home with their families, safe and well.

Dear Sir

Could you please give me any information concerning:

Roland Thomas Flavell, Pvte, A Company, 26th Battalion, 6th Brigade, 2nd Division NZEF.

Son of Thomas and Dell Flavell; listed as missing in action May 1940.

Yours sincerely, Betsy Nolan

Finding any information felt like looking for a needle in a haystack but Betsy had to try. She addressed an envelope to the army headquarters at Burnham Camp, hoping someone there would send it on to wherever it needed to be to find an answer.

Next, she penned a letter to Roland's parents, politely checking on their health before asking the many questions that scrolled through her head.

She considered a note to William as well, but it appeared he would likely be home before the letter reached him. What would she say? *I hope you are well;* not when he obviously wasn't. *I'm glad you are home safe.* She was glad, but anger and jealousy also festered beneath the surface. Why was it William and not Roland? Why, not both of them? Why any stupid war at all?

Black clouds rumbled angrily across the morning sky the day Duncan was scheduled to collect William from Christchurch.

"Take an umbrella," Nel suggested. "We don't want William to get wet."

"Dear," Duncan shook his head as he paused. "I think he will have experienced far worse than a bit of rain."

"Yes, but—" Nel protested.

"Yes, but nothing, Nel. I'd better get going." Duncan pecked his wife on the cheek, took the umbrella she held out to him and turned to leave. "Betsy, you'll need to check on the heifers. There are still a couple yet to calve. Take Rosey with you in case there is any trouble."

Betsy nodded without voicing her thoughts that Rosey was trouble. She didn't have a natural affinity with animals. The herd seemed agitated and unsettled whenever she was around. Duncan didn't seem perturbed the cows were producing less milk than Betsy remembered from the end of last season. She wouldn't speak out. She was living in Duncan and Nel's house now, she didn't want to cause any disharmony. And Rosey would be gone again soon. Her three months of training would surely pass just as quickly as Betsy's had.

She put her gumboots and jacket on and trudged up to the main house.

"Rosey!" she called out. "Duncan's given us a job to do."

"Coming," Rosey replied, as she opened the back door.

She was always bright and cheerful and that only served to annoy Betsy more. Rosey didn't seem to have a care in the world. *If only,* Betsy thought.

"We'll have to walk. Duncan's taken the truck to pick up William."

"Oooh!" Rosey shook her shoulders and her breasts jiggled from side to side. "So today is the day we finally get to meet the soldier boy."

"He's not a boy," Betsy snapped before she could stop herself.

Rosey stopped and turned front on to Betsy. "Are you sure there is nothing between you two? You're mighty touchy whenever his name comes up."

Betsy inhaled deeply to calm herself. "I just meant that he is a man and not a boy and I don't imagine that there is any soldier around that wants to be called a boy after the things they've had to witness and be party to."

"Point taken. Sorry. What have we got to do this morning?"

"Duncan wants us to check on the heifers. There are still a couple yet to calve."

The heifer paddock was close enough to the cowshed to be easily accessible. It was bordered on one side by a boxthorn hedge to provide shelter for the expectant animals from the southerlies, that at this time of the year, felt as if they transported some of Antarctica with them. Betsy and Rosey found the first of the heifers sheltering in the lee of the hedge happily chewing on its cud. The other was pacing, trampling the ground to create a muddy quagmire, on the opposite side of the paddock.

"I think we'd better take a closer look at that one." Betsy pointed across the paddock.

"She looks a bit angry to me," Rosey replied. "We'd best not get too close."

"She might be calving."

"Why is she pacing then? Why doesn't she just sit down and push it out? Aren't cows just like humans?"

Betsy giggled. This must be how Duncan felt when she or the other land girls asked silly questions that revealed their lack of experience.

"Let's pretend we're the midwives," she suggested. "We're just here to check everything is going to plan."

"Well, I hope so." Rosey stopped and put her hands on her hips. "Because I haven't a clue what else we can do."

As they neared the heifer, it stopped momentarily to stare at them, the whites of its eyes, were large orbs that signalled all was not going to plan.

"It's alright, girl." Betsy spoke softly to calm the animal while she slowly moved to get a look at her rear. "You stay there, Rosey, stop her from running away. Just stand there. Don't wave your arms. We're trying to calm her, not scare her."

All Betsy needed was someone to calm her. Her stomach rolled, her breathing faltered, and she had a sour taste in her mouth. What would she do if she needed to help calve the animal? How would she even know help was required?

The cow bellowed and arched its back.

"Oh, God." Rosey jumped back. "I never want to have children if that's what you have to go through."

Betsy had seen and heard that before. The heifer was calving. The tip of a hoof emerged but disappeared as the contraction passed. It happened so fast Betsy wasn't certain she'd seen it at all. Which way was it facing, backwards or forwards? Was it just the beginning of its journey or had it been doing that for hours? Did the heifer need help, or could she manage on her own? And if she needed help, the biggest question of all, would Betsy be able to provide it? Would she be able to save both calf and cow, either or neither? The responsibility of the situation settled on her shoulders like a weightlifting bar.

Another bellow, etched with pain. The cow spread its legs. Urine and excrement oozed, and the tiny hoof reappeared, like a child's innocent hand raised in a plea for help. Betsy knew then that she had to become Duncan. She looked across at Rosey as the blood drained from her face.

"I don't feel so good." Rosey wiped her brow with her hand.

"Quick!" Betsy yelled. "Go back to the cowshed. Get a bucket with some warm water. Go to the hayshed. Get a couple of pieces of baling twine. They're hanging on a nail on the wall. Bring them back here."

Rosey shook her head, as she backed away, trying to register the instructions being fired at her. Then she made the mistake of glancing at the heifer. That was the end. Rosey slumped to the ground where she'd stood.

"Aargh! Useless woman!" Duncan's words escaped Betsy's mouth.

She was momentarily torn. Who did she tend to first? It should be Rosey, but she'd only fainted. She would be alright. The cow and calf, on the other hand, they could both die. Betsy ran as fast as her gumboots would allow back across the muddy paddock. She grabbed the baling twine and headed for the cowshed. She filled the bucket halfway with warm water otherwise it would be too heavy to carry. She chucked the baling twine into the bucket and headed back to the animal.

Rosey had come to and moved herself over to the fence for support.

"I'd help you," she offered, her words slurred and her face still ashen. "But I don't think I can."

"You'll have to." Betsy knew this to be a two-person job. "I'll do the hard bits. You just come and pull on the twine."

Betsy took her jacket off and rolled her sleeves up, so they sat in her armpits. She washed her hands in the water, grateful she thought to warm it and folded the baling twine as Duncan had taught her. She waited for the next contraction and seized the hoof that appeared. She looped the twine above the knuckle, pulled it secure and handed the loose ends to Rosey.

"Now crouch down and pull just enough to hold it secure." Betsy avoided Duncan's bluntness and didn't explain there was a risk of ripping the hoof off if she pulled too hard. "Now breathe, and stay with me, don't faint."

She said the words to herself as much as she did to Rosey. She too, was breathing, long and deep, willing herself to stay calm and deal with what came next. Another contraction. Betsy prayed for the second hoof to appear. It didn't. She was going to have to do what Duncan had done, to put her hand inside the cow. She dipped her hand in the water again, rinsed her fingers and then squished them tight together.

She closed her eyes. Told herself she could do it. Told herself it was a medical procedure, not an invasion of the most private of spaces. Reminded herself that animals might die if she didn't. The cow's long deep moo was like a foghorn announcing her arrival and Betsy used the distraction to push her hand into the soft, warm cavity that held another hoof that she grabbed hold of and pulled out into the fresh air.

"Quick! Grab the other baling twine, make a loop, and pass it here."

"How do you do this?" Rosey gulped, swallowing all that threatened to leave her stomach.

There was no answer to the question. Betsy didn't know how she did it. She just knew she had to. And now she had to do it again, to reach in and feel for a head that needed to be freed, to be able to breathe for itself.

It was as if she was blind. Her sense of touch would mean success or failure. She reached between the two legs, her elbow disappeared into the warmth, muscle and sinew closed in around her arm, mucous coated her skin with a lubricating slime as her fingers searched. Two hollows were nostrils, hard bones were teeth, a protruding tongue all painted a picture of a calf's head, facing the way it needed to enter the world.

Betsy withdrew her hand and curled her fingers either side of the vulva, stretching the tightness of this first-time mother. "When the next contraction comes, pull," she instructed Rosey.

The combined effort of two women pulling and one cow pushing freed the calf's head. Adrenaline took over from there. Without a care for her arm covered in blood and slime, Betsy did as she had seen Duncan do. She flicked the mucous away from the calf's nostrils, put her fingers into its mouth and ensured its throat was clear. Another contraction and the shoulders came free. Another contraction, the hips were pushed clear, and the calf fell to the ground. It was like a replay of the movie Betsy had watched with Duncan and she was overjoyed it had the same happy ending.

She stood back, filled with a sense of pride as the heifer turned and tended to her calf.

CHAPTER

7

After stowing his kitbag under the hospital bed assigned to him, William made his way to the nurses' station in search of a telephone. Filled with dread for the ensuing conversation, he didn't take much notice of the other soldiers occupying the beds on either side of the long, narrow ward nor did he acknowledge the attractive nurse who smiled at him.

"How can I help you, soldier?"

William wished people would stop referring to him as a soldier. He might have the uniform on, but he was no longer capable of fighting, physically or mentally.

"Can I use the telephone please?" he asked. "I need to phone home to make arrangements to be collected when I arrive."

"There's one for patient use in the alcove, through those doors and along the corridor on the left."

"Thank you."

The wooden panelled alcove had a small seat William made use of. This was another first, another simple task that became more difficult with only one hand. He wedged the handset between his left ear and shoulder, dialled the numbers with his left hand and waited, his stomach churning as he contemplated who would answer and what he would say.

It was nearing suppertime. William hoped his father would have finished work for the day. He pictured him sitting in his chair beside the fire, reading the newspaper while his mother was busy at the sink preparing the meal. Domestic scenes, plain and simple. Normally comforting but William wasn't sure how he was going to fit back into this picture after what he'd experienced.

"Hello. McKnight residence. Betsy speaking."

William gulped. "B . . . B . . . Betsy. What are you doing there?"

"I live here," Betsy replied as if the question had insulted her. "Who's speaking?"

She didn't even recognise his voice. Had he lost part of that too, or had she forgotten him already? He needed to speak to his father. He couldn't have a conversation with Betsy now. He needed to sort out his thoughts.

"Is Dad, ah, I mean Duncan there? Can I speak to Duncan please?"

The line went silent. Nothing, then murmurings he couldn't decipher.

"Son. Son. Is that you William?"

William laughed. Most of me he wanted to reply.

"Yes, it's me. I'm in Wellington."

"You're in Wellington. That's good, son. Your mother was worried you were on that ship the Germans had sunk."

"No. I'll be on the Lyttleton ferry tomorrow."

"You'll be on the Lyttleton ferry tomorrow. That's good, son."

"I'll be on the train to Orari the morning after that."

"You'll be on the train to Orari the morning after that. That's good, son."

Annoyed at his father's repetition, William opened his mouth to growl. It was his right ear that was damaged not his left.

"Dad! Why are you repeating everything I say?"

"It's your mother, son, and Betsy. They're both standing here looking at me. They think I'm hiding something from them so I'm just repeating everything you say, so they know you are alright."

William nodded until the handset started to slip. He wasn't alright and they'd find out all too soon the extent to which he never would be.

"Right, I'll see you the day after tomorrow. At the train station. Alone."

"I could come and pick you up from Christchurch if you like," Duncan offered. "Save you another night."

"No!" The reply escaped before William could temper his tone. "No, I'll catch up with some of the lads in Christchurch and be home after that."

William sought to delay the inevitable, to hide the truth from them. As if another night would change the outcome.

William guessed the young boy, sitting opposite him, to be about six or seven. His socks were pulled up, his shorts and shirt neatly pressed and the part in his hair cut a straight line as if his mother had supervised his dressing. The boy's eyes were wide, taking in the excitement of the *Rangatira* ferry, curious about everything and everyone as they sat waiting to board.

"Mummy." He tapped his mother's leg to get her attention and pointed to William. "Is that man a pirate?"

"Sssh!" Embarrassment coloured the woman's cheeks as she swatted her son's pointed finger. "It's not polite to point. No, he's not a pirate. He's a soldier."

He was a soldier, William wanted to correct her. He wasn't any use as a soldier anymore. He tried to catch her eye, but she was already looking away, looking everywhere but at William. Was her reaction merely embarrassment or was she disgusted by his appearance, the ugly scar running down his face?

"Mummy." The boy persisted. "Why isn't he away fighting like Daddy?"

"He's come home for a rest." The woman leaned over to whisper her reply, but William still heard.

Rest was probably all he would be good for. He tried, each night when sleep eluded him, to figure what came next when you only had one hand. He hadn't come up with any answers.

"Mummy, why does he only have one hand?"

"Johnny. Be quiet." The woman stood and grabbed her son's hand, forcing him to stand. "Quickly. We're boarding now."

They were gone. William didn't have to feel her pity, watch her eyes look away.

A foghorn announced the boarding call. William gathered his things and followed the passengers making their way to the gangplank. There was no fanfare as there had been with the *HS Manganui's* arrival in Wellington. Nobody to farewell the soldiers taking this next leg of their journey home. This was an ordinary passenger ferry making its daily trip from Wellington to Lyttleton, albeit during the day in war times, rather than the usual overnight service, as it was deemed safer when foreign raiders and submarines were lurking in New Zealand waters.

At the top of the gangplank, a steward waited to greet William and usher him to his cabin.

"Good morning, sir." The steward saluted William before taking his ticket. "Welcome aboard the *Rangatira*."

William's automatic reaction was to return the salute, it was what soldiers did. He straightened his back, stood to attention, and raised his right arm.

"Fuck!"

He couldn't even salute. He couldn't return the sign of respect shown to him. He had no right fingers and thumb to straighten, no palm to face down and position to the right of his eye. Hell, he had no seeing right eye. What was he if he couldn't salute? Why was he even still in this uniform?

"Follow me, if you will, Private McKnight." The steward continued unperturbed by William's outburst. "We've reserved first class cabins for returned soldiers. The least we could do with everything you've sacrificed."

Sacrifice. William felt like he'd been sacrificed, an animal sent to slaughter. Bloody battle scenes, strewn dismembered body parts. He shook his head to dislodge the images.

The steward opened the cabin door and stood aside to allow William to enter. The single-berth cabin, was more luxurious than William had ever seen before. A space to himself. A space where he could be alone with his thoughts. The very thoughts he'd been trying hard to avoid.

"There is hot and cold running water if you wish to freshen up before joining the other passengers." The steward must have seen William's involuntary flinch, the boy and his mother had been enough of the other passengers for William and offered an alternative. "Or if you'd like to remain in your cabin and read, there is a reading lamp here above the bed."

William had never had much time for reading before the war and even less inclination now. His head throbbed with the concentration of focusing his single eye. The black and white images were blurred and no longer sat in organised lines on the page. He shook his head.

"On this deck, we have a Dining Saloon if you are feeling hungry and a Smoke Room with a bar." The steward glanced at his watch. "Both should be open within fifteen minutes. It's Thursday today so there will be poached eggs on toast for breakfast and roast beef and vegetables with gravy for lunch."

"Thank you." William read the steward's name badge. "Thank you, Sidney. It's much more than I expected, than I deserve."

"You soldiers, you deserve everything. Please call on me if there is anything I can do to make your journey home more pleasant. With this morning's fog it will be a slower trip, but you should be ashore in Lyttleton before dinner."

"That would be good." The words flowed as polite conversation was meant to, but William wasn't sure he meant them. Every leg of the journey took him closer to home and closer to the inevitable reunion with those he knew before.

"I hope so too," Sidney continued. "My wife is overdue to have our first child. She's fretting that it will all happen while I'm not there."

William was too absorbed in his own problems to show the steward any concern.

"I think I need a fag," he said. "Which way to the smoke room?"

William found a spot in the corner of the mahogany-panelled smoke room. It was a table for four, but his scowl ensured no one joined him except the barman who delivered his drink and lit his cigarette. He drew deeply on the cigarette staining the fingers of his left hand a dirty, telltale mustard. A malevolent laugh escaped with the realisation at least he'd got rid of the stains on his right-hand fingers.

He hadn't messed around with a beer; he'd gone straight to the top shelf. A crystal glass sat on the table, the third to be filled with a fine scotch whisky that burned William's throat each time he threw a swig back. It reminded him he was alive.

There was another group of soldiers gathered on the opposite side of the smoke room. William observed their banter and laughter from a distance, at times wishing he was part of it, remembering the camaraderie of his platoon. The brotherhood born of a shared experience. But he stayed in his corner, clung to his melancholy mood as if it was all he deserved.

He only moved from the space when an announcement broadcast lunch was being served and like a sheep being herded, he followed the lines of passengers to the dining saloon. There was no avoiding people here; the saloon was a bustle of activity, passengers hurrying to find a seat, chefs carving meat, stewards eager to serve. The clanging of cutlery, the clinking of plates accompanied the medley of conversations filling the saloon with noise.

"Let me cut that for you, sir." It was Sidney. He placed William's meal in front of him and leaned in to carve the meat as if it was a service he offered to every passenger.

William couldn't be angry. He felt like a child but when he glanced around the table, no one was watching. No one had witnessed Sidney's act of kindness but him.

"Thank you, Sidney. Thank you."

William was deep in his cups by the time the *Rangatira* had entered Pegasus Bay. On the starboard side, Christchurch peeked through breaches in the stubborn fog. The need to urinate had him stumbling down the corridor when the ship shuddered. A deafening boom, a scraping of metal on metal was followed by a sudden lurch that threw William off balance.

"What the hell was that?" He rubbed his head as he struggled back to his feet.

The ferry's siren blasted out its warning, followed by a call for passengers to move calmly and orderly to the top deck. The instruction was met with anything but calm and order. Passengers screamed and rushed past William.

"We've been hit."

"The Germans have got us."

"We're going to sink."

"Quick! To the lifeboats."

"Oh God, not the Titanic again. We're going to die."

In his inebriated state, William was incapable of sharing their panic. He waited until the corridor cleared. He felt the need for another cigarette but without the barman to light it for him had to abandon the idea.

"Private McKnight." Sidney tucked a guiding hand under William's elbow. "We need to get topside."

"What's happened? Have we been hit?" William slurred.

"Word is it's a torpedo, sir. Just nicked the bow. Nothing to worry about. We've been fitted out with a gun at the stern. We'll fire if required."

"The bloody Germans. Do I have to fight them here too?"

"Maybe not the Germans. Apparently, the Japanese are here."

William's foggy brain couldn't comprehend the Japanese presence in New Zealand. Were they trying to take over the Pacific while the rest of the world was distracted in Europe?

The lifts were out of action. They made their way into the stairwell. There was already a throng of panicked passengers clambering up the stairs, footfalls echoing on the steel steps. Sidney pushed William into their midst, and he had no option but to move with the group up two flights of stairs until they burst out onto the deck.

"Remain calm." The instruction booming out through speakers fell on deaf ears. "Follow the directions of your crew and lifejackets will be distributed."

Men rushed to get lifejackets for their wives, mothers grabbed them for their children. When it seemed the supply was exhausted, people snatched them from each other. William imagined the enemy laughing at the mayhem they had caused.

"The lifeboats. Where are the lifeboats?" A panicked passenger cried out.

Five white boats were suspended overhead on either side of the ship. Visible but out of reach, like a carrot being dangled, but what was required to be done to reach the reward remained elusive.

"There won't be enough for all of us." The man who made this comment looked at William as if to say he should stay behind, he wasn't worth saving.

William headed to the railing and scanned the ocean for the submarine. If the enemy were waiting to attack again, to finish them off, he wanted to know. Fog shrouded the ferry, holding tight to the disadvantage that had allowed the enemy to make their attack.

"Come away from the side, Private." It was Sidney, directing William as he placed a life jacket over his head and fastened the strap around his middle.

"Where are those bloody Huns? I went to the other side of the world to fight them. They're not supposed to bring the war here. How dare they?"

"I imagine they'll be long gone. Word is there is no damage. We're not taking on water, but they don't want the attackers to know that."

The ship started to move, inching its way through the fog as the engines cranked back into action. They were safe, they would be back on dry land soon. There was a collective sigh of relief. William's shoulders relaxed. Voices were lowered to murmurs, bewildered looks turned to smiles. But the ferry didn't head towards Lyttleton port, instead its bow pointed southeast and followed the coastline.

William made a beeline for Sidney who was now ushering passengers back inside.

"Where are we going?" he demanded.

"Pigeon Bay," Sidney replied as if it was the most natural thing to do.

"How long for?"

"Not long I hope, or my wife will have our first child without me."

"Oh, yeah, right, sorry." It dawned on William that other people had problems too. That he couldn't always focus on himself.

Life on the ferry continued as if nothing had happened, except once anchored in Pigeon Bay that was where it stayed, shrouded in fog, hidden from any enemy that still lurked in the Pacific Ocean. William spent most of the time in his cabin where he'd discarded the eyepatch that felt too tight around his throbbing head. The alcohol may have seemed a good idea at the time, but its after-effects weren't any better than the reality he sought to escape through imbibing it.

Sidney arrived at lunchtime. He didn't wait for his knock on the cabin door to be acknowledged. "Thought you might like today's offering," he announced placing a tray on the small table beside the bed and lifting a lid to reveal a plate of roast beef covered in a generous serving of gravy and accompanied by potatoes, pumpkin, and carrots.

"Thank you," William replied, grateful for the meal and Sidney's nonchalance towards his disfigurement. It was the first time anyone non-medical had seen him without an eyepatch. "Any news from your wife?"

Sidney's face lit up. "Not from her directly but my mother-in-law has sent a message through that my baby girl was born this afternoon, all six-pound of her."

"Congratulations!" William couldn't help but share the man's joy. He doubted it was something he would ever get to experience, now. "Does she have a name?"

"My wife wants to name her Joan, after Joan of Arc. A little battler with a mighty strength."

If a little baby could battle on, so could William.

"Let's hope we get home soon then."

"Yes, son, yes." Sidney left to continue with his duties, but his air of excitement and anticipation lingered in the cabin buoying William's mood.

And Sidney had called him son. He might no longer be a soldier, but he would always be a son. He pictured his own father but all he could see was his frustration at the waste of precious rationed fuel when he'd driven needlessly to collect William from a train he wasn't on.

Late the following day the *Rangitira* resumed its journey into Lyttleton port as if the preceding twenty-four hours never happened. The fog had lifted. Passengers, including William stood on the deck in the sunshine, their eyes scanning the water alert to dark shadows beneath the surface. William stood towards the stern of the ship, he was ready to yell the alarm and man the gun if needed. No enemy submarine was going to escape while he was on watch.

It was a pod of dolphins that accompanied the ferry past Adderley Head and into the harbour, surfing the swell, fins and snouts rising out of the water as if they too were on the lookout for unfriendly submarines.

CHAPTER

8

Everyone at *Whipsnade Farm* was on edge. Yesterday Duncan returned from the Orari train station alone. No words were needed, his downcast face and his glassy eyes communicated the despair everyone felt. There were a million questions and no answers that bore thinking about.

He was pacing about the cowshed this morning, impatient to collect the last of the milk cans for delivery to the dairy factory so he could be in time for this morning's train, certain it was all just a mix-up over days.

The cows must have sensed the tension and were as agitated. Normally quiet animals were bellowing, cows usually eager to be milked and relieved of the weight of full udders clung to the yard rails reluctant to enter the shed.

"Come on, girl," Betsy encouraged another cow into the bale. She tried to pretend she was calm, but her stomach churned. Fear, worry, anticipation, and anxiety, like components of a science experiment, festered and reacted in an explosive combination. Betsy remembered from her first day at *Whipsnade Farm,* this was when accidents happened. She carefully hooked a rope around the cow's back leg and tied it off against the post, ensuring no kick would be coming her way.

Rosey was out in the yard, giving a cow a hurry-up-whack on the rump. Betsy wanted to complain, to tell Rosey she'd get better results by being kind and assertive with the animal but with Duncan about, she assumed any berating would see her cast as the villain, so she stayed silent and concentrated on the cow in front of her, wrapping her fingers around the teats and repeating the squeeze and pull motion to encourage the milk flow.

She attached the cups and sat back on the small wooden stool, allowing the rhythm of the milking machine to lull her into a much-needed sense of security. She took comfort from the regular even pulse and willed her heart to do the same. Betsy wished waiting for news from overseas was this easy, that letters from soldiers arrived with such regularity, and like the fresh milk filling the cans the news was always good. Just how long it took until the cow's udders were empty was as unknown as how long it would take until the war office replied to Betsy's inquiry as to Roland's whereabouts but where milking passed in minutes, news from the war seemed to take months.

A high-pitched scream echoed off the rafters. Betsy jumped up and almost screamed herself when she saw Rosey. Fresh, runny excrement coated Rosey's hair and face. Her eyes blinked frantically from behind a mask of dirty green. She looked like a monster from the bottom of a loch; not that

Betsy nor anyone else could testify for certain what a loch ness monster looked like.

"Get it off me! Get it off me!" Rosey yelled as the excrement ran down her front, her ample bosom acting as a catchment area.

Betsy grabbed the hose. "Quick, come here and I'll hose you off."

Rosey screamed again. "That's freezing."

"Yes, but it's clean. Lean forward." Betsy aimed the jet of water at the top of Rosey's head. Gradually the excrement washed away until a faint hue remained.

"Bloody cow." Rosey shook her fist at the cow waiting in the bale.

"It's not the cow's fault." Betsy turned the hose tap off.

"Well, it's not my fault. I didn't poo everywhere."

"Yes." Thank goodness for that, thought Betsy. "But why did you have your head behind the cow's rear end."

"I was hooking up the chain so the silly thing wouldn't back out of the bale." Rosey scowled at Betsy. "Like you told me to."

Riled, Betsy planted her hands on her hips. "Don't blame me. It should be obvious to anyone with half a brain that you don't put your head beside a cow's behind."

Duncan coughed and stepped forward. "Now, now, ladies. I'll just go and check on Peggy and Jean, make sure they are getting on alright. You will be okay to finish up here, won't you."

There was no questioning tone to Duncan's words. They were a command but not one he stayed to ensure was followed.

"I can't keep milking like this." Rosey looked down at her saturated overalls. "I'll catch a chill. I'll go and get changed and you finish up."

Rosey was gone before Betsy had a chance to protest. "Humph! The cows and I are better off without you anyway."

Betsy had milked the cows before on her own and she quickly settled back into the routine, moving between the bales, setting the next cow up while the other one milked and remembering to check the milk cans and move the pipe and the gauze before the milk overflowed. She had six full milk cans lined up by the time the last of the cows left the yard and Duncan returned.

"You've finished. That's good." Duncan looked around the cowshed as if searching for Rosey but said nothing about her absence. He glanced at his watch. "I'll go get the truck and load up the cans. I still should be able to get to the dairy factory before I need to meet the train."

"Did you want me to come with you?" The question escaped Betsy before she had time to consider the consequences of a positive response. Did she really want to bring forward a reunion with William? Had she even had time to consider her feelings towards the man she hardly knew? An uncontrollable warmth deep inside reminded her of what she did know; William stirred in her feelings that no other man had ever done, not even her fiancé Roland.

"No." Duncan shifted uncomfortably.

"Are you going to take one of the land girls with you?" A tiny green monster whispered in Betsy's ear that the answer better be no, but she countered her jealousy and tried to appear nonchalant. "Show them where the dairy factory is and teach them to drive the truck like you did with Grace."

"No, not this time. Maybe tomorrow. I'll get Jean to shut the cows into their paddock. You hose down here and head home for breakfast."

Normally breakfast would have been a steaming plate of porridge. Not yesterday and not today. Nel had bacon and eggs frying in a cast iron fry pan. The delicious aroma greeted Betsy as she scrubbed her hands with soap and water in the washhouse tub. She'd learned Nel liked to celebrate special occasions with food. A mutton roast when the land girls arrived and to farewell William off to war and now bacon and eggs to welcome him home. Betsy hoped Duncan wouldn't return from the train station alone today.

"Nel, do I have time to check the letterbox before breakfast?"

"Yes, dear. I heard the mailman toot so I'm sure there'll be something today. Everything good is arriving today."

Betsy wanted to share Nel's optimism and headed down the driveway imagining the contents of the letterbox. She pictured the envelopes, their colour depicting the news, darkening with the severity of the contents. An innocent white envelope, oblivious to the war would likely bring news from home. A blue aerogram would deliver news from abroad, with the censored bits removed, blackened out like little blots on the landscape. At least Betsy would know the person who'd penned the words was still alive. It was the brown envelope that was to be feared. The officials probably chose brown to denote the seriousness of their communication. It was not a colour that conjured anything frivolous. It was not a rich brown, the delicious colour of chocolate but a dusty brown, not unlike the desert sand where

Roland may have been wounded, fatally or otherwise. Sometimes, in sleepless midnight hours Betsy almost came to terms with the fact he might be dead. At least that would bring certainty, allow her to move on with whatever life had in store for her.

The letterbox's metal door no longer squeaked. Betsy had opened it nearly every day since she'd been at *Whipsnade*, except for Sundays, even that day was sacrosanct for postal delivery, and winter days when the weather had been so foul, she only ventured from the house to do essential farming tasks. She faced skyward and closed her eyes, whispering a hushed please before reaching her hand inside. On top of the folded newspaper were two envelopes – one white and one brown. Betsy's heart skipped a beat. Both envelopes were addressed to her and that created a dilemma all its own. Which should she open first?

Countering her earlier thoughts, a postage stamp depicting the Egyptian pyramids adorned the white envelope. The handwriting was delicate, she assumed a woman's, maybe a nurse writing on Roland's behalf. Betsy flipped the envelope over and hooked her fingernail under the sealed flap. She snatched the letter from the envelope as quick as her trembling fingers would allow, unfolded the single sheet of paper, and devoured its contents.

She was right, white envelopes seemed oblivious to the war. It was a letter from her sister Irene, now stationed in Cairo as a Tui, socialising with soldiers, running errands, enjoying the sunshine, visiting the pyramids on days off. There was no news of Roland, no recognition anyone was in danger, just her sister appearing to be having a jolly good time.

Anger bristled Betsy's spine. War wasn't meant to be fun. War was hard work. She stomped her way back up the driveway. Betsy reached the house as Duncan pulled up in the truck. She stopped. Turned. And stared like a possum caught in headlights. William sat in the passenger seat.

Their eyes locked. It was the same as before, she couldn't tell what he was thinking. Except it was different, there was only one eye looking back at her. The other was covered by a patch – a black blotch as if the visions this eye had witnessed needed to be censored.

Momentarily stunned, Betsy stood rooted to the spot. She shook her head, needing her brain to tell her what to do next, how to react. She was still angry from her sister's letter, but she didn't want William to think she was angry at him. She stuffed both letters into her pocket, the contents of the brown envelope would have to wait until later. She raised her eyebrows, clearing the frown that furrowed her forehead and curved her lips into a smile. She didn't feel like smiling but she felt William deserved a cheerful greeting. She hoped he would think it was genuine.

She moved to open the passenger door but wrenched her hand back as if the door handle scorched her fingers. William's surly look told her no help was required nor wanted. Perhaps it was just his eyesight had been damaged. She stood back, watched, and waited as he climbed out from the vehicle. It felt like she was doing a mental inventory of his body parts: two feet, two legs, two arms, two … one hand. Betsy gasped and then clamped her mouth shut. William was missing a hand. Right? Left? No, right. Did it matter? Had William seen her reaction? She tried to fabricate another smile. She wanted to pretend everything was alright, even if it wasn't.

"Hello William, welcome home," she said as if he'd been away on holiday.

Betsy thought a holiday was the very thing he needed. He looked as if he'd aged ten years, but he hadn't been gone ten months. It was like the army had run out of uniforms of the correct size and William was having to make do with one that seemed two sizes too big. It hung loosely from his square shoulders, the bottom of one sleeve folded up and held with a safety pin. Even that sat askew as if all the military precision had been left on the battlefield with William's hand.

"Hello Betsy," he replied.

His voice sounded older, all his boyish humour erased to be replaced with a seriousness, a maturity that far exceeded his physical years. It was his eye that made her own want to tear up. There was no sparkle, no sign it would light up when he was teasing her. It was framed by darkness, not just the tan from the desert sun but a black shadow behind which terror lurked.

Betsy had to turn away. "Can I carry your bag for you?" she offered.

"No!"

The reply was swift, forceful, and filled with anger. Betsy flinched.

"I can do it myself." William slammed the door shut and wrenched his kit bag from the tray of the truck.

The message to not offer William any help was received loud and clear. Betsy looked across at Duncan who shrugged his shoulders and silently nodded. All three headed for the house. Betsy hoped William wouldn't be so abrupt with his mother.

Nel met them in the washhouse, her arms wide and welcoming. She didn't take no for an answer, she didn't even ask if William wanted a motherly hug. Nel wrapped her arms around her son, rested her face on his chest and breathed him in as her tears fell freely and silently.

"You're home. I'm so happy you're home, son."

In the end, it was Duncan's cough that hastened Nel to release William.

"Come in, come in." She stood aside, wiped her eyes on her apron and ushered them through. "I've got bacon and eggs for breakfast. You must be hungry after your journey. Come and meet our new land girls."

Rosey, Peggy, and Jean were already seated at the table tucking into their breakfast.

"Well, hello Billy," Rosey stood and beamed at William.

Betsy wanted to protest that his name was William not Billy, that Rosey had no right to be so familiar with him but the look on William's face said otherwise. Rosey got the smile Betsy had wanted.

"Sit down. Sit down," Nel urged. "Before it gets cold."

"Here, Billy, you sit here at the end of the table and us girls will squeeze up on the side." Rosey moved her plate and cutlery and nudged Peggy and Jean over.

Betsy sat in her usual spot next to Nel which meant she was opposite Rosey. She wanted to kick her under the table but restrained herself. Rosey filled William's plate, a slice of toast, several rashers of bacon and two eggs. Betsy waited, anticipated the fiery response that would surely come from William, the rejection of the help he needed but didn't want.

She felt her own rage boil when William simply picked up his fork and began eating, using the fork as a knife when required.

Fuming, Betsy clamped her mouth shut. If that was how William felt, at least she knew from the outset. He no longer had any feelings for her nor any need for her in his life. She was engaged to Roland, so it was better this way.

"We thought you'd been bombed by the Germans, William," Nel said.

"Bombed, torpedoed, shot at. That's what happens when there is a war going on." William's voice sounded world-weary and cynical.

"Your mother meant in New Zealand waters, son," Duncan added as if to shield Nel. "The newspapers have reported German submarines in the Pacific."

"It was a Japanese one that nearly scuttled the *Rangatira*. That's why we were delayed."

Nel gasped.

"I told you, Nel." Duncan patted his wife on the hand. "It's when, not if. We'll be fine, we've got those supplies stashed at the back of the farm. We can hunker down and now we've got our own soldier home to help protect us."

William scoffed. "I'll be discharged on medical grounds."

"Speaking of medical," Rosey interrupted the conversation, scratching at some spots on her hand. "I think there is something wrong with me. I've got these itchy spots."

William glanced at Rosey and then looked down at his amputation. His lips curved into a sneer as if he was comparing the seriousness of the two injuries.

"Have you been bitten by a sandfly?" Nel asked.

"Well, they're everywhere, the spots I mean, my arms, by body, they're even coming up on my face."

"Looks like you've been in the dugout with the boys." William laughed but Betsy thought it was a laugh laced with sarcasm, not joy. "Fleas. Fleas for Africa. Hell, probably fleas from Africa, blown all the way into Egypt in a dust storm."

Betsy swallowed quickly before the image of William's words prevented her from doing so. She glanced over at Rosey and noted the red splotches peppering her face. Glee that Rosey wasn't looking so desirable, now combined with guilt that Betsy could even have such thoughts, to colour Betsy's own cheeks.

"Perhaps you're allergic to something," Nel suggested.

"This has never happened before." Rosey abandoned eating, fidgeted, scratched her arms, and rubbed her face.

"What have you been in contact with that you haven't been before?"

William. She's allergic to William. Betsy wanted to say but didn't. He laughed malevolently as if he was thinking the same thoughts.

"Cow shit," Rosey replied. "The blasted cow covered me from head to toe this morning."

"It wouldn't be good for a land girl to be allergic to cows," the usually quiet Jean joined the conversation.

"Well, I've got a tin of Rawleigh's salve in the bathroom cupboard," Nel said. "We'll see if that helps and if you're no better in twenty-four hours then we could call Doctor Green."

"That would be good," Rosey replied. "Thank you."

"Maybe William, you would like the doctor to look at your injuries as well," Nel added.

William raised what was left of his right arm. "I don't think Doctor Green looking at this is going to fix it up like new."

Nel winced. "I … I … I just meant …"

Duncan cleared his throat. "Your mother meant that the doctor could check that your wound was healing as it should. There is no need to be rude to her."

William resumed eating with no acknowledgment of the hurt he had caused his mother. Betsy felt for Nel. It appeared William's homecoming was going to be more of a challenge than a comfort.

CHAPTER

9

The birds chirped their morning chorus as they had done before William signed up for the adventure of his lifetime. At least their cheerful sound signalled the end of the nightmares that plagued what little sleep he'd had. He was finally back in his comfortable bed, but it offered nothing other than further confirmation his life would never be the same.

William could hear noises from the room next door where Betsy was also stirring. She was as he'd remembered her. Beautiful. A pity he was no longer as she would have remembered him. He'd seen the look she'd given him, knew she'd tried to hide her disgust with a smile, but he was wiser now, he'd seen through it.

He assumed she'd be getting up to milk the cows. There was no point offering to help. What use was a one-armed farmer? He was no use for anything. He might lay in bed all day, keep the curtains drawn, keep the questions he didn't want to answer at bay and avoid the looks of pity and disgust. William's mouth twisted into a sour expression. What would that achieve? Nothing. Was all his effort for nothing? He couldn't let it be. He'd fought for King and country. He'd travelled to the other side of the world, lived in dugouts, eaten food that was barely edible, watched his mates die; that could never be for nothing. He owed it to their memory. He was one of the lucky ones. There would be others, men who knew what he'd been through, men he could share memories of the happy times with, men he could sit with in silence because no words were necessary or available to describe the horrors. That could be William's reason for getting out of bed, to find the other soldiers who'd come home. He knew Brian McPherson had to be one of them, there would be others, but he'd start with Brian.

Voices in the kitchen drew his attention, they were hushed murmurs, his father and Betsy, but he couldn't make out the words. Were they talking about him? Probably. He imagined more words of pity or perhaps they were angry with him, he had been a little rude. He'd have to try and be more polite with Mum, she was after all only doing what she'd done all her life, mothering him. She needed to realise though, that he wasn't her little boy anymore. If only he was. If only he hadn't seen the sights he'd seen. If only he'd never had to kill a man, a man as young and as innocent as him. The only difference between him and William being the colour of his uniform.

If only his sole concern was itchy spots blotching his skin like the new land girl. William scoffed. What was her name, the one with the breasts any man would like to bury himself in? Rose, Rosey. She even seemed to flirt with him. She probably saw a soldier she imagined was desperate for sex. Hell, he could deal with that problem himself, even left-handed. He didn't need to get involved with a woman who seemed so shallow. But he didn't know her, he shouldn't judge. He didn't want people to judge him so he should extend the same kindness to those around him. Betsy too.

William swung his legs out of bed, the coldness of the wooden floorboards bit into his toes like an electric shock to prod him into action. He swung his dressing gown over his shoulders and pushed his good arm into the sleeve as he left his bedroom.

"Good morning, son," Duncan said. "You'll need to change if you're going to get the cows in this morning."

William looked askance at his father as he digested the comment. It was true, he would need to get dressed. It was the 'if' William was stuck on. His life was full of 'ifs' and he was undecided how he should handle this one. As always, his father's face gave little away. Did he expect William to simply pick up farming where he had left off? Did he think nothing had changed? Or was his father testing him?

William cleared his throat. "Do you need my help?"

"Well, I thought you'd like to catch up with Patch and Jess."

The dog and the horse. Of course, William wanted to reacquaint himself with his pets. They wouldn't judge him or turn away from his injuries. As a child he'd taught himself to ride Jess with no hands. Surely, he could still do that, something he could do as well as before.

"Yes!" A happy smile crept over his face, the first he'd grinned since being home. "I'll be right there."

Before leaving the room, William glanced at Betsy. She was smiling too. He saw approval in her eyes, and he lapped it up before it disappeared.

"I'll go and set the cowshed up." Betsy was still smiling as she headed for the door. "See you there with the cows."

"You might need your eyepatch, son." Duncan suggested. "It's probably best to still protect the wound when you're outside."

William's left hand flew up to cover the scars that sliced through his right eye. He sucked in a breath, annoyed he'd forgotten to hide the ugliness. His reticence eased when he pictured Betsy's smile. She had seen his scars and still she smiled. That she hadn't cringed, filled William with a joy he hadn't felt for some time.

Back in his bedroom, he fumbled with his clothes and nearly lost his balance when he tried to step into his trousers. Adrenaline pumped the blood through his veins, and it felt energising. *Slow down, slow down*, William murmured to himself before sitting on the bed and pulling one trouser leg on at a time. The zip was easy to pull up, but the button at his waist still provided a challenge to his cumbersome fingers. Eventually between his thumb and forefinger the button edged its way through the buttonhole.

He threaded his stump into the sleeve of his checked farm shirt. It felt comforting to be out of his khaki uniform, the softness of the flannel fabric smooth against the tenderness of his amputated limb. William was in too much of a hurry, to neatly fold and safety pin the cuff of the sleeve up, so stuffed the loose, unused fabric into his trouser pocket. After struggling with the buttons of the shirt he decided in future he'd leave them all done up bar a couple at the neck so he could get his head through.

The eyepatch lay discarded on the dresser. It would have been preferable to not need it, but William retrieved the patch and hooked the elastic band over his head as he left the house.

Patch saw him coming across the yard, barked and wagged his tail excitedly.

"Gidday boy." William knelt and unhitched the dog from its chain, patted its head and ruffled its ears. He was rewarded with dog breath and a slobbery lick of his face. "Thanks, Patch. I've missed you too. Let's go and get Jess."

William, with his loyal dog at his feet went to Jess's paddock via the shed to collect the bridle. One-armed William had no way of getting the saddle as well, but he'd ridden bareback many times before. The horse whinnied and came to stand beside the stile, as if sensing this was where she needed to be for her rider. William scratched Jess in her favourite spot, just behind her ear, up under her mane. The horse's familiar smell felt comforting.

"Are you ready to go and get the cows, Jess?"

The horse raised her head ready to receive the bit. It took a little wangling but with patience, William got the bit in, and the bridle hooked behind Jess's ears.

"Right girl, stand still while I get on." William climbed up onto the top step of the stile. He was a little unsteady without two arms to balance himself but managed to swing his leg over the horse's broad back. "Feels like you need a good workout. Maybe not today though … but we'll get there."

He held the reins loosely in his left hand. Unconsciously he went to wrap his right hand over top. It was only a matter of seconds before his brain registered the futility and his right arm slumped dejected against his torso.

William cursed when they reached the gate. He should have opened it before he'd mounted. If he dismounted now, he'd have to go back to the stile to get back on. It was too low for him to reach down and stay balanced atop the horse. He kicked at the latch with his boot. It was third time lucky. Fortunately, the gate was loose on its hinges and swung open with a nudge from the horse.

William glimpsed his father over by the pig sty. The bucket in his hand seemed to be a decoy, to make it look like he was working when all he appeared to be doing was keeping an eye on William.

"Come on, Patch, let's go find the cows." William knew from years of experience, at this time of the year, when some were still calving, the herd would be close to the shed, calvers in one paddock and milkers chewing down the adjacent paddock. He pretended not to see his father, clicked his tongue to signal the horse and rode off towards the race.

He welcomed the cool morning air on his face. Comparing the New Zealand climate to Egypt's, William knew which he preferred even though his suntanned skin would likely fade. He inhaled the fresh air, filling his lungs without the risk of a dust storm.

The cows, eager to have their full udders milked, were bunched around the gate ready to go to the shed.

"Morning, girls." William greeted them as he reined Jess to a stop.

The latch on this gate was broken and someone had tied it shut with baling twine. William cursed; he'd have to dismount. He leaned forward, swung his leg over and slid off the horse, landing on the race with a thud. The gate opened inward, so the cows had to back up but once the gate was open, they knew the routine and set off down the race. William was left with the dilemma of remounting. He remembered an old tree stump down by the river and set off across the paddock, hoping it hadn't been eroded in the winter flood his mother had written about in one of her many letters.

Steaming cow pads dotted the paddock. Happy childhood memories filled William with joy but not so much he was tempted to remove his gumboots and socks and warm his bare feet in the excrement. He doubted it would do his still healing blisters any good.

The tree stump sat where it always had, visible where the paddock dipped away down to the river. The river water was a dirty-brown, evident of the recent rain. The current rushed by faster than he'd seen the water flow in the Nile. He left Jess by the stump and ventured over to dip his fingers into the water. William shivered. He'd miss the many swims he'd enjoyed with his platoon, cooling off in the warm waters of the Nile.

Back at the tree stump, with Jess on the low side, William was able to remount.

"Well, that wasn't so tricky, was it?"

Patch answered with a bark and the trio set off back across the paddock to tail the cows down the race.

Betsy and Rosey already had the first of the cows in the bales by the time William hurried the tail enders into the yard. He left them to it and took Jess back to the paddock.

William was halfway through a plate of porridge when a knock at the door turned everyone's attention to the washhouse.

"It'll be Doctor Green," Nel said, standing to go and answer the door. "I phoned him this morning. He said he'd be passing by this way and would call in."

William stiffened in his seat. He wasn't ready for another doctor to tell him any more bad news.

"Morning, everyone." The doctor walked in, removed his hat, and sat his medical bag on the floor.

"Morning, Doctor. Would you like a cuppa?" Duncan asked. "Nel, get the man a cup of tea please."

"No. No." The doctor raised his hand to signal Nel to stop. "I've just popped in to check up on our patients." The doctor looked at William and coughed awkwardly before turning towards the land girls. "I mean patient. How are you, Rosey, is it?"

"Worse!" Rosey groaned. Red blotches pocked her face.

"Mmm." The doctor leaned in for a closer look. "Itchy?"

"I can't stop scratching. I didn't get any sleep." Rosey's eyes teared up.

"Confined to your face?"

"No, they're everywhere." Rosey rolled up her sleeves, swung her legs out from under the table and hitched up her trouser legs.

William couldn't help but look. She did have shapely calves. They would have been nice if they hadn't been covered in spots.

"Have you ever had anything like this before?" the doctor continued.

"Never. It's just been since I started milking the cows. A few at first but when I got pooed on, they spread everywhere."

Doctor Green retrieved his thermometer from his bag, removed it from its case and shook it. "Open. Now close."

Rosey was silenced by the thermometer under her tongue while the doctor ran his fingers over her glands.

"Swollen," he murmured his observation. "Anybody else got any spots?"

Everybody at the table shook their heads.

"Not fleas then," William said.

"No, William, not fleas." The doctor retrieved a stethoscope from his bag. "I bet you had plenty of them in the trenches."

"Sure did. The little blighters were everywhere." It surprised William, the doctor seemed to have some knowledge of the conditions the soldiers lived in.

Doctor Green nodded as he placed the stethoscope on Rosey's back and listened. Then, seeming satisfied with what he'd heard, he slung the stethoscope around his neck, removed the thermometer and read it.

"Feverish as well. My initial diagnosis would be cowpox. It's rare these days and there'd have to be an infected cow, or a cat, for you to catch it. Or perhaps it's simply a bovine allergy. What have you been putting on it?"

"I gave her some Rawleigh's salve," Nel replied.

"As good as anything to quell the itching or if it's not helping then I recommend Calamine lotion. I suggest you stay away from the cows in the meantime. Rest up and I'll check on you again in a few days. We may need to get some blood tests done."

Rosey winced. "I'm scared of needles."

Just as well you didn't sign up to fight then, William wanted to say but didn't. Needles would have been the least of Rosey's worries.

William assumed he'd escaped any medical assessment as the doctor packed his instruments away, but he assumed wrong.

"And how are you settling back in, William?" the doctor asked.

"I only got back yesterday." There was a defensive tone to William's reply. Had his mother told the doctor he wasn't coping?

"And your injuries? Are you still under the care of the army doctors?"

William felt his temperature rise, the anger at the decisions made by the army doctors when he was incapable of arguing against them.

"Who'd want to be under their care? Look what they did!" William raised his right arm as he spat the words out.

"I'm sure they did the best they could in the circumstances."

"Yeah, that's right, you defend them. It's me that has to live with this." William thumped the end of his stump and then recoiled with the pain he'd caused himself.

"Calm down there, William. You don't want to aggravate it. Would, you like me to take a look? We could go to another room, somewhere more private."

"Ha. I've been living in twelve-foot square tents with seven other blokes. I don't need private."

William pulled the end of his sleeve out of his pocket and rolled it up to reveal the stump. There was a collective gasp from the women. A row of stitches, like the rungs of a tiny ladder, ran across the end, attempting to knit together the skin that should have covered William's forearm. The pinched skin was raised and red. It resembled an angry deletion, the removal of an error in the story of William's life.

"See, nothing to worry about," he mocked.

"It does appear to be healing well." The doctor ignored William's tone. "Just try not to knock it."

"Yeah, I'll do that."

"And remember, I'm only a phone call away if you need help."

The doctor was looking at Nel when he made this comment. William knew it was meant for his mother, not him.

"Right, I'll be on my way then." Doctor Green raised his hat in farewell.

"Thank you, Doctor." Nel stood to see him to the door.

"Thank you, Doctor," Rosey added.

William knew he should say thank you as well, but he didn't, instead he spoke to his father.

"Can I borrow the truck today, Dad?

"We need it to take the milk to the factory," Duncan replied.

"I can do that."

Duncan rubbed his chin, shifted uncomfortably and then cleared his throat.

"It's great that you can ride the horse but I'm not so sure driving the truck will be as easy."

"You mean you don't think I can drive with one arm?" William glared down the table at his father.

"Well … think about it William." Duncan paused as if he knew the truth wouldn't be welcome. "How are you going to change gears and steer at the same time?"

"I have been thinking about it, ever since the bloody Hun's bomb connected." William squeezed his eyes to shut out the pain. "I'll just brace the wheel with my thighs."

"Perhaps you could take one of the land girls with you," Duncan suggested. "Peggy needs to learn to drive."

Peggy shrunk down in her seat. "I've still got the pig sties to clean," she murmured.

"Betsy." Nel glanced mischievously at Betsy and smiled as she made her suggestion.

William didn't know how to interpret the blush that coloured Betsy's cheeks. He liked the thought of having her in the truck beside him, but he needed male company today, soldiers who in remembering, would help him forget.

"I did have some questions I wanted to ask you," Betsy added.

Curiosity almost had William changing his mind, but he doubted he had any answers that would help anyone.

"Some of the other lads are back in town, I want to catch up with them." He shrugged his shoulders at Betsy hoping she wouldn't think it was her he was rejecting. "I could be gone a while."

"I've got lots of jobs to do anyway. I'll go and get the milk cans ready." Betsy stood, took her empty plate to the sink, and left the house without giving William a second look.

"There's a new calf in the shed too," Duncan said. "It might need to be hand fed."

"William, you be nice to that girl," Nel chastised. "She's got a lot on her mind, with Roland missing and all. You of all people should know what it's like when soldiers disappear."

William felt ten-years-old again. That's probably how old he'd been when his mother last growled at him. She must have become fond of Betsy while he was gone. Betsy was easy to like; he knew how that felt and while he wasn't top of Roland's fan club list, he also knew no soldier deserved to have his whereabouts left unknown. The number of unmarked graves on the battlefield was far too high. If Roland was one of them, Betsy deserved to know.

CHAPTER

10

Sitting in the quiet of her bedroom, Betsy held the brown envelope in her trembling fingers for a good ten minutes before she found the courage to open it. Fighting back the tears that threatened, she told herself she was ready to deal with whatever news it delivered. She inhaled deeply, tucked her thumb nail under the edge of the flap and pulled it open. The typed words refused to sit still until Betsy flattened the paper and braced it against her thighs. She was ready for everything, but nothing …

Dear Miss Nolan

Thank you for your letter of 4th July.

We regret to inform we have no further information currently as to the whereabouts of Roland Thomas Flavell, Pvte, A Company, 26th Battalion, 6th Brigade, 2nd Division NZEF.

Please appreciate that there were some 50,000 allied troops in the area, and we are working to determine the whereabouts of those listed as missing in action.

The letter was signed off, but Betsy didn't bother to read who had left her hanging in limbo. Where was Roland? Someone must know. Someone would have seen him. William. He was there, he must know something. She'd have to ask William at the first opportunity.

Nel's suggestion she accompanied William to the milk factory brought a glow to Betsy's cheeks. The heat was echoed deep inside. Guilt, she liked these feelings too much, soon followed.

Then William had merely shrugged and the warmth and anticipation evaporated. Did she mean so little to him? Had other parts of his body also been damaged? It didn't matter, either way he'd decided he was going alone.

At the cowshed Betsy ensured the milk can lids were firmly shut and rolled the cans towards the door. It was a two-handed job; one she was certain William wouldn't be able to manage. She didn't want to bear his wrath, get glared at again for offering to help but she also wanted to seize whatever time she could, to ask him questions about the war, so she lingered at the shed until she heard the truck.

"Are the men you're going to meet up with from the same division as you?" Betsy tried to sound casual as she rolled a milk can onto the tray of the truck.

"Every New Zealand soldier is part of the 2nd Division," William replied. "Probably one hundred thousand in total."

Roland's designation was imprinted in Betsy's mind – *Pvte, A Company, 26th Battalion, 6th Brigade, 2nd Division NZEF.* If 2nd Division NZEF was everyone, then 'A' Company must be what she needed to ask about.

"Were you part of 'A' Company then?" she asked.

"No. 'C' Company."

It was like extracting teeth. Betsy took the frustration she was feeling out on a milk can and slammed it down against the tray of the truck. "Were 'A' company stationed at the same place as you?"

"Yes!" William's answer was peppered with impatience. "All of the 6th Brigade were tasked with defending the coast in northern Greece. Not that it did us any good. Why all the questions? I need to get going."

"I'm just trying to find out about Roland." Betsy's lips quivered. "He's missing in action. You might have seen him."

"I did early on, before … in Cairo before the fighting. But once we were out in the desert it was pretty hard to see anyone in a dust storm." William started to laugh but stopped abruptly when he looked at Betsy. "Sorry, didn't mean to make you cry. It's just that when we weren't fighting or moving base to fight somewhere else, we were hunkered down in our dugouts. You pretty much didn't see anyone other than those in your platoon. And then sometimes you saw too much of them." William's eyes glazed over. "Or too little of them."

"I'd appreciate you asking the soldiers you're going to meet up with if any of them are from 'A' company. Perhaps they knew Roland or could give me more information. Any information."

Their eyes met and Betsy was certain she glimpsed the old William, the one she knew before the war, but the look that made her insides do summersaults was gone in an instant.

"Sure." William's shoulders slumped with resignation. "The least I can do."

"Thank you."

"Is that the last of the milk cans?"

Betsy nodded and hitched a rope behind the cans to hold them secure.

"I'll be off then."

"Drive carefully," Betsy called out as William restarted the truck and shoved it into gear with a graunch.

He didn't acknowledge her comment. She struggled to drive the vehicle with two hands on the steering wheel, so she sincerely hoped he would drive carefully. Nel was having a hard time of having him home injured, let alone if something worse happened because of his stubbornness to prove himself.

With Rosey under the doctor's orders to stay away from the cattle, Betsy had to feed the calves by herself. Peggy and Jean were busy dealing with the pigs and sheep. There were two mobs of calves, the older ones out in the paddock and only receiving one feed of milk per day and the younger ones still in the shed on twice daily feeds. Betsy headed to the shed where the bellowing of hungry calves reverberated off the corrugated iron walls and the stench of fresh calf faeces assaulted her nostrils. Colostrum milk had been diverted from the milk cans and was stored in a drum. Duncan insisted the first two feeds had to be colostrum to ensure the new calves all got a good dose of antibodies. A second drum held another supply of milk which was diluted with water to feed the calves after that.

Betsy learned the hard way to get as many calves as possible feeding at the same time or otherwise; she'd get licked and bunted as if she was the mother cow. She filled the feeding bottles half fill with water, ladled in some milk, gave them a good shake, and pushed the teats hard on. There were sufficient bottles for all the calves, so Betsy set them feeding before she turned her attention to the new calf Duncan had mentioned to her over breakfast.

It sat huddled in the corner of the shed; sitting alone like a fallen soldier abandoned in the battlefield. Its legs were folded underneath as if trying to make itself as small as possible. Although in the dry of the shed, its black and white coat still had the moist sheen of birthing. A perfectly formed white heart marked the centre of its forehead and steered Betsy's thoughts to Roland. She hoped Roland wasn't lying alone and abandoned in a battlefield in Greece or Egypt or wherever he had been sent.

The tiny calf seemed bereft of energy, its head rested on the ground with eyes closed and ears drooping.

"Oh, you do look like you need a good feed." Betsy grabbed another bottle, dipped it in the drum of colostrum and put a teat on top.

She stood astride the calf and hooked her hands under its belly. "Come on, stand up, it's easier to drink standing up."

Betsy barely heard the calf's weak bellow. She couldn't encourage it to stand, neither could she lift its dead weight. *Dead.* She couldn't let the calf die; in her mind she felt as though saving the calf would somehow ensure Roland's survival.

"You may be little, but you're still heavy. Okay, have a drink sitting down then." Betsy moved to the head of the animal and offered the teat. "Open up."

There was no reaction from the calf. Betsy waved the bottle in front of the calf's nostrils and then pushed the teat against its lips. "Come on, it's good for you. You'll feel much better when you've had a feed."

"You'll have to open its mouth with your fingers."

Betsy jumped when Duncan's suggestion announced his arrival at the shed. He had that look on his face, the one that reflected his frustration at the land girls' lack of farming knowledge.

"Stand astride the calf," he continued.

"I was before." Betsy defended herself as she moved back to straddle the calf. "I tried to get it to stand but it's too weak."

"Hold the bottle in one hand and place your other hand over its snout. Use your thumb and fingers to open its jaw."

Betsy's fingers slid between the calf's lips, she felt the jaw still without back teeth, and forced it open. She cringed as she thought of the places, she'd put her hands since she'd been a land girl.

"That's it. Put the teat in and squeeze and release the jaw to encourage the calf to suck on the teat."

The calf's head flopped to one side.

"Wedge its head between your knees." Duncan continued to fire instructions at Betsy.

She closed her knees in behind the calf's ears, held its head upright and squeezed the teat. Milk poured out the side of its mouth.

"It's not swallowing." Panicked she was choking the calf; Betsy released her hold. "We can't let it die. Why won't it drink?"

"We'll have to tube feed it. Don't let it go," Duncan growled before he disappeared to the cowshed.

"Come on, little calf, don't give up on me." Betsy could just have easily been saying the words to Roland. She had to stay loyal to him, as he had been to her all those years ago. She couldn't be distracted by William's presence, by the feelings he ignited in her, her body's reactions when he was nearby.

"Push this over the end of the teat." Duncan had returned with a long tube and his command pulled Betsy's attention back to the calf as she followed the instruction. "Right, now open the calf's mouth again. Feed the tube in. On the lefthand side. It has to go into the oesophagus; not the lungs, or you'll kill the calf."

That was the last thing Betsy wanted to do. She needed to save the calf because it may be the only thing she could save. Panic churned her insides, urging the calf to hurry and drink.

"Don't force it." Duncan's tone made Betsy want to tell him to take over, but she already knew from experience his way of teaching was to let a person learn by doing. "Let the calf swallow it down. Lift its head up so the neck is lengthened."

Betsy did as she was told and slowly the tube edged its way into the calf's gullet.

"That's enough," Duncan said. "Tilt the bottle."

Milk flowed down the tube and much to Betsy's relief, nothing spilled out. The calf blinked its eyelids. The tiniest bit of milk seemed to be enough to spark the animal into life. Betsy wanted to lean down and kiss its forehead but knowing Duncan would think she was a silly woman, she resisted. She didn't stifle the smile that lit up her face though. There was hope, she needed to cling to the fact there was always hope.

"Now, don't you go and get all sentimental like Alice did," Duncan warned. "We don't name farm animals. This is just a calf."

Betsy knew she couldn't afford to be that sentimental.

Betsy called back in at the shed before the afternoon milking to check on the calf. It still sat in the back corner while the other calves pranced around the pen like children playing chase, but at least its eyes were open, and its head held upright. Betsy clapped her hands together with delight. A smile lit up her face and her walk to the cowshed gave way to a childlike skip.

She wanted to hurry through the milking and get back to give the calf another feed, but the herd were still ambling their way down the race with Duncan following. From the yard, Betsy could see the scowl that furrowed his forehead. He sat rigid on Jess, glaring at the track as if his look would make William materialise.

"Where is William?" Duncan demanded when he reached the yard.

Unsure why she was expected to know the answer, Betsy shrugged. "He's not back yet."

"He needs to focus on farm work, get back to how things were, not be gallivanting off with his mates."

It didn't seem possible life could or would go back to how it was before. Too many things had changed, physically and mentally for William. Surely Duncan could see that. And there was the presence of the Japanese, the war wasn't over. The threat that had been on the other side of the world was now virtually in their backyard.

"When he gets back, send him to me." Duncan stormed off to the pig sties.

Betsy got the first two cows into the bales and went to turn the milking machines on. William still wasn't back with the truck which worried her on two counts. She hoped nothing had happened to him and she hoped there would be enough cans to hold the afternoon milk.

She didn't want to be the one bearing the brunt of Duncan's bad mood so she set about the task assigned to her. The rhythm of pulsing machines and the calm of the cows chewing their cud soon allowed her thoughts to wander to happier times. She wondered how her friends were getting on at their new placements: Grace at the linen flax mill, Alice at Orari Estate and Moira over the road at Bill's. They hadn't caught up since the races. Perhaps there would be another dance at the Orari Hall now some of the soldiers were returning home.

At least William had both his legs, he'd still be able to dance, to hold her in his arms … Betsy's vision blurred as if trying to protect her from reality. How would it feel to dance with William now he no longer had two arms? Her chest tightened. Was this punishment for her disloyalty to Roland?

The cow in the bale bellowed and released its bowels; a timely reminder for Betsy to concentrate on milking. She removed the cups and opened the gate so the cow could leave the shed. She'd lost count of how many cows had been milked and thought it best to check the status of the milk can before it overflowed.

"Off you go, girl." Betsy patted the cow on the rump, shut the gate after her and went to the milk room.

She was just in time. Milk froth edged the rim of the can. Betsy quickly moved the gauze and the milk pipe to the next can. Behind her, the rumble of an engine, the screech of brakes and the slamming of the truck door announced William's arrival.

"I'm back." William sought support from the shed wall, as he drunkenly slurred his words. "Didja miss me?"

His eyepatch was missing but William's endearing grin melted Betsy's insides. His eye twinkled, with the innocence of a mischievous toddler. If only the sight of her put that look on his face and not too many beers.

Betsy smiled. "Not as much as your father did. You'd better watch out for him."

"Ne'er mind him." William burped loudly. "Oops, ne'er mind that either, sorry. He needs to lighten up, anyone would think there was a war going on." He laughed at his own joke.

"You had a good catch up with your friends then?" Even though he was drunk, it was good to see him smiling.

"Yeah, most of them." William's face dropped. "We've all got a bit missing. That's why we're home. You could probably make a whole one if you put us all together."

Betsy squirmed uncomfortably. "I'd best get back to the cows," she said. "Leave the truck there and I'll roll the milk cans into the shed when I've finished."

She regretted her offer as soon as she'd uttered the words. William stood upright, his shoulders drew back, and his smile became a defensive glare.

"I can do it." He stamped one foot. "I'm not totally bloody useless."

"I'll leave you to it then." Betsy's heartbeat thundered in her ears as she left the milk room. The old William, the before-the-war William she had liked so much came and went in the blink of an eye. Being around the post-war William was like walking on eggshells.

She went back to milking, seeking the calm it brought her, but the rhythm of the milking machines was interrupted by clashes and scrapes of milk cans and curses and blasphemy from William. Should she go back and help? Betsy shook her head, no, she'd likely get a short shift.

The slamming and crashing of cupboard doors reverberated, and angry voices greeted Betsy as she entered the kitchen.

"Where's the bloody beer?" William yelled.

"I think you've had more than enough already." Duncan spoke slowly and calmly as if to defuse the situation. "You shouldn't be driving with so many under your belt."

"Your truck made it home safely, didn't it?"

"It's not just the truck we're worried about." Nel joined the conversation, her tone kinder than her husband's. "There's no beer, but I can get you a lemonade."

"In case you haven't noticed, Mum." William gave up his search, yanked a chair out and sat heavily. He propped one elbow on the table and rested his head in his hand as if he'd lost another battle. "I'm not a little boy anymore. I can look after myself and I don't want a lemonade."

The room went silent. Peggy and Jean sat uncomfortably at the table, staring at the dinner that had been served up, avoiding eye contact lest they be drawn into the conversation.

Nel had made her delicious Shepherd's Pie for dinner, the mashed potato topping was perfectly golden, but William's mood had quashed Betsy's appetite. She picked at her serving, forcing herself to get the sustenance she knew she needed.

William wolfed down his dinner and dished himself up a second serving. Betsy hoped the food would sober him up.

"Oh, yeah, Betsy."

Betsy tensed, afraid of another 'William' outburst being directed her way.

"The lads reminded me." The clang of William's fork hitting his plate ensured he had Betsy's full attention. "About the time your fiancé disappeared, the 26th were covering the Aussies' backside. It was a full-scale withdrawal with the Germans hot on our tail. West of the Servia Pass."

Betsy's eyes lit up. "You think that's where Roland might have gone missing?"

"The lads said some, including injured soldiers, were taken prisoner."

"I could write again, to the authorities, request they check the lists of the prisoners." Betsy smiled.

"You could." William held her gaze but his was hard to read.

CHAPTER

11

William grunted and left the room when Duncan turned the radiogram on to listen to the nightly war update.

"He's probably just tired." Nel defended her son as Duncan shook his head.

"Well, it's from too much drink not from too much work," Duncan growled.

"Give him time, dear." Nel patted Duncan's shoulder. "He just needs more time to recover."

The conversation was interrupted by the announcement that to assist in the war effort all New Zealanders would be subject to butter rationing. The British had been surviving on two ounces of butter per person per week since 1940 and was heavily reliant on New Zealand as their main supplier of dairy produce.

"I make our butter so that won't affect us," Nel said.

Duncan quelled all chatter with a finger raised to his mouth.

Butter will be rationed to eight ounces per person per week. Cream is no longer able to be sold for personal consumption. Farmers are expected to ensure all cream is sent to the factory and all butter purchased using the ration book system. Any butter made at home is limited to the rationed amount.

"They could have waited another month," Nel grumbled. "It's the scone competition this month at CWI. How am I going to bake my prize-winning scones without butter?"

The mention of 'CWI' grabbed Betsy's attention. The last time she had gone with Nel to a Country Women's Institute meeting, she'd almost been roped into the end of year performance. It was time to make a quick retreat to her bedroom before the subject came up again.

"There'll be a black market for butter, just like there is for everything else," Duncan replied. "Just you wait and see. Perhaps you'll be able to make a little extra and swap it for some more tea. I'm sick of drinking weak tea. A decent brew would be just dandy."

"You're encouraging me to break the law?" Nel looked sideways at Duncan.

"Well, they say, everyone must make a sacrifice, I say we're making more than our fair share. What with William's injuries, the tractor gone, and rationed tea and sugar, and let's not forget the land girls we've got to have."

Nel mouthed an apology to Betsy. "Duncan, Betsy is here."

"Uh, what?" Duncan looked at Betsy. "Oh, sorry, I didn't mean you specifically. It's just I don't think the government should make women do men's work."

Betsy wasn't offended by Duncan's comment, but she took the opportunity to leave the room.

"Well, like it or not, I've got cows to milk in the morning, so I'll say goodnight."

"Duncan!" Nel growled. "Now look what you've done."

Duncan's ear was primed to the radiogram, and he didn't acknowledge Nel's or Betsy's remarks.

"No, it's alright. I've got letters to write anyway." Betsy smiled at Nel.

"Goodnight, dear," Nel said. "Sleep well."

Eager to contact the army headquarters again, Betsy hurried to her room. Any hope she may have had about getting more information out of William was dashed by the loud snoring that emanated from behind his closed bedroom door. At least he was asleep; bodies healed when they were sleeping. If his body healed, perhaps his mood would also improve.

Betsy had two letters to write, the first was a reply to her sister. She was still irritated by Irene's carefree attitude, enjoying her time in Cairo like it was a holiday in the sun but being stationed closer to the frontlines she might have access to information about Roland.

Although a couple of years older than Betsy, Irene had also known Roland since childhood. She squealed with delight when Betsy whispered details of her and Roland's 'honeymoon'. The forty-eight hours when they pretended, they were Mr and Mrs Flavell and only left the hotel for food. Betsy twisted the gold band on her finger. Would it forever be the only ring she wore? Betsy knew her sister would make the extra effort to find out all she could. Betsy rounded out the letter with news of what she'd been doing on the farm and signed off with her best wishes for her sister to stay safe.

Her second letter began with the name she'd not given a second look this morning. She worded the letter carefully, hoping a personal approach would appeal to the caring nature of the recipient. She relayed what William had told her about the prisoners of war taken by the Germans around the Servia Pass and requested prisoner lists be checked for Roland's name. A tiny speck of hope made her smile as she signed off and folded the single sheet into the envelope, she'd already addressed to the war office. She licked the flap to seal the envelope and raised it to her lips for a good luck kiss.

"Please find Roland," she whispered.

She turned out her bedside light and slipped between the sheets, exhausted but happy.

The confused threads of Betsy's dream were severed in the deep darkness of the night by screams that seemed too loud to be figments of her imagination. She sat upright, releasing the images of Roland that were so vivid, it felt as if he'd been lying beside her. She reached out, fanned her hand over the mattress, a single mattress that left no room for him had he been real. The noises were real though, and they were coming from William's room. He must be having a nightmare. Did she dare go to him? To risk being abused for offering to help? The screams were filled with agony and terror, she couldn't let them continue. Betsy climbed out of bed, turned on her bedroom light and tiptoed through to William's room.

The light filtering from her bedroom to William's was faint. His face screwed up as though he was in unbearable pain. His legs thrashed about, his sheets in a tangled mess on the floor. She hesitated.

"William?' She placed a hand gently on his shoulder. "It's alright, William."

His lips were white, closed tightly in a straight line as if zipped up. Was she brave enough to encourage them to speak, to reveal the horrors he'd witnessed? William stared vacantly at the ceiling, beads of perspiration dotted his forehead.

"You're safe. You're home." Betsy hoped her voice was reassuring. Her own heart thundered in her chest; she needed to calm herself if she was to be of any use to William. She inhaled deeply, exhaled slowly, and kept repeating the sequence until she felt her pulse slow.

It seemed like forever, but it was probably only a matter of seconds until his shoulder finally relaxed beneath her hand.

"That's it. Breathe. Nobody can get you here." She kept her voice quiet and gentle as her hand rested on his shoulder.

William reached up, his large rough hand gripped onto Betsy's and held tight as if his very survival depended on it.

"Don't leave me," he begged. "Like an angel, you're here to save me. Don't leave me."

Betsy sat on the edge of the bed. What had happened to William? What horrific sights had he seen to make him tremble with fear?

"I'm here." She lifted her hand and gently stroked his stubbled cheek. "I'm here."

"You're beautiful, Betsy." William's eyes closed as his breathing slowly calmed. "If only I was all here for you."

The words sounded as if they were meant for her, but it appeared William was still in the grips of a dream. If he was coherent and sober, she would have believed they were true. His fingers eased their hold of hers, but he continued to tremble. She was unsure if it was the cold of the night temperature or the chill of his memories. Replacing the blankets over him would warm his body but the memories of war could never be erased or forgotten. Betsy stood to retrieve the discarded bedding.

"Don't go."

"I'm just going to pick your blankets up."

She hesitated before covering William with the bedding. His pyjama shirt buttons were undone revealing his tanned chest. Betsy closed her eyes as warmth travelled through her body and sent a tingle down her spine. Her nipples hardened beneath her cotton nightie.

What am I doing, in the middle of the night, in my nightie, admiring the physique of a man who I have no right to look at? I'm engaged to another man.

A surge of guilt lodged in her chest.

"There you are." Betsy pulled the bedding up and folded the white sheet back over the blankets, so it sat neatly below William's chin. "That'll warm you up. Go back to sleep."

"You'll stay?"

The pleading in William's tone pulled at Betsy's heart. Like a frightened boy who needed protecting. All she was doing, comforting an injured man. That's all it was. Purely kindness, nothing else. She sat back down on the side of the bed with the bedding between them a barrier.

William rolled onto his side, freed his good arm from the blankets and rested his hand in her lap. She stared down at it, wishing he hadn't done that but did nothing to remove it. She leaned back against the headboard and absorbed the emotions his simple gesture brought.

A shaft of morning light edged its way through William's bedroom curtains and urged Betsy's weary eyes to open. Rain pattered on the roof, and she imagined the joy of staying warm and snuggled in bed. She sucked in a breath and tensed when the reality of where she was dawned on her. The barrier of blankets was still between them but during the night Betsy had moved. She was now lying next to William, their heads sharing the same pillow, his warm breath brushing her neck, his hand lying across her chest.

Noises from the next-door room told her Duncan and Nel would soon be up and about. She needed to move and fast. Being caught in this predicament wasn't an option. Betsy took one last look at the peacefully sleeping William. His facial scars were hidden in the softness of the pillow, his damaged arm under cover beneath the blankets. He looked like the William she had imagined sleeping with before the war had taken him away.

If only.

Holding her breath, Betsy eased out from under his hand, relieved he didn't stir. She pulled the door to and tiptoed back to her bedroom. She changed quickly, shaking knowing she had spent the night in his bed. Back in her farm clothes, she paused and inhaled deeply. She had to appear calm and composed, she shoved her still trembling fingers into her overall pockets.

"I'll get the cows in this morning." Duncan buttoned up his jacket and pulled a woollen hat down over his ears. "Nel doesn't want William out in this weather. That woman must stop mollycoddling him, he's not a little boy now."

Betsy bent to pull her gumboots on and hide her disbelief. That was a conversation Duncan should be having with his wife, not her. Last night William had looked like a little boy needing protection, but there was no way she could say that.

The rain had eased a bit, but Betsy still wore her raincoat to the shed, the rain drops splattering on the oilskin. Would the closeness she and William had shared last night be like the raindrops, dissipated in the light of day? Would he remember she was there? Hopefully he would think it had been a dream. It was better that way, she was, after all, engaged to Roland.

The milking went smoothly, and Betsy was finishing hosing down the yard, when the quiet morning was disturbed by the sound of raised voices. The loud yelling was Duncan and William disagreeing over something again. She hosed away the last of the cow effluent, rolled up the hose and hung it over the yard rails before venturing to the source of the noise.

"You can't keep taking the truck," Duncan growled. "We've got petrol rationing, we need it for farm work, you'll just go and get drunk again. You need to stay home and get on with your life on the farm."

"Get on with my life? Huh! What sort of life is it with one eye and one hand?"

"I know, I know." Duncan's voice was placatory.

"How the hell would you know? Did you go away and fight in the war? Did they sign you up too, while I was away?"

"No, that's not what I mean. I just think you're running away from reality."

"If you'd been in my reality lately, you'd know it's not the best place to be right now."

Having borne witness to that last night, Betsy wanted to defend William even more, but she stayed in the background like a fly on the wall. If was William so unsettled in his sleep, it was no wonder he was sullen and agitated in his waking hours. Her heart went out to him, to every soldier.

"I don't think you're going to find any sort of future in the bottom of a beer bottle." Duncan rubbed his forehead as if the battle was giving him a headache.

"Maybe not, but it certainly helps me escape the past." William grabbed the truck key from the ignition and stowed it in his trouser pocket. "Now if you'll just load the milk cans, I'll take the milk to the factory, so you don't have to worry about me wasting all of your petrol ration."

Duncan muttered under his breath as he rolled the milk cans onto the tray of the truck. Betsy snuck off to the calf shed, the need to avoid both of their grumpy temperaments stronger than the need to know if William was aware of what happened last night.

Betsy gave the calf its morning feed, relieved it was up on its feet and looking a lot healthier. His recovery gave her hope and she headed to the letterbox before breakfast with a lightness in her step. The trip to get the mail was more out of habit than any expectation that there would be any more letters for her.

She was pleasantly surprised by a white envelope with an image of a Maori woman on the postage stamp. It was Grace's handwriting; Betsy tore the envelope open and devoured Grace's news.

Dearest Betsy,

I heard that William has returned home, and I imagine that this is both good and bad for you. I hope that you are taking care and doing what you know to be the right thing to do.

Betsy laughed. Grace always had a way of saying something, without actually saying it. Betsy knew her friend was trying to protect her, as she always did. After last night, the reminder was timely, Betsy needed to take care and do the right thing. It was a pity her body, heart and head were in a three-way battle as to what the right thing was.

I hope William's injuries aren't too severe. Some of the soldiers I've seen stumbling from the pub on my ride home after work, bear horrible scars and some are missing limbs. It must be terrible for them.

Mrs McPherson, she's my supervisor at the flax mill, has been bringing her son into the factory. Brian is his name, not that he'd be able to tell you, he hasn't said a word since he came back. Apparently, it's called shell shock and there's nothing they can do for him but wait. She's terrified he'll do something awful to himself. At least at the factory, she can keep an eye on him.

Anyway, enough of war talk and injuries, my real reason for writing is to suggest a visit to Alice. We must all be due some time off soon. I thought we could drive out and see where she lives, have a good catch up and see how married life is treating her. Let me know what you think. Perhaps you could check with Moira since she's just across the road and she could ask if we could borrow Bill's truck.

What a good idea. A break away was just what Betsy needed to regain her perspective. She wouldn't have gone if her calf was still sick, but she was sure the others could give it a feed. Betsy smiled, thinking about how much she'd learned about farm life and how attached she'd become to a calf.

CHAPTER

12

"Bugger." William cursed as he climbed into the truck and slammed the door. Why didn't Dad just leave things alone?

He'd wanted to see Betsy before he left, to thank her for last night. He'd seen her standing in the machine room as they'd argued, but the argument with his father had left him rattled. Her caring had been what he needed, a reminder everyone could do something to help another, a prompt for him to get out of his wallowing state. In the early hours, as he'd lain there with her breathing steadily beside him, he decided he'd make Brian McPherson his project and he wanted Betsy to be the first to know.

When he'd first woken, her soft body against him, smelled the scent of her shampooed hair, and absorbed her warmth, albeit through the bedding, something stirred in him. A part of his body he'd worried would be as damaged as the rest of him was rigid, throbbing with a need for release, a need to scream it was okay, but it would be much better buried inside the beautiful woman who was so close, but so far away. At the time, he'd pretended he was asleep, sensed her watching him and felt her slip away. He did nothing except cling to the hope the feelings evoked; hope that one day the time and place to pursue them would be right.

William fumbled for the keys in his pocket. It was an awkward reach with his left hand to get the keys into the ignition. They dropped to the floor, and he banged his head on the steering wheel retrieving them.

"Bugger."

His day was rapidly deteriorating from bad to worse, but he wasn't going to let his father get the better of him. Duncan was still standing off to the side. William didn't make eye contact as he yanked the gearstick into first and pushed his foot down on the accelerator.

On the trip to the milk factory, William put thoughts of Betsy aside. For now, he needed to focus on finding Brian. William knew he lived with his mother; his father having been off the scene for some time. For a moment he imagined how good that would be, no father to argue with, to have to justify your actions to, but William knew deep down Duncan was acting out of love.

"Gidday, Billy," Jake greeted William at the dairy factory. "How long have you been back?"

If Jake had noticed William's injuries, he didn't acknowledge them, and William appreciated that.

"Just a couple of days," he replied. "I was wanting to catch up with Brian McPherson. He's back too. Do you know where he lives now?"

"No, sorry mate." Jake turned and yelled to the other men. "Any of you know where Brian McPherson lives?"

"With his mother," came the reply.

"Where does she live?" William asked.

"Don't know but she works at the linen flax mill."

William nodded. That was enough for him to go on. "Thanks, Jake, much appreciated."

He waited for the milk cans to be unloaded and replaced with empty ones, all the while planning what he could do for Brian.

The linen flax mill was still where William had remembered it to be and just as dirty. It didn't look like this area had the overnight rain Orari received, and the sun was shining on the group of women he spotted in the fields out to the side of the factory. He slowed, held the steering wheel steady between his thighs and wound down the window to feel the breeze and the sun on his face. Pre-war he would have waved to the women, but he didn't have a hand for that now. Pre-war and post-war, William needed to stop making comparisons, but it was proving difficult. He wouldn't be any use to Brian if he couldn't drag himself out of the doldrums.

A siren sounded as he pulled into the carpark. His immediate reaction was to duck, to shelter from the volley of gunfire that would surely follow. He laughed at himself when the skies remained silent, and he realised it was probably just the signal for morning tea.

An older gentleman exited the office and walked towards the truck.

"Can I help you there?" he asked.

"Good morning." William climbed out of the truck. "I believe Mrs McPherson works here. I was hoping to catch up with her."

William watched the man size him up. He wondered what thoughts ran through his mind.

"I'm the factory manager, Mr Cresswell." He proffered his hand but removed it quickly when he saw William's amputation. "It would be me you'd need to be seeing about a job but we're not hiring at the moment."

William wanted to add 'and we wouldn't be hiring a one-handed man anyway' but he kept his thoughts to himself.

"I wanted to see Mrs McPherson about her son, Brian. He was serving with me overseas and I'd like to catch up with him."

"Mmm, yes, he's not in a good way." Mr Cresswell stared at William's missing hand. "Not physical injuries like you, but definitely not one hundred percent." He tapped his index finger to his temple, a gesture that said more than required. "Actually, I was just going over to see Cathy, I mean, Mrs McPherson, she's with the girls in the field. Come with me if you like."

"Wasn't that your morning tea siren?" William asked. "I don't want to interrupt your cup of tea."

"No, no." Mr Cresswell chuckled. "That was the fire brigade siren. The goods train caught fire. The truck was dropped at the racecourse siding and the fire brigade are on their way to try and save it."

The pair walked across the field toward the women who were singing as they turned the piles of drying flax. A couple of them started with '*Pack up your troubles in your old kit bag*' and everyone joined in with '*smile, smile, smile.*' The lyrics had the desired effect, the women looked happy as they worked along their row and William couldn't help but smile too.

Next, one of the women tweaked the words from '*A long road to Tipperary*' and sang a long road to the row end. The others all picked up the change and repeated the chorus until they reached the end of the row of flax.

"Oh, no," the lead singer sighed, feigning despair.

"What's wrong?" asked a woman William recognised. Grace from *Whipsnade Farm*. She'd been one of the land girls with Betsy.

The lead singer splayed her hands over her heart. "My heart's not here at the end of the row," she said before folding over in laughter.

"But I'm the sweetest girl you know," another woman joined in on the joke, mimicking the song's words.

"You're sweet but I'm saving my heart for a man."

"Anyone in particular?"

The singer tapped the side of her nose. "That would be telling," she said with a grin.

"I reckon it's that fellow that works at the general store," teased another.

"What? The short one with glasses?" asked the singer. "No, it's Ronnie that likes him, that's why she's got silk stockings coming and not the rest of us."

Mr Cresswell looked uncomfortable and cleared his throat to announce their presence. William couldn't decide if the tone of the conversation was the source of Mr Cresswell's embarrassment or the state of dress of the women. Except for Mrs McPherson, the women's midriffs were bare, they'd rolled the fronts of their shirts up and tucked them into their bras to form a bikini top of sorts. William thought they looked good, and it made sense on a warm day.

"Nobody will be getting silk stockings any time soon," Mr Cresswell announced. "That siren, that's the fire brigade trying to save the goods train."

"That's a shame," Cathy said. "I hope no one was injured."

"No, no reported injuries but all the freight will likely be destroyed. The general store's order coming from Christchurch. Carpets, crockery, knitting wool and women's stockings."

"Oh, no." Ronnie's voice was laced with disappointment. "I had a pair of stockings on order, they were supposed to be arriving on the train today."

Mr Cresswell blushed and coughed again to clear his throat. "Right, I'll leave you to it then," he said. "Looks like you'll be finished today. You're doing a good job. I'll be off." Mr Cresswell turned awkwardly and almost tripped on some freshly turned flax. It jogged his memory. "Oh, I forgot, Cathy. This young man wants to talk to you about Brian. I'll leave him with you."

William had to introduce himself as Mr Cresswell disappeared back across the paddock. Grace smiled at him and he wondered if she and Betsy had already talked about him.

"What do you want with Brian?" Cathy asked, drawing him to the side and urging the others back to work.

"We were shipped home at the same time," William explained. "He was on the *HS Manganui* with me, but I never got to talk to him."

"Well, you can talk to him as much as you like," Cathy replied. "The problem is he doesn't answer, he hasn't so much as acknowledged anyone's presence yet." Her eyes glassed over. "My boy has locked himself away, he's in there somewhere hiding from whatever he must have borne witness to."

"The thousand-yard stare." William nodded.

"The what?" Cathy looked puzzled.

"Combat stress reaction is the official term, I believe. You're not allowed to call it shell shock like they did in World War I. Us soldiers call it the thousand-yard stare; like you stare off into the never-never."

"Oh, I see," Cathy replied. "I imagine you must have seen some horrific sights."

"Yeah, it wasn't pretty." William winced. "I thought I might be able to help." He raised his right arm up to his eyepatch. "I'm not much good for anything else."

"Nothing to lose." Cathy withdrew a hanky from her pocket and blew her nose. "You'll find him in the men's tearoom, sitting in the corner exactly where I left him at eight o'clock this morning and exactly where I'll find him at five o'clock tonight."

"I'm meeting up with the other lads in town later. I could take him with me if you like and drop him home afterwards."

Cathy's eyes dropped to where William's right hand should have been. "You can drive?" She blushed with embarrassment. "Sorry, of course you can, you drove here. Ignore me, just a mother being protective of her son, fat lot of good it will do me now though, the damage has already been done."

William touched his left hand gently to Cathy's. "I'll do what I can to help. It can't all be for nothing."

The meek smile that passed between them cemented their agreement; it could never all be for nothing.

"Where shall I drop him back to? It'll be after six o'clock, when the pub shuts, so you'll have finished here."

"Ours is the white house behind the picket fence where Lewis Street intersects with Cox Street," Cathy replied.

"I know the place. We'll see you later." William smiled. "Don't worry, I'll look after him."

Brian was where his mother had said he would be; sitting on a seat in the corner of the lunchroom, his bent legs hugged into his chest, his chin resting on his knees and his eyes appearing to stare out the window. William looked in the same direction, there was nothing to see but the wall of the factory, where paint peeled from the horizontal weatherboards. They needed repair work as much as the returned soldiers.

"Gidday, mate." William pulled up a chair and tried to emulate Jack, his Australian friend who'd persisted when William was at his worst. "It's good to be back on home soil, isn't it?"

Brian's head slowly turned towards William; his mouth opened as if he wanted to speak but nothing audible came.

"Did you have a good trip back? You were at the front of the ship, weren't you? My cot was in the middle, it got a bit rough in that storm, I nearly got thrown out of bed."

William rabbited on about whatever came into his head for another ten minutes. He thought he saw Brian swallow and possibly blink a couple of times but nothing more. William's throat was parched from all the talking, he needed a drink and after all his effort for nothing, that drink had better be a beer. He considered giving up on Brian, but an annoying Australian twang kept repeating words inside his head. *We can't give up because the alternative doesn't bear thinking about.*

He leapt up before he could change his mind. "Come on then, we'll go for a drive."

He had to unfurl Brian's fingers, lower his feet to the ground and hook his arm around Brian's back.

"Come on, Brian. Work with me, mate. Us soldiers have got to stick together. We're the only ones who know what it was like."

William opened the truck door and Brian climbed in without assistance. The simple action gave William a glimmer of hope, at least he was capable of doing something for himself. They drove into Geraldine and parked outside the agreed meeting place. The Crown Heritage Hotel, located on the corner of Wilson and Talbot Streets, had few patrons at this time of the day, other than the regulars who sat on stools at the bar, more for the company than the handles of beer they slowly imbibed, and the group of returned soldiers who had recently claimed a table in the corner as their own.

The high ceilings and subdued lighting gave the public bar a cavernous feel. After spending months in the dugouts no one wanted to feel confined. The soldiers' banter was already echoing off the walls and the smoke from their cigarettes coloured the air in both odour and haze.

"Gidday, Billy." Tom stood on his single leg to greet them, tucking a crutch under his armpit for balance. "And you've brought Brian, that's great. Welcome! Glad you could join us."

Tom's extended hand was left hanging. He noticed Brian's vacant look so grabbed his hand and shook it anyway. More chairs were pulled up to the table and the barman came over with a jug of beer and two more glasses.

"Now, pace yourselves today, lads," the barman cautioned. "I know you need to let off steam, but we don't want anyone getting hurt."

"More than we already are, you mean." The men laughed at the dark humour and the barman left them to it.

William took two cigarettes from his packet and leaned into the flame of Tom's match to light them.

"Here you are, mate," he said as he passed a cigarette to Brian. "A drag or two of this will help you feel better."

Brian took the cigarette, closed his eyes, and inhaled long and slow. William hoped the orange embers flickering at the end of the smoke were like a fire sparking inside of Brian. He wasn't foolish enough to think it would be easy to get Brian talking again but he had to start somewhere.

"Billy, did you hear Bob's got a job?" Tom steered the conversation forward.

"No, what doing?" William poured a beer for Brian and one for himself before looking at Bob and imagining what sort of job a man with the side of his face missing could have. Nothing to do with the public, he hoped for Bob's sake. William's scarring was minor in comparison, but still drew the attention of curious and ridiculing eyes. Bob's disfigurement would likely horrify.

"I'll be the one changing the reels at the cinema," Bob announced proudly.

"Congratulations! You'll get to see all the movies for free." It was a good outcome for Bob but William needed something more to give him the adrenaline they'd been living with the past few months.

"You'd better get them in order," Frank teased, garnering more laughter from the group.

"Hah, yeah, put the war news on last, no one wants to see that. It's all propaganda anyway. They don't show it how it really is, do they?"

"Hell no."

A despondent silence engulfed the group until Tom, who'd brought his officer status home with him and had become the self-appointed ringleader, changed the subject yet again.

"And Reggie here, he's already been very busy." Tom laughed. "Come on, Reggie, share your news."

Reggie was like William, blind in one eye but he was grinning from ear to ear. "I'm going to be a dad."

"I'll drink to that." William raised his glass. "Congratulations!"

There were cheers all around and even Brian lifted his glass before taking a sip.

"You'll have to keep your eye on a toddler," Bob joked.

Wherever the conversation went, someone couldn't help but bring it back to the war. It was like a fog hung over them, pervading every facet of their existence, seeping into every thought, and forever colouring their perception. They may have been home, but they would never return fully to the men they had been before the war took them away.

"And what about you, Billy?" Tom said. "You're the luckiest of the lot of us, you're surrounded by women. How many land girls are there at your farm?"

William almost choked on his mouthful of beer. He'd been hearing that word lucky ever since he'd woken in the patch-up centre near the frontline but now it was being related to the land girls. His thoughts immediately turned to Betsy as he remembered the warmth of her body next to his. He'd be a hell of a lot luckier if she'd been under the blankets with him, he could have buried his erection deep inside her. He'd never been one to get embarrassed easily, but the heat warmed his face. He took another mouthful while he thought of a response to deflect the conversation away from Betsy. He had no idea what was between them, and it was the last thing he wanted to share with this lot.

"Hah, yeah, I'm lucky alright. Four women dressed in overalls and gumboots. One of the new ones is allergic to cows. She's covered in spots and looks 'really' attractive."

"Can't look any worse than me." Bob replied with his self-deprecating humour.

"She's only been shat on by a cow, not shot at by a bloody Hun." William felt the anger boil inside him and sculled the rest of his beer, hoping the cool liquid was the calming elixir he needed.

The conversation was little more than a mishmash of slurred words and songs sung badly by the time Reggie stood to leave, late in the afternoon.

"You don't need to go yet," Bob joked. "You've already done the deed."

"Oh, he's got to keep in sweet with her or it might be the only kid he gets."

Reggie ignored their taunts. "I'll see you tomorrow."

"Not if you get your eyepatch on the wrong eye." Raucous laughter filled the bar.

Tom shook his head. He'd given up trying to keep the conversation positive, even joked about his own injuries, having a crotch and a crutch and being unsure which one to use.

"Right you are, lads." The barman gathered up the empty glasses. "Drink up. Closing time."

"I'd better get Brian home," William said. "His mother will be cursing me."

Brian's eyes no longer stared vacantly, mainly because they were half closed as he slumped in the chair in an inebriated state, but William had seen him smile several times. It wasn't much but it was a sign there was someone still inside, someone that with patience and encouragement could emerge and that was much better than the alternative.

CHAPTER

13

It was a case of *déjà vu* when William arrived home. The truck's tyres skidded on the gravel farm track and the bonnet stopped mere inches from the concrete steps into the cowshed. Betsy pretended she was busy in the machine room, as William stumbled from the vehicle and zig zagged his way towards her.

"Hello, my love," he slurred. "Are you going to be an angel and come and keep me company again tonight?"

Betsy stiffened. Her eyes darted around to check that no one else was close enough to hear the conversation. William's drunken words made everything sound so tawdry. Her kind actions had been cheapened and turned into something sexual. Or was she misinterpreting his words because that was what she wanted? She shook her head angrily. Any thoughts of that nature should be about Roland.

She ignored the comment. "You've parked the truck the wrong way around. How am I going to load the milk cans tomorrow?"

"Oh, don't be like that." William feigned a hurt look. "I'll turn it around in the morning."

"I imagine you'll still be sleeping off the beer when I need to load up." Betsy finished tidying the machine room, washing away the splashes of milk and lining up the empty milk cans.

"What's put you in a grump? Have you had a bad day?"

"What's put you in a good mood? Have you had too many beers?" Irked by William's remark, sarcasm laced her voice.

"I saw your friend today. The other land girl, Grace, I think her name is."

Betsy stood, her hands on her hips. She squinted and pouted simultaneously as a hint of envy pulled at her heart.

"Where did you see Grace?" she demanded.

"At the linen flax mill. What's she doing working there?" William asked.

"It's a long story." Betsy had no desire to explain Grace and Alice's placement swap. "What were you doing there?"

"Picking up Brian McPherson. Thought I could take him for a drive, meet up with the other lads, see if it would help him."

More sarcasm was on the tip of Betsy's tongue, but she swallowed it. William's kind gesture had her rethinking; he had thought of someone other than himself. It was the first time since he'd been home. The pub probably wasn't the best of places to take a shell shocked soldier but at least William had tried.

"That was nice of you." Betsy smiled.

"I can be quite nice; in case you hadn't noticed." William chuckled until a loud burp escaped. "Oops, sorry. I'd best go and get cleaned up for dinner."

He turned and left Betsy smiling to herself. Yes, William could be very nice, and therein lay the problem.

Rosey was back at the dinner table, her spots all but gone except for the ones she'd been unable to resist scratching.

"You're looking much better, Rosey," Nel said, bringing a beef stew to the table.

Betsy watched Rosey glance at William as if she wanted his confirmation he'd noticed the change. To Betsy's relief, William appeared oblivious, more concerned with dishing up the stew than listening to their conversation.

"You'll be back milking in the morning then." It was a statement, not a question from Duncan.

"I guess so," Rosey replied.

"That's good." Betsy seized the moment. "I had a letter from Grace today. She's suggesting her, Moira and I go and visit Alice and see how she's getting on. Now that Rosey's back, would you mind if I had a day off?"

"Erm." Duncan took his time to consider Betsy's request, his thumb and forefinger rubbing his chin.

"One day won't matter, will it?" Nel supported Betsy.

"No, I guess we can manage," Duncan conceded.

"Rosey, you'll have to make sure the new calf gets fed," Betsy said. "It's only just coming right."

"It's up and about," Duncan said. "It'll be fine."

Betsy worried about Duncan's casual attitude, but he was agreeing to time off, so she kept her concerns to herself.

"Thank you," she replied. "I'll give Grace a call to check when she can have a day off and pop over to see Moira after dinner and ask if we can borrow Bill's truck."

"Where have Fergus and her moved to?" Duncan asked. "Staveley, isn't it?"

"Yes, the very end of Winterslow Road," Betsy replied.

"Bit of an extravagance to use Bill's petrol rationing on a joyride that far, if you ask me." Duncan frowned his disapproval.

Just as well Betsy was only asking Duncan for time off and not the use of his truck or they wouldn't be going beyond the end of the driveway. William stayed silent but the look he gave Betsy indicated he didn't approve either. He was wasting Duncan's precious fuel everyday so it couldn't be for that reason.

"Bill might need us to collect some things on the way," Betsy suggested.

She hurried to finish her dinner, excused herself from the table and went into the passage to phone Grace.

The women at the linen flax mill were all being allowed a day off before the busy harvesting season started again. Grace said Ronnie had tomorrow off, so she'd ask Mrs McPherson for the day after that.

"We can pack a picnic to take with us as we're going to be arriving unannounced," Grace suggested.

"Can't we telephone Alice and let her know?" Betsy asked.

"According to the letters I've received from her, there's no power or telephone out there and it'll take a week for any letter to arrive and another for a reply to come back. We're better off just turning up with our picnic."

"What if she's not there?"

"She'll be there," Grace assured Betsy. "There's so much work to do and nowhere to go."

"Okay, I'll check with Moira and if you don't hear back from me, we'll pick you up the day after tomorrow, first thing in the morning."

"I'll be waiting."

Bill and Moira were still having dinner when Betsy walked past the window to knock on the back door.

"Come in, Betsy," Moira called out. "No need to knock and I'm too tired to come and open the door."

"Sorry," Betsy apologised. "Hi Moira, hello Bill. Have you had a busy day?"

"Every day is a busy day around here," Moira groaned. "We don't have the luxury of four land girls like *Whipsnade*."

Betsy stepped back. Perhaps asking Moira to join them was a bad idea, it would leave Bill managing on his own and Moira might be too grumpy and tired, to be good company on the trip. Then she realised there wouldn't be an outing if they couldn't use Bill's truck.

"Oh, they're all newbies though, even worse than us." Betsy chuckled. "At least we aren't allergic to the animals. Rosey broke out in spots when she got cow poo on her. Oops, sorry, you're still eating your dinner."

"I'm finished." Bill used a slice of bread to mop up the last remnants of gravy on his plate. "I'll go and make a cup of tea and leave you ladies to talk. I guess you've got a lot to catch up on."

"Well … actually … the reason for my visit concerns you," Betsy said.

"Really?" Bill frowned and sat back down. "Best you take a seat then."

"What is it? What's happened?" Moira looked worried.

"Grace—"

"Of course, it would be Grace," Moira interjected. "Whose life is she trying to organise now? Not Bill's?"

Betsy hesitated. Moira was right, Grace was trying to organise all of them, but it was in a nice way.

"She's just suggesting that we—you, me and her—might like to visit Alice, that's all."

"That's a nice idea," Bill said. "She's probably feeling quite isolated. How are you planning to get there?"

Betsy swallowed. "Umm … well … we were wondering if you might lend Moira your truck to drive us?"

Bill straightened in his chair and his eyes went wide but then he looked at Moira. Betsy knew he'd probably give Moira his right hand if he thought it would make her happy. She wished she had a man who looked at her like that … Roland … William …

"We could pick up any supplies you might need from Geraldine on the way back so it's not a wasted trip," Betsy suggested.

Bill smiled. "That's a good idea. There are some things we need. I'll make a list. When are you planning to go?"

Moira cleared her throat. "No one has even asked me if I want to go yet."

"It'll do you good to have a day off farm work," Bill replied.

"The day after tomorrow if it suits." Betsy ignored Moira's complaint and answered Bill's question.

"Right then, I'll fill the tank and check the truck over, make sure it's all good for the trip. You'll be wanting to leave early morning if you're going all that way in a day. The Home Guard meeting is that night so I'll need the truck back by six so I can get to the meeting on time. It wouldn't look good if I was late for training."

"Early morning?" Moira's eyes looked like marbles now.

"We'll just have to tuck you into bed early the night before." The smile Bill directed at Moira told Betsy more than she wanted to know.

"Thank you, Bill. I'll see you, Moira, not tomorrow, but the next day. Early!" She stood to leave and chuckled. "Don't worry about getting up, I can see myself out."

Betsy spent the next day ensuring Rosey knew how to do all the tasks that needed doing, especially feeding the calves. One in particular.

"Now make sure this calf gets a feed," she said. "He had a bit of a rough start."

"They all look the same to me," Rosey replied. "How am I going to know this one from any other?"

Betsy frowned, the calves all had different markings, how could Rosey not see that?

"He's got the heart on his forehead," she continued, pointing to the calf's head.

"Oh, that's cute, I hadn't noticed that before."

Betsy turned away and rolled her eyes. She knew a little how Duncan must feel.

"I can help her," William offered.

Both the presence of William at the calf shed and his offer startled Betsy. Now he chooses to turn up and offer help. To Rosey, not her. And when she wasn't going to be there. What was he playing at? She eyed him suspiciously. She'd heard William again in the night, groaning as if he was in pain, cursing like the enemy were in the room with him but she resisted the urge to go to his room and offer him solace. If he was going to cheapen her presence, then he would have to manage without it.

"Right," she said trying to sound calmer than she felt. "I'll leave you to it then. I'll go and pack the picnic for tomorrow."

Betsy strode away without looking back. She didn't want any images of William and Rosey to torture her imagination.

When Betsy arrived at Bill's the next morning, Moira was downing the last mouthful of the cup of tea Bill had made her. She had a glow to her cheeks and the look Bill gave her bore a familiarity Betsy wished for. It was the way Roland had looked at her, the first morning they'd woken in the same bed, their honeymoon night, except they weren't actually married.

Betsy waited until her and Moira were on the road before she sought confirmation.

"It looks like you and Bill are getting on a lot better."

Moira's lips curved into a dreamy smile. "We did this morning," she purred.

"That's good." Betsy tried to say the words like she meant them. She did mean them; she was happy for Moira; it was just she wished the same for herself.

"But he still doesn't acknowledge our relationship in public."

"Anyone can see though," Betsy said. "The way he looks at you."

"Mmm, I'm not sure if that's love or lust." Moira looked across at Betsy as if she might know the answer.

With the driver distracted, the vehicle veered towards the edge of the road. A bump jolted their attention and Moira pulled on the steering wheel to face the truck in the right direction.

"Best watch where you're driving." Betsy held firmly onto the door's arm rest until she felt safe. "I'm sure lust can turn into love."

"What about you and William?" Moira asked. "Is that lust or love?

"I'm engaged to Roland." Betsy swallowed loudly, grateful Moira needed to keep her eyes on the road and not see her cheeks redden with guilt.

"So, you keep saying." Moira slowed to check for traffic before she drove onto the one lane bridge before Geraldine. "Do you have any news of his whereabouts?"

"I've got the war office checking the prisoner of war lists," Betsy replied. "William said some soldiers were taken prisoner at Servia Pass about the time Roland went missing."

"And if he's a prisoner of war, you're going to stay loyal to him until they free them?"

Betsy had already asked herself that question many times. The only answer she had was the one her head kept telling her was the right thing to do. Every time, she heard the word 'loyal', you must remain loyal, you owe it to Roland to remain loyal; it felt like a tiny piece of her heart fragmented.

"They're saying the war should be over by Christmas," she answered with a feigned positivity.

"They said that last Christmas."

The double-storey boarding house where Grace was staying rose majestically on the left, surrounded by foxgloves in whites and pinks and a blending of both. Moira flicked the indicator lever. The loud ticking sounded like a time bomb counting down to the moment Betsy would have to decide how loyal she really was.

Grace wore a blue dress, and her blonde hair was tied back with a matching scarf. Betsy shifted into the middle of the bench seat to make room for her long-legged friend.

"Morning, girls." Grace was bright and cheery. "A lovely day for a drive into the country."

"Aargh," Moira groaned. "What's that stink?"

"Oh, it's just me." Grace chuckled. "You get used to it. It's just from the retting room."

"You're going to stink us out. Put the window down."

"Hang on. I'll just go and pick some flowers from the garden." Grace was back out the door before they could respond. She disappeared behind the white picket fence and soon returned with a handful of freesias. "There that'll do the trick."

The cloying scent soon filled the cabin of the truck. Betsy wished she still had the window seat and a breath of fresh air.

"Who is going to catch me up on their news first?" Grace asked when they were on the road again.

Betsy steered the conversation away from her. "Moira and Bill are getting on well. Really, really well."

"Oh, tell us more, Moira." Grace leaned forward to look past Betsy at Moira. "Mmm, second thoughts, maybe you'd better not. I might get jealous."

"Aren't there any men at the flax mill? You'd probably smell as bad as one another." Moira laughed.

"Mrs McPherson's son, Brian, has come home from the war," Grace replied. "She's been bringing him into work."

"And?"

"Well, he's rather nice-looking," Grace said. "But he's shell shocked. Hasn't said a word since he got back. Mrs McPherson is beside herself. As if she doesn't have enough to worry about."

Betsy could have added to this conversation but that would mean talking about William again, so she stayed quiet and let the other two catch up.

"And Grace needs another project? Someone to try and fix?" Moira was never one to mince her words. "What happened to Ben, your escaped soldier? Last time I saw you, he was in a detention centre. Is he still there?"

"Yes, he is. Some of them are on a hunger strike to protest the conditions. Not Ben though, he tries to not do anything to lose his privileges. He just wants to get out of there and on with his life."

"A life with you?" Moira continued her prying.

"Well," Grace hesitated. "I don't know. We hardly knew each other. While I can understand his point of view and admire him for taking a stance, it's hardly what you build a relationship on, is it? And, who knows how long it will be before he's freed. If there is anything I've learned from this war, it is that life is short, and you never know what is around the corner."

"Did you hear that, Betsy?" Moira nudged Betsy with her elbow and glanced her way.

"Keep your eyes on the road." Aloud the words were directed at Moira. Internally Betsy directed the caution to herself.

CHAPTER

14

"Surely we must be nearly there." Betsy's bottom was numb, except for the spot where an errant seat spring poked her every time the truck hit a bump. She wanted to growl at Moira and demand she drive more carefully but the road was in such a state of disrepair avoiding potholes was impossible.

"Alice wrote in her letter their cottage was the last at the end of the road," Grace said.

"There's one coming up." Moira raised her hand to point but had to quickly grab the steering wheel as a pothole jerked the vehicle off track. "Look, there on the left. You can see the smoke rising from the chimney."

The smoke didn't have to rise far before it blended with the fog that sat low in the valley like a heavy blanket. Not a blanket that offered any warmth but one that kept the morning dull and dank, denying any penetration by the sun's rays.

Betsy sighed with relief, when Moira eased off the accelerator, thinking they'd arrived at their destination.

"The road keeps going," Grace pointed ahead. "I don't think it's this one. And look there's an old man waving from the veranda." Grace waved back and laughed. "That's not how Fergus looked last time I saw him."

Betsy shifted uncomfortably as they continued until the end of the gravel came into view.

"I hope that's not it." Moira sounded incredulous. "That's not a cottage, that's a tin shed."

"It's got windows and a door," Betsy observed. "And look the chimney's smoking too."

"By the look of it, that could mean it's about to burn down." Moira turned into the driveway and shut down the engine.

"That's Fergus's truck, isn't it?" Betsy asked.

The little truck that had taken Fergus and Alice away on their wedding day sat at the back of the cottage, grass growing up around its tyres as if it had sat in the same spot since they'd arrived.

"Come on, hop out, hop out." Betsy spied Alice peering out the window and was eager to see their friend and stand and relieve her pain.

The front door opened, and Alice ran out to greet the trio.

"What a lovely surprise!" she squealed. "Come in, come in, Fergus will be home for morning tea soon. I'll show you around."

Alice's home might be a tin shed at the end of a long, narrow, bumpy road but she seemed delighted with it. She had a luminescence to her cheeks and a lightness in her step that exuded happiness. Married life appeared to agree with her. Betsy felt a tiny twinge of envy and twisted the ring on her finger. It kept her bound to Roland but felt more like a life buoy she was desperately clinging to than a commitment that brought love and comfort and filled her with the joy that Alice was clearly thriving on.

"You're looking wonderful," Grace enfolded Alice in a hug. "Married life agrees with you."

Alice's cheeks coloured scarlet and Moira roared with laughter.

"I think I know which parts Alice is enjoying the most," she teased.

"Moira!" Grace growled. "Come on, Alice, show us around."

Alice showed them through the front door into the short passage that led to the living area. There were two rooms off the passage, the one to the right held a double bed, and the room to the left was empty except for several cartons.

"You haven't finished unpacking yet?" Betsy asked.

"We don't have any furniture to put the things in," Alice replied. "Fergus has been busy."

"He's probably been way too busy in here," Moira continued her teasing as she poked her head into the bedroom.

Alice ignored the taunting, cleared her throat, and tried to maintain a ladylike manner while she ushered them into the living area. Heat emanating from the coal range raised the room temperature and drew Betsy to it. She stood back on to the range and wiggled her bottom to get the blood flowing.

"He's milled some trees and is waiting for the timber to dry before he makes some shelves," Alice explained. "Come, sit down at the table, I'll make a cuppa and you can tell me all the news."

"I need to use the toilet first, please," Moira said.

"It's out the back. A long drop," Alice sounded apologetic. "There shouldn't be any spider webs though, I brushed them away this morning."

"Oh, it's a bit different to living in the luxury of Captain Boyle's house, isn't it," Moira observed before darting out the back door.

"That was luxury for all of us." Sitting at the table Betsy reflected, it seemed she'd been a guest at other people's tables for some time now. She gazed around the room; even with its faded curtains, worn arms on the settee and patinaed table, the living area was homely. It would be nice to have something to call her own, even something as humble as Alice had.

"I love your flowers." A glass jar in the centre of the table held fresh flowers. Betsy leaned in, anticipating a bubble gum aroma from the vibrant array of pink, orange, and yellow blooms.

"They won't smell," Alice said. "They're zinnias, they don't really have a scent. They're too busy looking pretty to worry about smelling nice too."

"I assume they're out of your garden," Grace said.

"Yes, the vegetable garden." Alice giggled. "I found an unlabelled paper bag of seeds in the back shed and put them in with the other veges, thinking they might be carrots or something edible. They grew."

If it was possible, Alice's face lit up even more as she talked about her flowers.

"You must have been listening when Nel taught us all about gardening that day," Betsy said.

"It's such fun to plant a seed and watch it grow but now I've got so many of them I don't know what to do with them all," Alice said.

"You could sell them," Grace suggested. "Set yourself up as a flower farm. Fergus can farm the animals and you can farm flowers."

"That's a lovely idea but there's a slight problem," Alice replied. "Nobody's going to drive all the way to the end of the road just to buy my flowers."

"Mmm, true." Grace frowned as she sought a solution to Alice's dilemma.

"But I can give you all some to take home with you," Alice offered. "We'll pick some before you go, so they stay fresh until you get them home and into water."

"Look what I found out the back." Moira chuckled as Fergus followed her in the door. "Looks like he's almost as woolly as those sheep we passed back down the road."

"Fergus has broken the blade of his razor and we haven't been to town yet to get another," Alice explained as if she felt the need to defend her husband. He leaned in and kissed her on the forehead.

"Doesn't seem like you mind," Moira continued her teasing and Alice coloured scarlet.

"Have you told them?" Fergus asked.

"Have you told us what?" Moira glanced around at the group. "Did I miss something when I was in the loo?"

"No, no, I haven't." Alice fidgeted, swaying from one foot to the other, twisting her hands together.

Fergus put his arm around Alice and kissed the top of her head. His eyes lit up as his quiet voice shared their news.

"We're going to be parents."

"No! How? When?" It was Betsy's turn to blush and she giggled awkwardly. "Forget the how. When is the baby due?"

"Well, we're not exactly sure." Alice and Fergus stood side by side, grinning from ear to ear. "I think I'm about halfway."

"That's wonderful news." Grace leaned in to hug Alice. "No wonder you're looking so good. You've got the glow of impending motherhood."

"Did you have any morning sickness?" Moira asked. "I could never handle that, vomiting at the mere smell of food. Come to think of it, I don't want any part of it. Pregnancy, childbirth, parenting. Uggh!"

"Well, you and Bill had better be taking precautions then." It was Alice's turn to tease.

"So, you'll be making a cradle, Fergus, when you've finished the shelves." Moira deflected the conversation away.

Fergus straightened and glanced around the women as if he'd been caught out. "Yes, I'm just waiting for the timber to dry."

"Sit down," Alice encouraged the group while she busied herself placing cups and saucers, freshly-baked scones, milk, butter, and jam on the table.

"Lovely! Scones!" Moira licked her lips. "I'm too busy doing farm work to bake scones."

"Alice does farm work too." Fergus winked at Alice as he sat at the table.

"And poor Fergus is sick of scones." Alice stood behind Fergus and rubbed his shoulders. "But until the chickens start laying again, we don't have any eggs and I can't cook his favourite carrot cake."

"Nel keeps a supply of preserved eggs especially for baking," Betsy said.

"How does she preserve them?" Alice asked.

"Norton's Liquid Preservative, I think it's called," Betsy replied. "Thickens over winter, like a gravy. I had to fish them out with a ladle but once we washed the stuff off, they just looked like an ordinary egg."

"We'll have to get some next time we go to town." Alice added to her shopping list, a small notepad hanging on the side of the cupboard with a pencil attached by string.

The cups of tea were poured, and scones sliced, buttered, and spread with generous dollops of jam.

"Have you had any news about Roland?" Alice asked Betsy.

The bite of scone Betsy had taken served as a welcome reprieve to catch her breath and her emotions.

"I'm waiting on the war office to check the prisoner of war lists." She closed her eyes and tilted her cup to conceal the tears that threatened. Just why she suddenly felt overwhelmed, she couldn't fathom. Was it merely the excitement of the day? Hardly. Was it the futility of her search for Roland allowing desperation to swamp her? Possibly. Was it the guilt that it was William's face and not Roland's that she saw when she imagined herself having what Alice had? Probably. Betsy hoped her explanation would cover her feelings.

"William was told there were prisoners taken at the Servia Pass around the time that Roland disappeared. The war office is still working to get their names. William said they were helping the Australians, backing them up while they retreated from the German invasion into Greece. William had gone by train but said others went by truck and they were bombed. William said there were deaths but there were also injuries and soldiers taken prisoner," she jabbered until she needed to stop and take a breath.

"William certainly has a lot to say," Moira observed.

Betsy lowered her gaze and swallowed. All she'd succeeded in doing was accentuating the feelings she was trying to hide. Trust Moira to notice.

"Grace," Alice was kind enough to turn the conversation away. "What about Ben? Have you heard from him? Is he still in the detention camp?"

"Yes, he is. I was telling the girls on the way out, some of them are on a hunger strike but he's not doing anything to jeopardise getting out of there as soon as possible."

Fergus and Alice looked at one another. "We've been lucky so far," Fergus said. "Hopefully the ballots won't find me out here and if they do, I'll be able to argue that I'm in an essential industry, married and a father."

Alice touched her hands to her stomach and looked down. "I hope so."

"Well, you are miles from anywhere," Moira said. "It's not like the Japanese are going to invade you all the way in here."

"The Japanese?" Fergus's eyes went wide.

"Yes, coastal areas have been instructed to stow supplies in forty-four-gallon drums in case we need to hide if they invade. All the farmers have them stashed over the backs of their farms. They've set up a Home Guard as well, so those who haven't gone away to fight can help protect us at home."

"Let's forget about the war." Betsy wanted to steer the talk towards happier topics.

"It's fairly easy to do that out here," Alice replied. "The newspaper only comes once a week, and we only go to town when we have to."

"Tell us what you've been doing on the farm," Grace suggested.

"Fergus has rebuilt the yards, given me a covered area to milk Daisy, the cow. He and Jericho have been pulling out the overgrown gorse bushes and ploughing the land to re-grass."

"Alice has got the vegetable garden up and running, pruned all the fruit trees, helped me with the shearing and drenching and looked after the abandoned lambs of course."

They were like a mutual admiration society, full of praise for one another. What wasn't communicated by their words was conveyed by a look or a touch. Betsy sat quietly and envied their relationship. What they had built in such a short time was what she wanted, what she would have to wait years for if Roland was held captive by the enemy and unlikely to be released until the war was over. Could she wait that long? Was her loyalty strong enough to give her the patience required? Or should she listen to her friends' advice, acknowledge that life was too short, and opportunities should be embraced, especially when they were right in front of her on a daily basis.

Moira's laughter broke Betsy out of her reverie. "What, what's so funny?" she asked.

"Alice!" Moira replied as if that was all that was required.

"Alice what?"

"Alice and Daisy and Jericho and all the animals she's named and is yet to name."

"Alice's heart is so big." Fergus kissed his wife on the cheek. "She has room in there for everyone."

Perhaps that was the message Betsy needed to hear. There was room in a woman's heart to love more than one person.

Alice blushed.

"I'll leave you ladies to have a good chinwag." Fergus stood, kissed Alice again and prepared to go back to work. "I'm sure there's lots to catch up on without me hanging around."

It wasn't the sun that told the land girls it was late in the day, for that still hadn't been able to penetrate the clouds but their cheeks aching from laughter, throats dry from talking despite umpteen cups of tea and Daisy bellowing to be milked.

"I'd better get on with my evening chores," Alice said. "Before it gets dark."

"And we'd best get on the road," Moira added. "So, we can get home, before Bill starts to worry, I've crashed his truck."

"And, so he can make it to the Home Guard meeting on time," Betsy said.

"Oh, I almost forgot." Alice plonked the last of the cups on the kitchen bench. "We'll do a quick tour of the garden and I'll pick you some flowers to take home."

It was easy to ignore the rundown facade of the building Alice and Fergus called home. A row of brilliant yellow dahlias stood proudly on spindly stems, their spiked petals radiated as if they were miniature suns capable of lighting up the world, their green foliage hiding the wooden piles that supported the cottage. Opposite the dahlias, a line of hydrangeas provided an equally impressive but contrasting display of tiny white petals gathering to form full moon orbs. Between day and night sat a broken concrete path that led the group to a netting fence separating the section from the orchard. A climbing rose in the palest of pinks ambled its way along the fence sprinkling its subtle perfume.

Stepping through the gate into the garden was like walking into another world. The grass was soft under their feet as they followed Alice single file between the neat rows of cabbages, silver beet plants, carrots, and radishes. They had to duck under the branch of a lemon tree laden with ripening fruit to reach the zinnia's standing in a row itching to be picked.

"Help yourselves," Alice offered.

"I feel like a little girl in a lolly shop." Betsy giggled and pointed to each of the different colours. "Eeny, meeny, miny, moe …"

"Just take a bunch of all of them," Alice suggested. "It's not like I'm going to run out."

Betsy's and Grace's eagerly picked bunches were tied with string, just tight enough to keep them from escaping.

"Don't you want any, Moira?" Grace didn't wait for Moira's answer and picked another bunch for her.

"They make me think of Bill putting flowers on his wife's grave." Moira crossed her arms across her chest. "I seem to be forever haunted by the ghost of his dead wife. I'm sure I'd not just be his land girl if it wasn't for her."

"Well, these are from Alice especially for you." Grace held the bunch while Alice tied a piece of string around their stems.

"Thank you." Moira's eyes glazed over as she stared into the flowers as if the answers she sought were hidden in their tiny centres.

"Thank you so much for visiting." Alice gave each of them a hug. "It's been wonderful to have female company."

"Perhaps you'll have a little girl of your own," Betsy suggested.

"Oh, I hope so." Alice wrapped her arms around herself. "But a boy to be Fergus's little helper on the farm would be nice too. So long as the baby is healthy."

"You look after yourself and I'm sure the baby will be fine." Grace spoke with her motherly tone.

Despite the annoying seat spring, Betsy was happy to sit in between Grace and Moira for the return trip, allowing their conversation to flow past her while she contemplated life and relationships that had the power to elevate living to another level. By the time they'd made it to the end of the gravel road, she'd concluded everything came down to choices, choices only she could make. How long was she prepared to wait for answers about Roland? What was she prepared to sacrifice in remaining loyal to him? Would she even be able to have the sort of relationship she desired with William, the post-war William because the only thing that was clear was that the pre-war William no longer existed?

CHAPTER

15

It was to offer an apology to Betsy, that William headed over to the calf shed when his pounding head told him to keep his hangover under the bedcovers. He thought his offer to help Rosey would earn him the smile he craved from Betsy but instead she scowled at him again. He'd felt that piercing look before, like her brown eyes were firing deadly spears direct at his chest, when he'd helped Moira after the dance. Betsy had misjudged him then and she was misjudging him now. Yes, he'd help Rosey but not for any other reason than the poor woman didn't have a clue what she was doing and would surely kill the calf Betsy had become attached to. How would he convince her otherwise? He'd have to start by ensuring the calf survived.

William never got the chance to explain his intentions to Betsy, she was gone the next morning, long before he managed to drag his damaged body from his bed. He'd endured another rough night, the bedding looked as dishevelled as he felt, sheets and blankets strangling one another, his pillow flung to the far side of the room like it was a grenade he'd hurled at the enemy.

"Good morning, sleepyhead," Nel greeted him as he entered the kitchen. "Betsy dropped this off for you."

William's pulse quickened. Betsy had left something for him. His excitement quickly deflated when he realised it was merely some mail, she must have collected from the letterbox. He scuffed the chair legs across the floor and slumped down at the table.

"It's from Australia." Nel's cheeks coloured when she realised her comment gave away her nosiness.

Knowing the letter had to be from Jack, William grabbed it, eager to see how life was for the Australian.

"Bugger," he muttered, shaking his head. The simple task of opening an envelope was no longer easy.

He wasn't sure whether Mum had been watching him or heard him swear but she appeared at his side with scissors in hand. He appreciated her silence, the simple offering of assistance. He held the envelope up while she snipped the end. His left hand and her right hand, together they got the job done and Jack's familiar scrawl fell out onto the table.

Gidday cobber. William heard the words as much as he saw them, the familiar twang that had often pulled him from his self-pity, served to do so again.

Maria says gidday too. I've told her that's all she's allowed to do after I showed her that photo of us up on deck. She thought you were handsome and wouldn't believe me when I said you didn't have a sweetheart waiting for you at home.

William smiled as the memories of Betsy's body tucked in beside him sent blood to regions, he didn't want his mother to see. He'd be a happy man if Betsy was his sweetheart but the oblong timber-framed mirror that hung on the wall above his dresser and greeted him each morning was another reminder he wasn't whole. It reflected the ugly scar that ran through his useless eye. He fought the internal argument his injuries were all Betsy saw; that she could no longer be attracted to him. She might sidle up to him under darkness but the looks she gave him in the cold light of day said otherwise.

I hope your welcome home was as good as mine and Orari has whatever it is you need to move on. It's taken a bit for me to settle down, the pace of life at home is a lot slower, just as well, since I'm now one-legged, couldn't keep up otherwise.

William laughed, even on paper Jack's sense of humour lifted the mood.

Not complaining though. Those poor buggers that will never make it back. Even worse – the unlucky sods stuck in prisoner of war camps – they might be wishing they were dead. I bet the Huns aren't offering them any five-star accommodation.

Images of lifeless bloody bodies blurred the words on the page. William scrunched his eyes closed until darkness blotted out the memories. Roland's face replaced them. The man that stood between he and Betsy. Was he one of those lifeless bodies or a prisoner of war? Either way William needed him gone if Betsy was ever to become his.

Our government have got a land allocation scheme for returned soldiers and I'm thinking of making an application for some farmland. You being a farmer and all, I thought I'd write and see what you reckon is the best way to go. There're so many options – dairy, sheep, pigs, fruit, or grains. What do you think would make the most money? I hope you've kept up with the writing practice and I'll get a letter from you soon.

What did William think? He couldn't envisage himself being a farmer with one arm. How the hell did Jack imagine he was going to become a one-legged farmer with no prior experience or knowledge? But that was Jack. In the short time William had known him, he'd always looked on the bright side. What was it he said? The alternative didn't bear thinking about.

William smiled and folded the letter back into its envelope. He hadn't been practising his writing; he hadn't seen any need to, but he'd at least make the effort to reply to Jack. He'd try to look on the bright side while he was drafting his response.

"Good news, then?" Mum asked.

"Just an Aussie mate I met on the ship asking for advice about farming," William replied. "He's thinking of applying for some farmland under the allocation scheme for returned soldiers."

"They have that in New Zealand too." The excitement in Nel's voice dissipated when she must have realised any scheme application by William would see him moving away. "But you don't need to do that, there's plenty of farmland right here for you. Do you think it's a good idea for your friend?"

"Well, he's only got one leg so anything is going to be tricky but if anyone can give it a go, Jack can."

His mother hesitated as if she wasn't certain her thoughts should be voiced.

"If a man with one leg can give farming a go." She placed her hand on William's shoulder. "My son with one hand can give it a go too."

William turned and stared at her for the longest time. His mother, the woman who only ever wanted the best for her son, often knew what that was before he did. This seemed like one of those occasions. He'd never liked to disappoint her. He sighed; the long, slow exhalation released a bevy of emotions. Frustration, anger, fear dissipated like a weight being lifted from his shoulders.

"No time like the present." William stood, wrapped his good arm around his mother and squeezed her shoulder. "Everything is going to be alright, Mum."

"I know," she whispered as tears welled up.

Everything being alright had to start with helping Rosey, look after the calf Betsy had rescued.

"I'll go and make sure Rosey's got everything under control at the cowshed," William said.

"Wait." Nel took the loose cuff of William's right sleeve and neatly folded it up until it sat just below his stump. She grabbed a safety pin from her knitting bag and secured the sleeve. "It'll be safer out of the way."

It would be safer if he still had two hands! Feeling his anger festering again, William breathed long and slow, nodded and feigned a smile for his mother's benefit before escaping out the door.

He found Rosey in the cowshed, running between the bales, excrement splattered all over her overalls and on her arms and face. The remaining cows, yet to be milked, looked as panicked as her and were pushing back against the yard rails as if there was someplace else, they'd rather be.

"Stop running," William yelled. The words echoed through the cowshed and his own head, repeating until the message was received. Far more important than Rosey rushing in the cowshed was William's own avoidance of the truth of his situation.

"Well, help me then!" Rosey looked as if she was about to burst into tears.

William stared from his left hand to the space where his right hand should have been and pondered the options. What could he do when the limb his brain most wanted to communicate with no longer existed? He couldn't put cups on the cow's udders nor remove them, he couldn't change the milk cans, but he could usher cows into the bales, he could wash their teats, and he could hand milk to finish them off. Each of the tasks would take him longer but they could still be done one-handed.

"Which cow is nearly finished?" he asked Rosey.

"That one." Rosey held her head between her hands, oblivious to the filth she was spreading, and looked from one cow to the other. "No, that one … arggh, I don't bloody know. How the hell does Betsy do this by herself?"

William touched his fingers to Rosey's forearm and stilled her. It was easier to assume a calm demeanour when the other person was a blithering mess. He'd noticed that on the battlefront as well. The ones who made officer status were always calm under pressure.

"You can tell by the tightness of their udder." William moved between the two cows and ran his hand down the back of their udders. Pointing to the cow whose bag was saggy he asked Rosey to remove the cups. "I'll finish milking her by hand. You go and sit with the other one and catch your breath."

The rhythm of pulling and squeezing of the cow's teats came naturally to William, albeit one teat at a time took longer but it was still something he could do with the same outcome, milk squirting into a metal bucket. He sat on the small stool beside the cow and rested his forehead on its belly. He'd missed the even-paced rise and fall of the cow's belly, a welcome reminder there were some things in the world the war hadn't touched.

When the milk flow ended, William carefully moved the bucket out of the way, stood and released the cow from the bale, giving her a thank you pat on the rump.

"Hello, girl," he greeted the next animal that came his way chewing on its cud.

William smiled. His presence had created a sense of calm. Having a purpose raised his spirits. Perhaps what he'd told his mother wasn't just a lie to pacify her; perhaps everything would be alright. When William had washed the cow's teats in clean water, he swapped places with Rosey, and they repeated the cycle.

The army functioned on cycles, routines that began at dawn and continued until lights out. William was happier knowing what would happen and when. Maybe it had been nothing more sinister than the lack of routine since his injury that had thrown him off kilter.

An hour later, Rosey stood, hands on hips and surveyed the empty yard. "Thank goodness for that. You saved the day, Billy."

William puffed out his chest, as if ready to receive a medal bestowed on him. He closed his eyes and savoured the good feeling of having a purpose. He smelt Rosey's closeness before he felt her lips on his. His eyes went wide, and he stumbled back.

"Sorry, sorry," Rosey stammered. "I just wanted to say thank you. I couldn't have done it without you."

William swallowed and glanced around the cowshed hoping Betsy hadn't returned unexpectedly. "I'm sorry … you caught me by surprise." William turned away so Rosey wouldn't see guilt colour his cheeks. "I'll go and shut the cows in, and you go feed the calves."

The walk up the race was long enough for William to get his thoughts in line, make them stand to attention so he could inspect them and decide which to discard as pure foolishness and which to retain. Rosey's kiss and what it could possibly lead to fell into the first category despite the protestations from his groin. He had to stop living day to day and cast his eyes further ahead. The future he imagined would include Betsy not Rosey. Rosey would be nothing more than an indulgence, a satisfaction of his physical needs that would cause more trouble than good.

His father must have readied the paddock for the cows, and they were happily munching on the fresh grass when William reached the gate and closed it. He decided to put some distance between himself and Rosey. With his future in mind, William hurried back down the race. He avoided the calf shed and headed straight for the house. He had a letter to write. Jack was with the Australian battalion that fought in the Servia Pass. Perhaps he had met Roland and knew of his fate.

"I suppose you want the truck again?" Duncan was at the table, his normally broad shoulders slumped with resignation.

Aware of his father's disappointment, William rephrased his response.

"If you like, I could take the milk to the factory and pick up any supplies you'd like in town. I've got a letter I'd like to write and get in the post, and I thought I could bring Brian McPherson out here for a visit. His mother takes him to work every day and he sits in the tearoom from eight till five. A bit of fresh air would do him good, I reckon."

Duncan sat up with a start, almost choked on a piece of toast and coughed until he drank from the glass of water Nel handed him. Eventually he was able to nod his assent.

William finished his porridge, borrowed pen, ink and paper from his mother and went to his room to craft a reply to Jack. His enthusiasm was short-lived. Writing left-handed with a fountain pen wasn't easy. The side of his hand, resting on the paper for stability, smudged every word he scrawled. He screwed up the paper and threw it against the wall and went in search of a pencil.

The note that eventually got folded and stuffed into an envelope was barely legible, short, and abrupt but asked the important question about Roland's whereabouts and offered advice about farming, suggesting dairy farming would be the most profitable assuming Maria could milk cows.

William found his mother in the washhouse scrubbing clothes in the tub and asked her to address the envelope so he could be sure it would get delivered.

It was with a sense of purpose that he drove down the track, the full milk cans loaded on the back by Duncan, the addressed envelope on the seat beside him, a smile on his face and an image of Betsy in his mind.

CHAPTER

16

The return journey from Staveley to Orari seemed shorter and conversation was exhausted by the time Moira and Betsy reached *Whipsnade Farm* after dropping Grace off in Geraldine. The last of the sun's rays lingered on the peaks of the Southern Alps and in the half-light, Betsy could see the silhouette of people in the calf shed.

Her grip on her posy of zinnia's tightened as alarm bells triggered. Farm chores should have been completed by now and everybody inside cleaning up for dinner. Why were they still at the calf shed? Who were they? She squinted to get a better view and recognised the side profile of Rosey; her buxomness giving her away as it always did. The other person was as tall and had short hair so wasn't Peggy or Jean. It was a man. He moved to stand back on, arms hanging at his side or in this case only half an arm on one side. William. Betsy's breath caught in her mouth.

"Right, here you are then." Moira stopped the truck beside the path to the house.

Startled, Betsy dropped the flowers, and they splayed across her lap.

"Blast," she cursed as she scrunched the zinnias into an untidy bunch, one eye still on the pair in the shed and a sense of dread churning her stomach.

"Best you get them inside and into some water before you kill them," Moira warned.

The flowers were the least of Betsy's concern and inside was the last place she was going. She clenched her teeth and muttered under her breath. "Bloody Rosey."

If the day with Alice had taught Betsy anything it was that you held onto the things, be they human or otherwise, that were precious to you. All Betsy could imagine in this instant was that Rosey was doing her best to steal both William and the calf from her.

She opened the truck door and climbed out ready to stride across the yard and confront Rosey.

"Bye," Moira said. "Thank you for the lift, it was nice spending the day with you, see you again soon."

Moira's sarcasm was lost on Betsy. "Yes, bye," she said, closing the door without glancing back.

The crunch of the departing truck's tyres on the metalled track drowned out any conversation Betsy was eager to hear. She stopped mid-stride, her head jerked back, and she sucked in a breath as the silhouettes merged into one.

Time stopped in that moment. Like the silhouette, the emotions racing about Betsy's head all blended into one confused blackness. She blinked; perhaps the image wasn't real, but the same sight greeted her opened eyes. What should she do? Confront them? Demand Rosey let go of William? Scream that William was hers?

As she stood in the middle of the track, an evening breeze blowing her fringe across her brow, reason and rational thinking slowly edged its way in. William wasn't Betsy's. Roland was. It was just a hug; it didn't mean anything. And even if it did, it was none of her business.

Betsy looked down at the zinnias, each one unique but beautiful, cupped petals, pointed stamens, delicate filaments in a rainbow of colours all needing some water. She needed to take care of the things she had control over and let everything else look after itself. She turned and headed for the house.

"Oh hello, dear," Nel said. "I thought you might be William. He went over to the shed when he got back from dropping Brian home. Rosey was having a spot of bother with the calves. Have you had a lovely day visiting Alice?"

Nel had either been lied to by William or Betsy had jumped to a lot of unfounded conclusions in the short time she'd been home. She was unsure which point to address first and her confusion was compounded by the staring eyes of Peggy and Jean. The land girls sat at the table with Duncan; his head was hidden in the folds of the newspaper, but their eyes were fixed on Betsy as if she had food stuck on the end of her nose. She didn't but went cross-eyed to check and brushed her hand across her cheeks and chin to ensure there was nothing else askew.

"What?" she demanded.

They dropped their eyes to the flowers.

"They're zinnias."

"Here's a vase, dear." Nel handed Betsy a jar from the cupboard. "Looks like they need some water."

When the flowers' stems were submerged, Betsy put the jar on the windowsill.

"Why was Brian here?" she asked Nel.

"William thought it might be nice for him to have some country air. He picked him up when he dropped the milk at the factory. Brian's been here for the day. It seemed to brighten him up. He was quite jumpy though. Any loud noise and he must think he's back at the front."

Duncan lowered the newspaper and spoke. "He will be back at the front if these newspaper reports are correct. The Japanese are on our doorstep."

Nel ignored her husband, as if not acknowledging his comment would lessen its seriousness and continued. "Brian didn't speak but I saw him smiling and nodding."

"That's good." Betsy was going to say that was very kind of William, but he and Rosey burst into the room together as if they were conjoined twins and left her stunned into silence, mouth gaping like a clown in a sideshow stall.

She looked Rosey up and down, sizing up the opposition and had to raise a hand over her mouth to hide the grin that formed. Rosey was covered from head to toe in excrement, her hair, her clothes and where skin was exposed, green splotches intermingled with red spots. She was clearly allergic to cows and that knowledge brought Betsy more joy than it should.

William's arm was wrapped around Rosey, but it fell away when he saw Betsy. He shifted awkwardly, putting space between them like a demarcation line he hadn't crossed.

"Rosey needed help," he offered in explanation.

It was then Betsy noticed Rosey's eyes. She'd been crying or more correctly, she was crying. Any glee Betsy had been feeling was now replaced with dread.

"What's wrong?" Betsy wrapped her arms across her chest, for protection or comfort, or both. Silence engulfed the room, and she repeated her question, demanding an answer. "What's wrong?"

William and Rosey glanced at one another. Betsy imagined it was a signal to ensure their stories matched, that the truth they'd conspired to hide would remain undisclosed.

"It's your calf." William spoke on their behalf. "It's got scours."

"Scours?" Betsy turned to Duncan hoping her query wasn't one of those dumb questions Duncan would shake his head at.

"Diarrhoea," he answered, no head shake, no further explanation.

"It's poorly," William continued. "I don't think it will make it through the night."

"I've only been gone for a day." Betsy felt the heat rise inside her; her face reddened. "How can an animal die from diarrhoea in less than twelve hours?"

"If its weak to start with." Duncan shrugged as if it was an everyday occurrence.

"Can't we get the vet out to it?" Desperation and panic squeezed Betsy's voice into a high-pitched squeal.

"That would cost more than the calf is worth," Duncan replied.

Betsy searched for solutions. "I'll go to the shed. I'll tube feed it again."

"I think it's beyond that," William said.

Unsure whether it was pity or guilt she saw on William's face, Betsy lashed out. If he wanted to protect Rosey, then let him bear the brunt of her anger.

"What would you know? You're not a farmer or so you keep saying. You're no good for anything remember."

William flinched and Rosey stepped forward as if she was about to defend him.

"And what would you know?" Betsy redirected her barrage. "You're allergic to cows."

As soon as the words left her mouth, Betsy regretted them. It was a silly statement, clearly nonsensical.

"Now, now," Duncan tried to defuse the tension. "These things happen. I did warn you not to get too attached."

Betsy stormed from the house as the words hit the mark.

Too attached. That was the crux of the problem. She was too attached to Roland who was God knows where. She was too attached to William who was everywhere he wasn't supposed to be, and she was too attached to the damn calf whose death could only be a signal *everything* was beyond her control.

She reached the calf shed in double quick time. Despite the warnings, she had to try and save the animal … Roland … William. The calf lay cast in a separate pen; its stomach hollow, its breath raspy, a trail of milky discharge caked its tail and behind. But it was the stench that assaulted her nostrils. Was this what death smelled like?

She wasted no time in making up a bottle of milk, attaching the feeder tube while she stepped outside for a last inhale of fresh air. Holding her breath, she straddled the calf, heaved its dead weight semi upright and wedged its shoulders between her legs. She lifted its head and held it, so the calf's neck was extended while she fed the tube into its mouth and down, what she hoped, was the animal's oesophagus.

"Oh, God, don't let me be the one who kills you."

Betsy needed to breathe but she needed to concentrate more, not much longer, she just had to get a small amount of milk into the animal. It had perked up the first time she'd done it, surely it would work this time too. She lifted the end of the bottle and watched the milk run down the tube, praying it really was the nourisher of life she'd learned about in Sunday school.

There was no acknowledgement from the calf. As soon as Betsy removed the tube and stepped outside for fresh air, the calf flopped lifelessly back down. Feeling defeated Betsy slumped down to the floor at the entrance to the shed. It was far enough away for the stench to not engulf her but close enough to watch the calf for any miniscule hint that her efforts had made a positive difference. Her temples throbbed and she rubbed the back of her neck in a futile attempt to ease the tension that had her in its grip.

Cold seeped into Betsy's bones, seeming to freeze them at the awkward angles at which she found herself in darkness, still slouched against the corrugated iron walls of the calf shed. Outside, a smattering of stars provided the only illumination in an otherwise charcoal sky. Everything was quiet except for the distant hoot of a Morepork. Too quiet. Betsy scrambled to her knees and crawled in the direction of the calf. Her stomach spasmed and she dry retched at the stench, but she kept going, she needed to hear the calf's raspy breath. Silence. She felt around for its head, placed her fingers in front of its nostrils and willed for a hint of breath to signal life. Nothing. In the darkness, she couldn't see whether the animal's chest rose and fell. She cursed herself for not bringing a torch.

Dejected, she sat back against the shed wall. She'd failed. She let her tears fall. Whether they were for the calf, for Roland or for the mess her life was, it didn't matter. In this moment, she was alone, and it wasn't a feeling she enjoyed. Betsy sat, hugging herself, until her tears exhausted themselves and her. She leaned her head back, closed her eyes and sighed

Chin up, girl.

Betsy had drifted off, but she was wide awake upon hearing those three words as if whispered straight into her ear. Her wide eyes scanned the darkness, seeking the truth. Could it be possible or was she merely dreaming? The encouragement Roland always gave her right when she needed it, sounded too clear to merely be a figment of her imagination.

Was he here?

Had he come back from the war and found her in the middle of nowhere in the middle of the night? It sounded too bizarre to be true, but the effect was the same. Betsy stood, inhaled deeply, and lifted her chin before leaving the calf shed for the warmth of her bed before the sun brought another day.

That day arrived all too quickly with the piercing ring of Betsy's alarm. Her eyes ached from crying; her limbs ached from sleeping in the calf shed but worst of all her heart felt numb. She wanted to pull the bedding up over her head like protective walls around her heart but noises from outside her bedroom reminded her there were jobs to be done, cows to be milked and people with expectations of her regardless of how she felt.

Chin up, girl! She repeated Roland's words to herself as she climbed out of bed and dressed. It became her adopted mantra for the foreseeable future.

"You look like you're fresh from battle," William observed when Betsy entered the kitchen.

His words stopped her in her tracks. She hadn't expected William to be up and about at this early hour. The irony of the remark, from a battle worn soldier more scarred than she would ever be, made her laugh.

"Not a battle I won, unfortunately," she replied.

"The calf died?" William moved towards her as if he anticipated the answer and wanted to console her.

Betsy felt the tears, she'd thought she'd exhausted, quiver beneath a thin veneer that would crack if she allowed William to be nice to her.

"I've got cows to milk." She shook the tears away and stood straight with a determined slant to her chin.

"I'll come and help you," William offered.

"Not necessary. Rosey will be there." Betsy buried her clenched hands deep into her pockets.

"Ermm, no she won't." William winced as if the revelation caused him pain or guilt.

Betsy assumed it was guilt. "Why not? What have you done?"

William huffed with indignation. "She has a bovine allergy."

"In more ways than one." Related to cattle and slow and stupid. Betsy didn't like the sneer that coated her comment, but it escaped before she had a chance to rein it in. "I'd best be going."

"I'll come with you," William repeated his offer.

Betsy stared at William's missing hand. She felt the surge of his anger boring into her, an accusation that was matched by the heat of her guilt.

"I can milk, even one-handed. I helped Rosey while *you* weren't here."

Betsy was grateful this was a battle of words and not weapons for surely William would win. She was wise enough to acknowledge the loneliness she'd felt last night would be with her forever if she didn't concede defeat.

"Thank you. You get the cows in. I'll set the shed up and we'll take it from there."

She didn't wait for a response and only released the breath she'd been holding when she left the confines of the house. She paused on the concrete step, registered the warning written in the sunrise painting the swathe of clouds a fiery red. There was a battle brewing. Was it the one she'd just endured or was there more to come?

William had the cows at the shed quicker than Betsy anticipated. She exited the machine room, after setting up the first milk can, to find him squatted on a stool washing a cow's teats with water, he scooped one-handed from a bucket. Her first urge was to offer to help but she checked herself as he looked up at her.

"The other one is ready for the cups," he announced. "I can start and finish them; I just can't do the middle bit."

Thus, the routine for the milking was set. The pair swapped bales as each cow came and went. Betsy made sure the full milk cans were swapped for empty ones and those cows that didn't come into the shed willingly were chased up when their turn arrived. The rhythmic pulsing of the milking machines eased everyone: man, woman and cattle, into a sense of calmness which felt more like a ceasefire than a skirmish at the warfront.

Betsy and William kept their thoughts to themselves. There was no conversation but alone was the last thing Betsy felt. Knowing William was there, gave her comfort. The feeling wasn't what she was certain Alice had with Fergus, but it felt like the next best thing and that filled Betsy's heart with a contentment she hadn't felt for some time.

CHAPTER

17

William walked back to the house, shoulders back, a happy grin, confident and contented. He'd helped Betsy and he'd seen enough through her tough veneer to know she'd appreciated his efforts. He held no expectations she would voice it aloud, but it was a start.

The noise of a vehicle on the driveway drew his attention. He assumed it would be the mailman, but he'd have stopped at the letterbox unless the delivery was something important like a telegram. These days telegrams weren't welcome arrivals, but the war office's means of delivering bad news. William's heart thudded, and he registered this is what it must have felt like when the bad news about him had been delivered.

It was Bill's truck that came into view.

"Good morning," he called through the open driver's window, his forearm resting casually on the door. "Just the man I wanted to see."

"Morning, Bill, come inside, we're about to have breakfast."

"Already eaten," Bill replied. "I just need to talk to you."

"Well, come inside for a cuppa," William headed for the washhouse. "I can't talk on an empty stomach."

The kitchen was a hive of activity with everyone seated at the table passing about the milk jug to pour a share of the fresh cream over their plates of steaming porridge.

"Morning, Bill," Duncan greeted his neighbour. "You're out and about early, do you need a hand with something?"

Bill's eyes darted from William's hand to his face and a laugh escaped before he shifted awkwardly, cleared his throat, and took on a serious demeanour.

"I've joined the Home Guard and think William should consider volunteering too."

Twigging to Bill's sense of humour, it was William's turn to laugh as he raised his amputated limb.

"I think you need two hands to help with something like that." William joked about his injury.

There was a collective inhalation, the room went silent, and everyone stared at William. He couldn't decide if they were shocked or pitying him, but he felt the need to fill the silence.

"Well, it's true," he continued. "I can't hold a rifle anymore."

"Yeah, but you can teach those who've never held one in their life how to do it properly, so the recoil doesn't smash their shoulder to bits," Bill said.

William slowly nodded. That much was true. He'd thought his time in the cowshed was over but the last couple of days had proven he'd just had to learn what he could do and let others pick up the slack. Perhaps he could apply the same to soldiering.

"And you've got two legs," Bill added. "You can teach us the drills. They've put out a training manual, we're just waiting for our copy to arrive in the mail."

Memories of hours and hours of marching, backwards and forwards across the fields at Burnham, made William sit and take the weight off his feet. Left, right, left, right, in sun, wind and rain had seemed futile at the time but it meant when they reached the front, the soles of their feet were hardened like a farmer's calloused hands. Treks between camps seemed like mere strolls not miles advancing from one battlefront to another.

"And you've had the army discipline drilled into you." Bill must have assumed William needed further convincing. "God knows we need to be arranged into some semblance of order."

"Why?" It was Nel that joined the conversation with a simple question and a demeanour that demanded an answer.

Bill looked from William to Duncan and back again as if he thought this was a conversation best held away from sensitive female ears.

"Because, dear," Duncan answered. "As I keep saying, it is a matter of when the Japanese arrive, not if."

Nel huffed. "We're in Orari not on the coast like Christchurch or Timaru." She stood and hurried over to the kettle bubbling away on the coal range. "Would you like a cuppa, Bill?"

"A cuppa won't save anyone if we're invaded, Nel," Duncan continued. "If the Japanese want to take over New Zealand, they might start with the coastal towns but I'm damn sure they won't stop there."

"Why ever would they want to take over New Zealand?" Nel's tone indicated she thought the idea preposterous. "We're just a little country at the bottom of the world."

"A little country with lots of resources," Duncan answered. "Fertile land, fresh water, coal, forests."

"But we've sent our men to help Europe," Nel countered. "Surely they would come and return the favour if we were invaded."

"That relies on the Japanese waiting until the war in Europe is over." Sarcasm peppered Duncan's voice. "That's the very thing they're not going to wait for. We're an easy target while everyone else is occupied on the other side of the world."

"Their king is our king too." Nel had always been a royalist. "We're British subjects. They'd have to come."

"Mum," William attempted to stop his mother's train of thought. "It took weeks for us to reach the war on the other side of the world. It would take them the same time to get here, and it could be too late by then. We need to defend our own shores."

"The Home Guard might have a chance if someone like William can give them some training and guidance," Duncan added. "What do you say, son? Are you going to make a contribution?"

"He's already made a contribution." Nel looked on the verge of tears. She moved to stand behind William and placed her hands on his shoulders as if the action would anchor him permanently. "Surely they can't ask any more of my son."

William lay his hand across his mother's. "Mum, they're not asking, I'm offering."

"That's great." Bill didn't wait for Nel to counter William's offer. "What about Brian? He can join too, the more of you with experience, the better."

"That poor boy can't even speak," Nel said.

"Yes, Mum's right about that." William patted his mother's hand. "Brian either jumps with fright or runs for cover at the slightest noise. I don't think he'll be up to being around firearms any time soon."

"One's better than none," Bill said. "They've scheduled a training day for the weekend. Can you make that? I can pick you up."

"I can drive one-handed." William noticed his father's frown and decided it was wise to accept the offer. "But sure, that would be good."

"Great, I'll see you right after breakfast on Saturday."

"Your cuppa, Bill?" Nel remembered the kettle and brought it to the table.

"No time for that, Nel." Bill headed towards the door. "Moira and I have a big day of fencing to get done. The bloody river has undermined the fence line again. I've got posts suspended in mid-air thanks to Mother Nature."

The washhouse door was no sooner shut when Duncan steered the conversation back to farming.

"Right, we'll need to re-organise things," he said. "Rosey can't milk cows anymore."

"Rosey's leaving?" Betsy asked.

William couldn't tell if her expression was one of surprise or delight.

"No, unfortunately not. You land girls are assigned for three months of training so that's how long we've got to have you for," Duncan replied.

"Duncan," Nel admonished her husband, but he continued undeterred.

"Well, Nel, it's bad enough we must have women working on farms but now the powers that be insist we have a land girl who's allergic to cows. Heaven forbids, if she's allergic to pigs and sheep as well."

"Betsy and I milked the cows this morning." William looked across at Betsy and smiled hoping she'd agree it was a good idea for them to continue working together.

Duncan shook his head in disapproval.

"We managed fine," William countered his father's negative response. "We can keep doing that."

"This is a training farm." Duncan continued to shake his head. "The whole point is to train the land girls in all facets of farming so that no matter where they are assigned to next, they have some inkling of what they're meant to be doing. It's my reputation on the line here and I don't want to be made to look like a fool."

William had seen the look on his father's face many a time. It was usually futile to argue with him when his eyebrows drew into a continuous brow and a furrow creased his forehead.

"Peggy." Duncan's gruff tone had Peggy sitting to attention. "You continue with the pigs for another week and show Rosey what to do, while Betsy teaches Jean how to milk and then we'll swap over."

"I could teach Jean how to milk." If William couldn't work with Betsy, he figured he could do her a favour instead but the glare she fired his way was like a lightning strike which would have scarred his other cheek if it had been real. He regretted opening his mouth. Two steps forward and one step back. William hoped he'd make more progress in training the Home Guard than he was with Betsy.

"We've got to wean and dock the lambs so that could work." Duncan rubbed his forehead. "William, you head out on Jess and bring the mob of ewes and lambs into the yards. If we haven't finished by milking time, then you and Jean can do the milking while the rest of us finish the docking. That'll sort today at least, and I'll worry about getting the weaner pigs to the abattoir and the bull out with the cows another day."

"What about getting the milk to the factory?" William asked.

"Blast! Yes, we'll need to do that too."

"I'll take it," William offered. "I can pick up Brian again and he might be a helping hand in the yards."

"Or another hindrance," Duncan muttered before swallowing the last of his cup of tea.

"Good, you're back. William, we want to separate the lambs from the ewes as quick as possible." Duncan looked relieved when William and Brian arrived at the yards. "You go on the gate, so we don't have any mess ups."

The expression on Betsy's face told William she didn't appreciate Duncan's insinuation the land girls would make mistakes, but he had no choice but to take his place at the gate. Quietly he was glad to have another job he could manage.

Working a gate with one hand was all very well, left for ewes, right for lambs, a simple task once some oil was applied to the gate's hinges. The adjacent pens began filling with sheep and with the ewes still visible to the lambs there was less stress from the separation. What William didn't appreciate was the way his eyesight was also divided. One hundred percent vision from the left, zero from the right.

"Watch out," Betsy yelled as a sheep decided to bound over the rails and rejoin the mob still in the race.

It came at William from the right and caught him unawares, slammed into his bad arm and threw him off balance. He kept hold of the gate's handle as it smashed into the railings, jammed his knuckles, and wrenched his thumb.

"Bugger." Stars circled; shards of pain filled William's head. He leaned back on the railings and inspected the damage. Blood, torn skin, flesh and bone meshed with wood splinters and tufts of wool.

"Are you alright?" Betsy was at his side, and he appreciated the concern in her voice.

Duncan showed no such patience as he wrangled the escaped ewe back into the correct pen and glanced at William's hand. "Just a surface wound. You will have seen worse at the front. Wash it off under the tap and take up the whistle."

It was true, compared to he'd witnessed the enemy inflict on his fellow soldiers, this was a mere scratch. The hurt went deeper than skin though. It went right to his worth as a man. A man who couldn't be a soldier; a man who was unable to carry out simple farming tasks; of what value was he to anyone? It was with leaden feet that William made his way into the yards to take up the menial task of whistling the dogs.

Wallowing in his own misfortune, William had forgotten about Brian. When he finally looked around, he realised that the smile Brian had worn on the trip back to *Whipsnade Farm* had vanished in the cacophony of the sheep yards. The shrill commands whistled to the dogs, their excited barks as they jumped between pens and nipped at the heels of belligerent sheep who bleated in protest, all blended in a racket reminiscent of a battlefield. Brian's eyes were wide with fear as he cowered behind a Kauri tree, saved from sacrifice as timber for the yard construction. If only the tree could have shared its towering strength, Brian may have ceased shivering like leaves in the wind.

William shook his head. Another mistake. He should never have brought Brian today. The progress he'd made was clearly negated. Responsibility weighed heavy on William's shoulders. He should rescue his fellow soldier but would have to abandon his post to do so. The task he'd been reduced to, ensured the separation of lambs from ewes flowed continuously and evenly, minimising the sweat that beaded the brows of the land girls and easing the frustration his father wore in a scowl.

He glanced up at the sun and judged by its angle in the sky his mother would soon arrive with a basket of sandwiches, baking, and fruit for lunch. Her mothering instincts would present the solution to William's dilemma, she'd want to take Brian back to the house and mollycoddle him. It wasn't what he needed either, but it would have to do.

William's eyepatch caused a pounding throb at his temples. The band holding it in place collected the sweat that oozed from his pores but seemed tighter than normal, like a tourniquet cutting off the blood supply. Beneath the patch, where jagged scars ran through his eye socket, salty perspiration accumulated, dried, and started to itch. His need to remove the patch and scratch until the desired relief was delivered was tempered by the tiny hope William carried; a chance he clung to, that his sight may return. A hand covered in the lanolin of sheep's wool, coloured the khaki of excrement and dirt was no hygienic instrument and he kept it far away from his face.

Nel's arrival was welcome. The land girls washed off under the tap in clean rainwater captured from the roof of the sheep shed before finding spots in the shade to enjoy the proffered sandwiches and a cool drink. William rinsed his hands, flicked off his eyepatch, and splashed his face with water, revelling in the instant relief. He glanced across at the land girls. Would they be disgusted by his appearance? Did he have to replace the patch, or could he enjoy the freedom? His head ached too much to worry about appearances.

After a dip in the water trough, the dogs shook themselves off before skulking away to lay in the settling dust. With no dogs to rustle them along the sheep also calmed and the only bleat was of a separated lamb crying out for its mother.

In the quiet lull, William attempted to coerce Brian from behind the tree but what fingernails he hadn't chewed off were clawing at the cratered bark of the Kauri. There weren't many soldiers William knew whose fingernails had survived the war, chewed down to the fingertips, sometimes as a futile attempt to calm frayed nerves but more often merely as a safeguard against infection. Germs couldn't survive where there was no crevice for them to hide.

The aroma of egg sandwiches helped William push aside the images of flies landing on the slices of tinned corned beef, the staple of a dugout diet. He wrapped his fingers around two sandwiches and walked over to sit down beside the Kauri tree. It was impossible to eat and hold Brian's sandwich at the same time, but William avoided the broad leaves of the foxgloves growing within arm's reach. They would have made a good plate had they not been poisonous. He placed the spare sandwich on his thigh and started eating his in the hope Brian would be tempted to do the same. Eventually, William's patience was rewarded, and Brian edged his way to the ground. William was careful to speak quietly.

"It's alright Brian, you're safe here." William's comforting words appeared to fall on deaf ears although the smile he saw Betsy sending his way indicated it was only Brian who was oblivious to his kindness.

Gingerly, Brian took the sandwich from William and his tension appeared to ease with each mouthful he ate.

"How about you head back to the house with Mum?" William asked. "It'll be quieter there; she might need help in the vegetable garden. We'll head in for a beer later. God knows, I need one."

Brian nodded and there was only a slight tremor in his hands.

CHAPTER

18

The sun was low in the sky by the time the land girls finished docking the lambs and released them into a paddock beside the woolshed so they could lick their wounds, so to speak, while the ewes remained within sight but separate.

Betsy wiped the sweat from her brow with the back of her hand and arched her spine to counter the bent position she been in for most of the day. Her stomach echoed her eagerness to get home and tuck into the dinner Nel would most certainly have cooking.

"Come on, Rosey." Peggy ushered Rosey towards the pig sties. "We've got to feed the pigs now."

"Oh, I hope I'm not allergic to them too," Rosey replied as the pair veered off.

"Are you going to teach me how to milk, Betsy?" Jean asked. "It doesn't look like William has made it back in time."

"What?" Betsy snapped. Jean bore the brunt of her anger, but it was William she wanted to swear at. Where, the bloody hell was he? Milking was the last thing she had energy for.

She searched all the places the truck could have been parked. Her tired shoulders slumped even further when it was nowhere to be found. Damn him, he was probably at the pub getting drunk again. All very well for him to drown his sorrows with beer, forcing her to keep working.

Following their body clock, the cows had made their own way down the race, waddling around their full udders, and stood ready to enter the yards. It wasn't the cows' fault and Betsy felt for them.

"Open the gate and let them in," she instructed Jean. "I'll set up the milk room. I'll teach you that another day. There's no time and I'm too tired today."

Fortunately, unlike Rosey, Jean seemed to have a natural affinity with animals and the instructions Betsy gave only needed to be said once. She oversaw Jean milk the first cow and confident she wouldn't make any major errors Betsy would get the blame for, left her to it. She finally sat, grateful to catch her breath while the cups drained the milk from the cow's udder. Resting her head on the cow's belly, Betsy's thoughts wandered. Why was it men couldn't be relied upon? Roland and William were both now missing in action, obviously not to the same extent but definitely with the same effect. Betsy was made to struggle on alone. How long was she supposed to carry on like this, with her life in limbo?

Wallowing in self-pity didn't suit Betsy, she always tried to look on the bright side so it was herself she was admonishing when she discovered the milk can was about to overflow.

"Wake your ideas up," she growled as she quickly moved the milk pipe and gauze to a fresh can.

I'm just tired. Everyone else has done the same work as you and they're not moaning. William said he would milk the cows. Well, William's not here and you are.

The silent debate continued inside her head until the milking was finished. Betsy wasn't left with any answers just a head that throbbed. Frustrated, she ran her hands through her hair and pinched her lips together.

"I'll go and shut the cows in. You hose down the yard and head back for dinner," Betsy instructed Jean.

Despite her tiredness, a quiet walk back up the race would allow Betsy's thoughts to clear. As much as she wanted to throttle William, she had already lambasted him, and it wouldn't achieve anything positive to do it again.

Her steps fell in time with the plodding of the cows ambling their way back to the paddock and her heart rate lowered to a similar pace. Early morning and evening were the times of the day she enjoyed the most. It was when nature was either unfolding or enclosing itself, like a peeling back to begin the day and a tucking in to retire at the end. Birds chirped with excitement at sunrise or serenaded their repletion at sunset.

By the time Betsy reached the gate the last of the cows had selected its resting spot for the night and lowered itself to the ground to join the others chewing their cud.

"Goodnight, girls," she called out to the herd as she latched the gate and headed back down the race. "At least you're sturdy and reliable."

They were traits Betsy needed to tether herself to in this time of world upheaval. What would William do if he exhibited those characteristics? He would be at home joining them for dinner without a slur to his words. He would be a gentleman, pull out her chair for her and apologise he wasn't home in time to milk the cows. He would offer to milk in the morning so she could enjoy a well-deserved sleep in.

With these thoughts in mind, Betsy smiled as she entered the farmhouse, inhaling the aromas of dinner. Nel placed a platter of pickled pork in front of Duncan for carving. Peggy, Jean, and Rosey passed around the vegetables, filling their plates with boiled potatoes, carrots, and cabbage. William was nowhere in sight. Betsy stopped and swallowed the realisation there was no sturdy and reliable in the post-war William.

She sat at the table, took each bowl of vegetables as it was passed to her and piled her plate high with generous servings. She sought solace in the food and allowed it to assuage the hollow feeling in the pit of her stomach.

William's seat remained empty for the duration of the meal. Betsy certainly wasn't going to be the one to ask after him and nobody else mentioned his name. It was almost as if he'd never returned from the front. She pondered how different her life would be if William wasn't there as a daily reminder that she was engaged, that her loyalties must lie with a man nobody knew the whereabouts of. In a way it was torture, but Betsy didn't for a second imagine it was anywhere near as bad as the torture Roland may be subjected to as a prisoner of war. She shook her head, chasing the thoughts away to concentrate on the meal before her.

Conversation was absent from the dinner table; exhaustion took its place. Even Betsy's nourished belly stayed silent when she patted it after settling her knife and fork side by side to signal, she'd had quite enough.

Duncan moved from the dining table to his armchair beside the radiogram, a habit since war had been declared. Static filled the room until he adjusted the dial to the correct position to receive the nightly war update.

The hollowness edged out of Betsy's stomach by food now sat like a weight on her chest. Another war report was more than she could handle.

"I think I'll go to bed early tonight." She stood and took her plate to the kitchen sink.

"Erm, what, yes, another day in the yards tomorrow," Duncan said, his ear glued to the radiogram. "Best you all have an early night."

Betsy glanced into William's bedroom on the way to her own with wishful thoughts she had no power to prevent. Its emptiness didn't stop the warmth simmering deep inside her as memories of his body close to hers filled her with a longing.

She hurried past and into her bedroom, shutting the door with more force than required as guilt quashed any arousal.

Roland. Roland. Roland.

She repeated her fiancé's name and summoned his image to her mind. It emerged, as if from a smoky haze, blurred at the edges like it was being slowly erased. Betsy swallowed, slumped to the edge of her bed and bit her lip to stop her chin from quivering.

"What am I when I can't even picture your face?" she muttered tearfully to herself. "Sleep, I just need sleep, come to me Roland, come to me in my dreams."

Betsy undressed, slipped her nightie on, and climbed between the sheets. Their softness enfolded her like the physical embrace she longed for but without the danger of a male presence. She closed her eyes and let sleep claim her.

It was dark when Betsy woke with a start, certain she'd heard someone about outside her bedroom door. It felt like she'd received the requisite dose of eight hours asleep but the hands of her bedside clock, glowing in the darkness, told her it was only eleven-thirty. Unsure whether the noise was real or imagined, Betsy remained still and quiet, her ears peeled. Perhaps it was William finally making it home, banging about the house in his drunkenness. He must have found a party to go to as the pub would have closed hours ago. Annoyance at being woken was countered with curiosity, it was a long time since Betsy had been to a party.

Her eyelids grew heavy as she waited. There were no more noises and it must have simply been the weatherboard cladding of the old house creaking as the outside temperature lowered. At least if William wasn't home sleeping, he couldn't be having nightmares again.

Several hours later, the clock's hands had blended into one and lay horizontal as if they were snuggled in together and asleep. They were everything Betsy wasn't, her eyes wide, a sense of dread churning her stomach. It was a quarter past three. When she should have been able to hear William next door, there was still silence. His drunken snoring or even his screams of nightmarish terror would have been more welcome than the silence.

Betsy crept out of bed and tiptoed across the cold floorboards. Gingerly she turned the handle of her bedroom door, grateful it didn't squeak in protest. She could hear Duncan's snoring from the bedroom at the far end of the passage but nothing from William's room even though the door remained wide open.

She crept along the passage, remembering to avoid the floorboard that always protested when trodden on, and allowed her eyes to adjust to the darkness. She stopped at William's room, willed for a vision of him sleeping peacefully to soothe her heartbeat. An empty, unused bed sat in the middle of the room, like an exclamation mark. Betsy sucked in a breath. Where was he? Should she be mad or worried? What if something happened to both William and Roland?

Lost in her thoughts, she stepped back to lean against the wall, forgot the loose floorboard and shuddered as it creaked in the quiet of the house.

"Is there something wrong, dear?" Nel emerged from the bedroom, sleepy-eyed and knotting her dressing gown belt around her waist.

"Oh, um, no …" Betsy didn't want to lie to Nel, neither did she want to admit she'd been awake, worried about William. "Um, I'm not sure. I was just going to go to the toilet when I noticed William's not home yet."

"Oh." Nel rubbed her eyes and peered into William's bedroom. "What time is it?"

"A quarter past three."

"Oh." Nel turned to look wide-eyed at Betsy. "He should be home by now. Perhaps he's staying at Brian's house."

"Yes." Betsy seized hold of the simple explanation. "Of course, that's what it will be. Sorry, for waking you, Nel. You can growl at him in the morning for not letting you know."

"Yes." Nel's mouth curved into a knowing smile. "I'll let him know we were both worried about him."

Betsy hoped the darkness would conceal her blush; she turned back towards her bedroom to be certain.

"I'd best get back to bed," she said. "Another big day tomorrow."

"Weren't you going to the toilet?" Nel asked.

There was no choice now, Betsy couldn't let Nel catch her out twice. She turned again and tiptoed past Nel, out to the kitchen, through the washhouse and across the porch to the toilet. Wind rattled the tiny room's glass louvre window. From its position high on the wall behind the cistern, the small window allowed the moon to cast an eerie glow around the tongue and groove walls. Betsy generally avoided the toilet at nighttime, except when she couldn't hold on a moment longer. She could have pulled the string that hung to the right of her face and illuminated the area but that would have meant she was eye-to-eye with the Daddy Long Legs that made the room their home despite Nel's constant cleaning.

"You might as well while you're here," she told herself.

She tensed and sucked in a breath when her bare skin touched the cold wooden seat. Deliberate slow breathing was required before what was meant to happen occurred. Her relaxed state remained only for a matter of seconds. Her spine went rigid when she heard a knock at the door.

It would be William. No. William wouldn't knock. He would know the door wasn't locked. Perhaps she'd imagined the tapping sound. Betsy finished her business and sat quietly; ears once again peeled to the noises of the night.

The knocking came again, louder this time, confirming there must be someone at the door. Betsy flushed the toilet and hurried to the door, reaching it the same time as Nel who'd turned on the washhouse light. Betsy squinted until her eyes adjusted to the brightness.

The look they gave one another held all the doubts, worries, and concerns they were hesitant to voice. It also gave Betsy strength to turn the door handle, the pair of them together were better placed to deal with whomever the visitor was.

A man stood side on to the door, the moon cast light on the metal buttons that ran down the front of his black uniform and illuminated the white of the police decal that adorned the hat he politely held in his hands.

"Good evening, ma'am," he said tilting his head. "Sorry to disturb you at this time of night but unfortunately I have to report there has been an accident."

Nel's scream pierced the night and brought Duncan stumbling to the door in his crumpled pyjamas, rubbing his eyes.

"What is it? What is it?" he asked in a voice still croaky with sleep.

"There's been an accident, Mr McKnight," the policeman replied. "A vehicle we believe is registered to you."

"William!" Betsy and Nel gasped in unison.

The officer pulled a notepad from a pocket inside his jacket. "Yes, William McKnight was the name of the driver," he read from the opened pad.

No. Betsy mouthed the denial and backed away from the door. William couldn't possibly be 'was'- that was past tense. That would mean he was no longer. That he was d…. She couldn't bring herself to think let alone voice the word.

"I'm afraid your truck is in a bit of a mess," the policeman continued. "We've had to have it towed."

"What about William?"

Betsy imagined her face would mirror the look of despair she saw in Nel's pained stare.

"He's a little worse for wear," the policeman answered.

He was already that before he crashed the truck.

"How much worse for wear?" she asked.

"Oh, nothing that a night in the cells won't cure." The officer shook his head. "He shouldn't have been driving in that condition, might have a headache in the morning, but the alcohol he'd quite clearly been consuming, probably saved his life. He was thrown clear of the vehicle. The first driver on the scene found him unconscious in the bracken at the side of the road."

"He could have a concussion." Nel expressed a mother's worry. "I should get dressed and come with you."

"No need for that. The doctor is there checking him over as we speak, and we'll monitor him overnight. We don't believe he needs to be transferred to the hospital at this stage."

"Will he be charged?" Duncan asked.

"I can't tell you that sir. The sergeant will make that decision. I can say there does seem to be a bit of leniency towards the returned soldiers, with all they have had to deal with and all. That's not official, of course."

"Thank you. Thank you for letting us know," Duncan said. "We'll let you get home to your family. We'd better get back to sleep so we can deal with this mess in the morning."

"Duncan!"

"Well, Nel, there is nothing we can do at the moment." Duncan's voice was firm. "Good night, constable."

"Good night, sir, ma'am, miss." The policeman returned his hat to his head, turned, and walked off into the darkness.

Nel opened her mouth to speak but her words remained unspoken when Duncan raised his hand to quell any protest.

"Nel, William is a grown man. You've got to stop treating him like the little boy I know you'd still like him to be. He got himself into this mess, from which we will all now suffer without a truck to help with the farm work, and he needs to pull his socks up, stop wallowing in self-pity and get on with life."

"But–"

"I'm going back to bed." Duncan turned his back on any further protest. "I suggest you do the same. It will be an even busier day tomorrow now, thanks to William."

Tears welled in Nel's eyes. "But–" she murmured again.

Betsy took Nel's hands in hers and squeezed them. She wanted to say William was all right, but she wasn't convinced herself.

"At least William has no more injuries," she settled on.

"Yes." Nel shook her head. "Yes, you're right. It could have been a lot worse. We'll get him home in the morning and everything will be all right."

Betsy hoped so.

CHAPTER

19

The jangling of keys woke William; their ring was like an alarm clock chiming in his ear but the throbbing in his head said it was too early to wake. He must have had one beer too many last night. Again.

If he'd set his alarm clock though, it must mean he had something important today, somewhere he needed to be. If only the fog would clear from his head and allow him to remember. He rolled over, squinted through his good eye, and reached his hand out from beneath the itchy grey blanket that covered his chest, to shut the alarm off. His arm fell through nothingness to brush his fingers on a cold concrete floor. The realisation he wasn't in his bedroom made William's heart pound as loud as his head.

Where was he? How did he get there? He scoured his scrambled memories but found no coherent answers.

He rubbed the sleep from his good eye and sat up, all too quick, to scan his surroundings. The stars that circled his head weren't those of a night sky, there to help him find his way, and the room he was in wasn't about to let him go anywhere. Iron bars embedded in a concrete wall covered the only window, a small square of frosted glass let in muted light with no view of the landscape and no air flow

Air was what William needed most. An acrid stench absorbed whatever fresh air had been in the room. A combination of urine and vomit signalled whatever he'd been doing wasn't good.

Two feet from the end of the cot, floor to ceiling iron bars held him captive. His tiny cell was mirrored across a passageway. Its occupant snored loudly, his belly rising and falling with each rumble.

William's first question was answered. He knew he was in the police cells but how he got there still eluded him.

"Anybody there?" William moved to stand by the bars.

There was a snort and a grumble from the opposite cell but no answer to his question. He strained to peer through the bars and down the corridor that extended out to his left. If his right eye had been functioning, it wouldn't have been a problem, but bars and concrete obstructed his view.

William found the source of the stench, a toilet that jutted from the wall opposite the cot. His need to urinate was more urgent than avoiding the soiled bowl. He held his breath until he was able to flush the toilet.

Feeling useless, William lay back down on the cot and tried to reassemble the actions that brought him here. He noticed the injury to his thumb and vague memories of sheep, gates, land girls, and Brian, struggled to find a semblance of order.

He closed his eyes, and the image of Brian's terror confronted him: glaring pupils, trembling limbs, cowering behind a tree. That's right, William had failed on all counts. He'd let his soldier mate down, been useless at the job asked of him and thereby increased the workload for the land girls. A farmer he was not. A soldier he was not. He was incapable of being anything useful. Was that why he was in prison? It hadn't been an officially punishable offence that he knew of.

The memories edged their way in. He told his mother he'd take Brian home. They went via the pub. Tom, Bob, Reggie, and Frank; they were all there. Joking. Laughing. It was just what William needed and with each beer Brian's trembling eased a little more. Each mouthful of the brown ale was like an anaesthetic numbing the pain. Perhaps he'd had too many. The walk to the truck seemed to take forever as if the ground under his feet were a moving carpet. The key played tricks too and William dropped it several times before finding the ignition. He had to rev the engine loudly, to check it was running. The lads cheered as he drove off, screeching the tyres.

He could do this. He could get Brian home safely. He needed some fresh air and wound the window down to feel the cool night air on his face and inhale its sobering qualities. Landmarks came at him too quickly, trees rushed by. Sometimes it seemed the branches were growing into the cab of the truck. And then they were.

"Shit!"

Realisation he'd crashed his father's truck hit William like a punch to the stomach. He'd have to brace himself for the fallout from that but there was a more urgent concern gnawing into William's guilt. Brian. William was in a police cell but where the hell was Brian? He raised his still throbbing head and looked across at the other cell to check whether the snoring man was Brian. The man's face was hidden behind a rotund stomach that two gnarly hands could barely reach around and didn't belong to Brian.

William attempted to swallow the feeling of dread that parched his throat more than the alcohol had dehydrated it. Had his actions injured Brian? Was Brian hospitalised? Was Brian dead? How could he have been so stupid as to risk the life of a fellow soldier? To survive the war only to be killed on the road by a drunk who should know better. William vowed he'd never touch another drop of alcohol, if only, if only Brian was alright, safe at home with his mother. William wished he too was safe at home with his mother, that none of the nightmare unfolding was true, but he knew this wasn't a problem his mother could fix, try as she might like to.

The keys jangled again. Closer this time.

"William McKnight," a deep serious voice summoned him from the door of the cell. "Lucky for you, your father is here to collect you."

Lucky. William kept hearing that word, from the day he was injured until now when it was the last thing he wanted to be if it meant Brian hadn't been so fortunate.

"No time like the present," he muttered to himself as he swung his legs off the side of the cot and pushed himself up to stand.

He followed the police officer from the cell and down the corridor bracing himself for the bollocking that lay behind the closed door. What he got was far worse. His father's head was lowered, his shoulders slumped, he didn't make eye contact with William, just nodded to the police officer, and turned to leave. The silence was deafening, the disappointment cast in his father's stony expression said everything.

William stopped before the sergeant's office door.

"Sir," he said. "Could you tell me if Brian McPherson is alright?"

The sergeant peered over the rim of heavy black glasses to look William up and down as if he was assessing his worthiness for a reply.

"No thanks to your actions, young man." The police officer removed his glasses and rubbed his forehead. "You're free to go only on the good standing of your father in this community. I thought the army would have drilled some discipline into you soldiers, but it appears not. Driving under the influence, careless driving causing injury, careless use of a motor vehicle. I could throw the book at you but instead I'm releasing you into your father's care under a good behaviour bond. You've had your warning, don't mess up again."

William hoped the sergeant would take his silence as remorse. He nodded quietly and followed his father from the station. The only glimmer of hope was the officer had said injury, not death. Brian was still alive.

Outside Jess was hitched to the cart, the farm's only mode of transport, thanks to William's actions. Empty milk cans on the cart were evidence they'd already been to the milk factory and now there was the long journey back to *Whipsnade Farm*. The horse neighed as they climbed aboard the cart; not a friendly whinny but a nostril flared, high-pitched, toss-of-the-head cry of protest.

"Sorry, Jess," William whispered to the horse. "I've made things harder for you too."

It wasn't until they'd set off that William sensed the brightness of the morning sun on his damaged eyelid. He felt for his eyepatch, but it was missing. His head had been so sore he hadn't registered its absence. He couldn't test his father's patience further and ask him to return to the station.

Duncan headed the horse and cart in the opposite direction from home and stopped after a few hundred yards, outside the local garage.

"Gidday, Duncan." A greasy-overall clad mechanic exited the garage wiping his hands on a rag. "Have you come to inspect the damage?"

Duncan nodded and climbed down. "Hopefully it's not too bad. She's sorely needed."

The mechanic led Duncan out to a yard at the back of the garage and William dragged his feet along behind. Cars and trucks with dented and rusty panels and smashed windscreens sat haphazardly amongst overgrown grass. It was almost a graveyard for dead vehicles and William hoped that wasn't the fate of the farm truck which sat closest to the gate. With the front of the truck stoved in, the bonnet buckled, sitting askew, no longer able to close and a smashed headlight which wouldn't be able to shine any light on what had happened, the truck looked worse than William felt. Whatever he'd hit, had been stronger than the truck.

"We'll have to order a new light and a radiator in from Christchurch. They should be here by the end of the month, and we'll have her back up and running. No panels available though, I think they've been requisitioned for the steel. I haven't had time to search through this lot yet but I'm sure there's another truck the same over in the back corner. I knew I kept it for a reason." The mechanic chuckled as he cast his eyes and hand over the yard. His weather-beaten skin said he'd been around longer than the wrecks. "There's bound to be something here we can panel beat into shape or if you're worried about how she'll look I can phone around for a second-hand bonnet."

"I'm not worried about how it looks," Duncan replied.

"So, all is not lost then," William dared to suggest.

His father's glare indicated it would have been smarter to say nothing at all.

"I appreciate you giving it priority," Duncan said. "Give me a call when we're able to pick it up."

Each clip clop of the horse's hooves on the road was like a time bomb counting down. Duncan remained silent all the way home and William imagined the reception at home would be as cold. If only he could turn back time. Not just to reverse last night's damage but back before he'd been injured. Hell, he'd even reconsider enlisting if he had his time over again. Imagine the life he would have been living if he'd still been whole. He could have taken over the lion's share of the farm work, allowed his father to ease up a bit. But then the land girls wouldn't have been recruited, he wouldn't have met Betsy. He wondered how she'd look at him this time; with disgust for his actions, with anger at his irresponsibility or with pity for his uselessness, a mixture of all three or worse still, she might never look at him again.

They reached the *Whipsnade Farm* gate all too soon. As Duncan urged Jess and the cart into the driveway, two vehicles arrived from the opposite direction. William recognised Bill in the first and gave him a sheepish wave, hoping he'd continue home and not decide to visit. The second vehicle looked like the doctor's; they both followed the cart and stopped outside the house.

"Morning," Bill called out as he approached. "I heard the news."

William sighed. The joys of country living, news travelled quicker than a brisk easterly wind. By the end of the week, everybody in the district would know how stupid he'd been.

"Morning, Doctor. Bill," Duncan greeted the visitors. "Come in, I'll get Nel to make us a quick cuppa. I've got a big day in the sheepyards."

William wanted more than one cuppa to soothe his parched throat. He'd have to drink them quick and make amends by helping in the yards.

"Morning, Duncan," the doctor replied. "I've just come to check on William."

Duncan glared at William as they walked inside. William imagined his father saying he needed to harden up, there was nothing wrong with him. He couldn't decide if the throbbing that persisted in hammering his forehead was merely trying to knock some sense in or he had been injured in the crash. The doctor solved that mystery.

"I attended the accident scene last night. William was unconscious when found. We were unable to establish for how long. The police officers monitored him overnight while I took another patient back to my surgery."

With the land girls and Nel already at the table the room was now full. William dropped his chin to his chest avoiding everyone's gaze. He heard their collective gasp and wasn't ready to receive whatever judgements lay instore for him and he was too busy wondering and worrying if the other patient was Brian.

The doctor pulled a chair out from the table and signalled for William to sit while he retrieved some instruments from his medical bag.

"Excuse me, ladies." The doctor shone his ophthalmoscope into William's eyes. "I'll just check for brain function and be out of your way."

"You'll be lucky to find anything there." Duncan's tone held no hint of humour, but a collective giggle circled the table embarrassing William.

"Mmm, a little slow to constrict," the doctor observed, swapping the ophthalmoscope for a stethoscope, and listening to William's chest. "How are you feeling William? Any pain?"

"Just my head." William spoke quietly hoping only the doctor would hear, but not quiet enough.

"That'll be a self-inflicted, serve-you-right hangover," Duncan diagnosed.

"There is evidence of concussion and I think it best you rest up for a few days," the doctor prescribed.

William heard the groan that resounded around the table, beginning in Duncan's baritone voice, and ending with a higher, but none the less unimpressed, feminine tone. He had to apologise.

"Sorry everyone." William looked up but shame cast his eyes to the safety of the view outside the kitchen window, beyond the disappointment he would surely see in the eyes he felt boring into him. He wished he could be as light and carefree as the cottonwool clouds floating by.

"He'll be right by Saturday though, won't he, doc?" Bill asked. "We've got the Home Guard training and I've only just recruited him to lead us."

"You won't want him leading you to the pub," Duncan's jibes continued.

"He'll be right by Saturday," the doctor reassured everyone. "He's pretty right now but it's not worth doing anything strenuous and risking another knock."

"Here, doctor, sit and have a cuppa." Nel pushed a cup and saucer across the table.

"I think I just might today," he sat, added a heaped teaspoon of sugar to the cup and gave it a quick stir. "Unfortunately, the night's events only let me get in a few hours' sleep."

William decided not knowing was worse than any compounded guilt he would feel upon learning Brian's fate.

"Was Brian injured?" he asked. "Will he be alright?"

The doctor paused to drink his tea as if he needed the time to contemplate an answer.

"He'll recover from his physical injuries. Not by Saturday though. I don't imagine you recruited him for the Home Guard, did you Bill?"

"No," replied Bill. "We didn't think he'd be up to being around gunfire anytime soon."

"Correct. Good. And now he has a broken leg to heal as well," the doctor said. "Unofficially, I'd diagnose he's recovering from a hangover too."

"No doubt, that's thanks to William as well." Duncan wasn't about to forgive his son.

"Brian is a grown man. I'd assess him still to be capable of making his own decisions about having a drink or not."

It wasn't an excuse, but William appreciated the doctor stating facts that attempted to defuse his father's anger.

"Well, I'll be going then." Bill stood to leave. "Thanks for the cuppa, Nel. William, I'll pick you up on Saturday, straight after breakfast. And ladies, the hall committee are arranging another dance, at the end of the month, to raise funds for the Home Guard. I hope you'll all come along. If William is no good for dancing by then, I'll be sure to accompany you on the floor."

"Only if Moira lets you," Betsy teased. "Nobody could separate you two last time."

Bill coloured, shifted awkwardly, and cleared his throat. "Umm, yes, well anyway it's all for a good cause so I hope we'll have your support."

While everyone said their goodbyes to Bill, William dared to look across at Betsy. She was even more beautiful when she smiled. If only her smile was for him. He'd have to ensure he was recovered by the dance so he could hold her close, breathe in the fresh scent of her hair.

"And how are you doing, Rosey? Has the allergy eased?" The doctor asked the question before he glanced in Rosey's direction. "Erm, no, I can see your allergic reaction hasn't healed at all."

"Well, it had." Rosey's voice quivered and her eyes went glassy. "But now it's back and even worse."

"Have you not been staying away from the cows?" the doctor asked.

"Yes. I've been helping with the sheep and the pigs."

"Have you had anything like this before? As a child?"

"I'm from Christchurch." Rosey sniffed back the threatening tears. "We don't have cows, pigs and sheep in the city."

William saw his father roll his eyes and was glad his frustration was directed at someone else.

"No." The doctor put his cup down, rested his elbows on the table and his forehead on his steepled fingers as if he needed to pray. The silence that ensued seemed to last forever. "What about pets, dogs or cats?"

Rosey's face flickered. "When I was a little girl, we had a cat. *Toscar* was its name. It used to sleep on my bed until … until I broke out in spots, just like these ones." A tear trickled from the corner of her eye. "We had to give *Toscar* away, to another family. I missed him but I didn't miss the spots."

"Well, Rosey, I think you're destined to be a city girl in a house without pets," the doctor said. "It appears you have a general allergy to animals. Duncan, you'll have to release Rosey from her training."

Duncan grunted before swallowing the last of his cup of tea. "If that's the case and we're another man down then I haven't got time to sit here and chat. We've got sheep in the yards that need dealing to." Duncan stood. "Come on, Betsy, Peggy and Jean, there's work to do and lots of it."

What came around the table this time and stopped like a firing squad aiming their guns at William's forehead was the glare of three women who reluctantly stood, already fatigued and angry at the man who'd increased their workload.

If only the doctor had ordered William straight to bed to recuperate.

CHAPTER

20

Rosey was leaving. The loud 'yes' that wanted to escape from Betsy was tempered by the guilt she felt. The buxom woman who felt like a threat to Betsy's relationship with William was being sent home for reasons beyond her control. She was upset and in pain from the welts that covered her from head to toe. Betsy shouldn't feel such glee, she should feel empathy towards Rosey but in this instance what she should do and wanted to do were not aligned.

That seemed to be the predicament dominating her entire life. She should remain loyal to Roland however long it took for him to return from the front, but she wanted to move ahead with her life, to feel like she was doing more than just existing. She should see William as merely the son of her employers, a colleague to undertake farming tasks with, but she wanted their relationship to be more than that, much more. She should be angry with William for his stupidity, his drunkenness, his crashing the truck which has added to their workload, but she wanted to hug him, and tell him everything would be alright.

In the end she decided she'd better concentrate on the task at hand and stay as far away from him as possible. Yesterday, they'd finished dealing with the sheep and released them back to the paddocks, the weaned lambs now at one end of the farm and the ewes at the other, all newly docked, crutched and drenched.

Now the focus was back on the cows and one that seemed to be out-of-sorts as Betsy went to the paddock to fetch the herd for the milking. There was a bite to the morning air that seeped into Betsy's bones; she imagined the cow to be suffering from the same aches and pains as it shivered.

She recognised the cow, even though Duncan detested the naming of animals, Betsy had called this one, *Panda*. It was the only cow in the herd with a white head except for black circles around each of its eyes. The cow had calved a healthy calf the day before, but now appeared to struggle to walk. Betsy wondered if the cow's legs were stiff from waddling around a full udder or there was something else going on.

"Come on, girls," Betsy rallied the herd towards the gate.

Panda wobbled on unsteady legs but otherwise stayed put, like a tree rooted to the ground with its branches blowing in the wind.

"I think I'd best get Duncan to come and have a look at you."

Betsy got the rest of the herd into the race and moving towards the cowshed. They ambled at the same steady pace at which they always walked but this morning it wasn't fast enough for her. She wanted to yell and hurry them along, but Duncan's warning rang loud and clear, the cows' milk wasn't to be churned before they reached the cowshed. The well-being of most of the herd versus the health of *Panda*, Betsy debated what to do. She glanced back at the paddock as *Panda's* legs gave out and the cow fell heavily to the ground. Spurred in to action, Betsy pushed past the herd and ran down the race, hoping Duncan was up and about, hoping he would know what to do for *Panda*, hoping it wasn't too late.

The cold air burned her throat, compounding the sense of urgency that throbbed at her temples. She neared the pig sty as Duncan left the building, bucket in hand. She was panting too much to speak so raised her hand and waved to catch his attention. He came across the track, a grumpy look on his face.

"What on earth has happened?" he asked. "Where are the cows? Why aren't you milking yet?"

All the questions gave Betsy time to catch her breath.

"It's *Pa* …. one of the cows." Betsy caught herself. "There's something wrong. It's gone down in the paddock."

"A newly calved cow?" Duncan strode towards the cowshed.

"Yesterday," Betsy replied. "But it was fine at milking last night."

"What's it doing with its head?" Duncan continued firing questions while he grabbed a bucket and half filled it with boiling water from the cylinder. He dropped a syringe, a rubber hose and bulb into the water.

Betsy thought back to *Panda*. "She kept turning it to the side."

"Milk fever. Blast." Duncan shook his head. "We'd better hurry before it's too late. I suppose it's one of the best cows too. It's always the good ones that go down."

"Milk fever?"

"Parturient Apoplexy to be precise," Duncan explained. "What was the breathing like, noisy?"

Betsy didn't notice the cow's breath any noisier than usual. She hoped she hadn't missed something so important.

"No, I don't think so."

"Eyes?" Duncan, bucket in hand, left the cowshed and headed towards the race. "Damn, William, I'd get there a lot quicker in the truck," he grumbled.

Betsy tried to keep up, with Duncan's urgent stride and with the question, what did he mean by eyes? Yes, *Panda* had two of them, they were open but what else they might be that was relevant to milk fever, Betsy hadn't a clue.

"Were the eyes clear or glazed over?" Duncan growled.

"I'm sorry, I didn't notice," Betsy had no choice but to apologise. "But the cow was standing when I reached the paddock, and I ran straight here when I saw it go down."

"Well, at least that's something."

"Will you be able to save it?" she asked.

"I hope so." Duncan kept walking, the water in the bucket sloshing about like a choppy sea. "I damn well hope so. Captain Boyle won't be pleased to hear if I can't."

They passed the herd still ambling its way to the cowshed and reached the paddock to find the cow cast on its side, legs flailing wildly and head twisting from side to side as it tried to stand.

"At least it's still got some fight left." Duncan knelt close to the cow and rinsed his hands in the bucket before removing and assembling the apparatus. "Rinse your hands and use the rest of the water to clean the cow's udder."

Betsy did as she was told, grateful the cow seemed to give up its struggle to stand so a kick from a hoof wasn't a concern.

"What is that and what are you going to do with it?" Betsy pointed to the contraption Duncan held.

"It's an air syringe," Duncan replied. "I'm going to pump air into the udder. It's an old method but I've never had it fail. You must milk the cow out first."

"Shall we stand her up to do that?" Betsy knew as soon as she'd asked the question, Duncan would roll his eyes and he did. It was obvious the cow was incapable of standing. "I'll just milk her here then."

Duncan nodded and moved to the side so any milk would squirt onto the ground.

There was no obvious improvement by the time Duncan had finished pumping air into each of the teats, but he seemed satisfied.

"You'd better get back and milk the rest of the herd," he said. "I'll keep an eye on this one. Good spotting, we may have got to it in time."

Betsy lapped up the rare praise from Duncan and headed back down the race with a smile.

Heavy grey clouds had rolled in by the time Saturday arrived at *Whipsnade Farm*. Betsy told them to remain at bay as she made her routine trip to the letterbox after the morning milking but before breakfast. Her heart skipped a beat. There were two white envelopes resting on top of the folded newspaper inside the letterbox. She grabbed them, eager to devour the good news they must surely deliver. She recognised Grace's handwriting on the first envelope, its arrival was appreciated, but not what Betsy was waiting desperately for. Her expectations buoyed when she noticed the second postage stamp depicted three soldiers in different uniforms standing to attention with the head and shoulders of a nurse faded into the background. The war image could signal a letter from Roland. Betsy sucked in a breath, closed her eyes, and wished her dreams would come true.

She checked the envelope for a postmark. Was Roland still in Egypt? Had his captors shipped him elsewhere? Australia. Betsy blinked to clear her eyes. The postmark was Australia and when she studied the stamp closely, she noticed Australia printed in white capital letters across the bottom. Disappointment stopped her in the middle of the driveway, she'd got so caught up in possibilities she failed to see the letter was addressed to William.

She hadn't spoken to him since the accident. He'd kept mainly to his bedroom avoiding his father's wrath. She was going to have to talk to him now. The letter wasn't from Roland, but it could hold news about Roland. Or had William met someone else while overseas? Someone like the nurse in the postage stamp, a woman who had been there when William needed comforting the most

Either way, Betsy had to move through the jealous twinge tightening her chest and get the answers she needed. Meanwhile, she opened the letter from Grace and read it on the way back up the driveway.

Dearest Betsy,

It's not the same - writing letters, I mean. I miss you, and our chats, but pen and paper are better than nothing. If only I had energy at the end of a day in the flax mill to bike out to

Orari to visit but I barely have enough to scribble this note, and the one I'll do next to Ben.

Anyway, I wanted to let you know that Cathy, Mrs McPherson, Brian's Mum is chuffed with what William is doing for Brian, taking him out instead of him staring at the four walls of the lunchroom. She's noticed a marked improvement since he first returned from the front and has even got a couple of one-word responses to her questions.

Betsy glanced at the date at the top of the letter, the day before the accident. Mrs McPherson's opinion of William would surely have plummeted now. Betsy folded the letter back into the envelope when she reached the house, she'd write back to Grace later.

A clean-shaven, smartly dressed William was seated at the table and a wolf whistle nearly formed on Betsy's lips. His appearance in army uniform was a first, since he'd returned home battle worn and injured and Betsy's insides reminded her of the physical attraction, she was unable to deny. She coughed to clear her thoughts and her throat before speaking.

"There's a letter from Australia for you, William." She offered him the envelope.

"Oh, it might be from Jack." Nel came to stand behind her son, taking the envelope from him in an unspoken, pre-arranged offer of help. She flicked a small knife under the flap and sliced the paper to release the letter.

The subtle gesture wasn't lost on Betsy. It was a reminder William wasn't the same man he'd been before the war. His missing limb would always make even the simplest of tasks more difficult. Perhaps, Betsy should be more like Nel, aware when help was needed and become the extra limb without a need for prompting, certainly not waiting for William to ask for help as he wouldn't do anything that highlighted his inadequacy.

Betsy released the breath she didn't realise she'd been holding and sat down. Jack was the soldier William had met on the ship transporting them home. There was no nurse to rival for William's affection. There was just Roland, she reminded herself.

William's eye moved forwards and backwards across the page. Eventually he looked up and their eyes met. She tried to interpret his expression, he'd always been a difficult book to read and now the scars were like creases in the pages, distorting the message. She waited patiently until he spoke.

"The 26th battalion were attached to the Australian 19th while they were staging a withdrawal manning the lines to the west of the Servia Pass. The journey took much longer than it should have. There were frequent bomb attacks." William paused and looked at Betsy before continuing. "Jack distinctly remembers Roland because he wouldn't let the boys coerce him into a trans-Tasman arm wrestling challenge. He insisted he had to write a letter home to Betsy, his childhood sweetheart and he had to do it that night. It was like he had a sense of foreboding, a premonition the next day would bring the worst attacks of the withdrawal."

Betsy nodded. She was grateful for the information but urged William to get to the crux, where was Roland?

William's eye glazed over as if he'd disappeared back into a closet of memories and was deciding what to keep and which to discard.

"The Germans had numbers. They swooped in." The hitch in his voice evidence he remembered them all too well. "Jack believes Roland was injured. He wasn't in the dead when the stretcher bearers were finally able to search the aftermath."

"So, he must be in a hospital somewhere?" Betsy was desperate for answers.

"Everyone was evacuated after that. Some boarded the train for Thermopylae and the rest went by truck." William hesitated, looked reluctant to continue. "Jack doesn't think it is one of our hospitals. Some of the injured were taken prisoner by the Germans."

"They'd offer him treatment in a German hospital, wouldn't they?" Betsy's voice trailed off as doubt swamped it.

"Compassion isn't a trait the Germans have in any great quantity," Duncan joined the conversation with his diplomatic way of saying all hope was surely lost.

A knock at the door made everyone sit up with fright. Bill didn't wait for an invite but walked straight in, oblivious of the conversation he brought to a premature close.

"Are you ready, William?" he asked. "We'd best not be late for your first training. We want to set a good standard for others to follow."

William folded Jack's letter. He held the envelope still on the table with his elbow, the scarred stump of his amputated arm declaring to everyone he could manage. He stuffed the letter back into the envelope and passed it to Betsy. Their fingers touched briefly, just enough to convey a silent message before William stood ready to leave.

"And Duncan," Bill turned back from the washhouse door. "I was thinking, when I don't need my truck, I could get Moira to drive your milk cans to the factory. It'll help you and give her the practice she needs."

"That's a generous offer, Bill. One I'd be a fool to turn down," Duncan replied. "It takes so long with the horse and cart and adds to an already long list of things to do."

"Right then, I'll send her over after breakfast tomorrow," Bill said. "Might need to use some of your petrol coupons though or I'll exhaust my ration."

"Of course." Duncan stood and shook his neighbour's hand. "I wouldn't expect anything less. It's only temporary. Our truck should be up and running by the end of the month."

Betsy clutched the two letters to her chest, stood and left the room in the opposite direction. She fled to the safety of her bedroom, flopping on the bed to let the tears that fell be absorbed by her bedding.

Emotional and physical exhaustion carried Betsy into a deep sleep. Someone must have checked on her as her bedroom door was closed and a crocheted blanket covered her back when she finally woke to see the hands of the bedside clock had moved time into the afternoon.

She felt comforted, the blanket like a mother's hand, something her own mother would have done when she was a child. Betsy missed her Mum more in that moment than she had since leaving home. She needed to write to her parents, to check on their health, to reassure them she was safe.

Letters. She was reminded letters had brought her to her bedroom. The morning's mail sat beside the clock, the open envelopes like an invitation, an inkling of a possibility that perhaps William, with his one eye, had misread Jack's letter and Roland had been evacuated on the train to Thermopylae.

With renewed enthusiasm, Betsy sat up and withdrew the letter from its envelope. She skipped over the bits William hadn't read aloud, something about farming that held no interest for her. She stopped, ensured the sheet of paper was taut between her hands, and read each word about Roland slowly, interpreting it as a singular word and combining it with those either side to gain further meaning. It was like piecing together a puzzle she hoped would create a beautiful picture but there were still puzzle pieces missing when Roland's name was mentioned for the last time.

"Please, Jack, please give me what I need," she begged as she continued to read.

Her eyes went wide, and she sucked in a breath when she saw her name penned in Jack's handwriting.

'And about that woman, Betsy, that you mentioned in your last letter, I reckon you need to tell her how you feel. If you love her, let her know. Women like that sort of thing. And as we well know, life is too short. Maria accepts me. She sees past my injuries, knows I'm the same man inside, except for having seen a few things I'd rather not have seen and having done a few things I'd rather not have done. Not that I'd ever tell her about any of that. I'll take those memories and images to my grave. Sure, life is different without my leg, but we adapt. You can too.'

Betsy stared at the ceiling while she gathered the thoughts that raced about her head, she needed some semblance of order, so she knew what took precedence: guilt for reading a letter that wasn't addressed to her, delight that William had feelings for her, frustration he'd written to a man he hardly knew and not spoken to her.

All that flooded in, were questions. Had William read this part of the letter? Did he know what Jack had written when he handed the letter to Betsy? Was this his way of telling her his feelings? Or was he totally unaware and now she had invaded his privacy and would never be able to reveal what she'd read?

Betsy swallowed and drew her shoulders up to her ears.

Roland.

All the questions raised were irrelevant. It didn't matter how William felt about her while there was the slightest possibility Roland was still alive. She twisted the thin gold band around her ring finger. In the past it had been like a life buoy she'd clung to but now it felt more like a handcuff restraint.

CHAPTER

21

What had William let himself in for? His was the only uniform amongst overalls and gumboots, worn farm trousers and rolled-up sleeves on shirts that would offer no camouflage if they were under attack. His attire would either give him the authority he needed to order the men, who'd gathered on a chilly Saturday morning at Orari Hall, or make them think he was a complete twat.

"Great turnout." Bill grinned with enthusiasm.

"It is?" William recognised most of the assembled group as the fathers of the men he'd enlisted with. Would they have the stamina required to be a soldier? He was certain some of them had served in the First World War. Then there were a couple of lads who would have been at school if it wasn't a Saturday. They had to be at least fifteen to volunteer, but William judged from their bumfluff they only just made the cut-off.

"Well, they sign up, all keen but then they never turn up to trainings," Bill explained. "At least there's a good number here today."

"Yes," William had to agree, he estimated there were about twenty volunteers. "It would be better if we all had a uniform."

"We've got the armbands." Bill's enthusiasm was not to be tempered as he pointed to a pile of white cloth armbands sitting on the seat between them; they were embroidered with a red crown and 'H G' in blue capitals.

Bill parked the truck and grabbed the armbands. Most of the men were smoking, he lit his pipe and offered William a light as they approached the group. Standing with the men, huddled against the wind, a cloud of smoke wafting skyward, the combined murmurings of morning chatter almost made William feel he was back at the front but there was no sand blowing in their faces, no sounds of battle on the horizon, and no imminent threat making the hairs on the back of his neck stand to attention.

When the last of the cigarette butts were stomped into the ground Bill chose to speak.

"You all know William McKnight," he said. "As you can see, William has learned the hard way the dangers of an enemy attack. He's kindly agreed to share his soldiering skills so that we can protect our families and properties should the worst-case scenario eventuate."

"Right," William said. "Apparently, the powers-that-be have produced a manual that will tell us the drills we're supposed to practise. Bill says it hasn't arrived yet, lucky for us, neither have the Japanese."

Stilted laughter told William his attempt at humour was appreciated by some, if not all.

"Anyway, I thought I'd get you doing what they made us do at training camp, starting with how to hold your gun. Did everyone bring a gun along?"

"I've got a pistol." One of the men waved a German Luger above his head. "My brother got it from a bloody German he shot in the First World War. I'll get the bastards."

"It's a Japanese invasion that we're concerned about," William replied. "And you're more likely to get one of our own if you keep waving it about like that. Anyone else?"

Another man stepped forward holding a .22 rifle out in front of him. "I have this for shooting pesky rabbits that get to my ripe fruit before I do. Not sure how much use it will be if we do get invaded but it's all I've got."

"I've got this." Another man held out a double barrel shotgun. "Only buckshot though, good for about thirty-five yards but I hope I don't have to get that close to any Jap."

Bill had his shotgun so that made four armed men out of the group. They weren't going to present an effective defence at that rate.

"We'll have to pressure the army or the government to supply us with arms or it'll all be pointless," Bill said. "What shall we do in the meantime?"

"We could make some bombs." The teenager's face lit up.

"Yeah, Fred," the other lad chimed in. "That'll be grouse."

"We'll have to leave that for another day." William wondered what the boys planned to blow up but couldn't dispel the idea completely. "Maybe next weekend when we've had time to gather some old tins, nails, and scraps of metal. If everyone brings along anything they have, Bill could try and source some gelignite and fuses."

"We might as well go home then," one of the older men spoke up. "That wind is fair howling through the trees this morning and a cuppa wouldn't go amiss."

Bill leaned over to William and spoke in a hushed voice.

"Don't let them go. Get them doing something so all is not lost."

"We can warm up with some basic drills, standing to attention and marching in formation," William suggested. "It's all part of discipline, being able to follow orders when necessary."

"I've got the key to the hall; we can stop at morning teatime for a hot drink. We'll hand out the armbands first," Bill suggested. "Everyone, take one, and pass the pile on. It goes on your upper left arm."

William at least had a left arm for the band to go on but without his right hand he had no way of getting it there.

"Bugger," he swore under his breath. What sort of leader would he look like if he had to ask the group for help for such a simple task?

Fortunately, Bill saw the source of his frustration and without speaking put William's arm band in place. William kept an eye on the group ready to shut down any jibe directed his way, but everyone was too involved in sorting their own arm bands to even notice.

"There's some old bits of timber and battens under the hall," Bill said. "We could improvise, pretend they're rifles in the meantime."

"There'll be some sticks amongst the trees," yelled one of the lads as they both ran off towards the macrocarpas bordering the field.

The men who were without a weapon rummaged around amongst the piles under the hall until they found a substitute. The exuberant teenagers could be heard yelling from across the field as if they were already in hand-to-hand combat with the enemy. Eventually, they returned with sticks whose bent barrels would be incapable of firing real bullets.

Despite a personal demonstration, which William was proud he could still manage, it took some time for the men to organise themselves into a nearly straight row, standing as upright as their age-worn backs would allow, eyes facing forward and with the butts of their rifles—real or pretend—cupped in their left hand with the barrels resting over their left shoulder.

As William yelled the commands to forward march, halt, mark time, and about face, he stood ahead and slightly to the side so the men could see his movements. They made their way up and down the field. Their line of marching wasn't always in time, and neither was it straight but most of the time it was at least in the same direction. William needed to teach them how to present arms, but that required two arms. He looked down at his right arm which hung by his side like a comma in the middle of an unfinished sentence, waiting for something to complete it. Rather than admit his inadequacy he decided that procedure could be left until next time. He directed the men towards the hall.

"Halt," he commanded. "At ease. That's pretty good for our first day. I think we deserve a cuppa."

The wind rattled the sash windows, but it was much warmer inside. Bill put the jug on, and others helped by getting enough cups and saucers from the cupboard under the servery.

"Any cake?" Fred asked. "I'm starving."

William chuckled. His Mum always claimed, *those hollow legs of yours, you'll eat us out of house and home* when he was a teenager.

"I'll have to get my wife to do some baking for next time," one of the men offered.

"That'd be good, thanks for the offer." Bill poured the cups of tea. "I remembered the milk, but my cake tins are bare. Perhaps we need to share the provision of morning tea around, we don't want to use up all your sugar ration."

On the hall notice board, beside the servery, was the poster advertising the upcoming dance. The last time William had been in the hall was for a dance, the final hoopla before they'd shipped out. He could still remember how good it felt to hold Betsy close, spin her around the dance floor and watch her face light up, well, at least until she misinterpreted the help he gave Moira, after Bill disappeared without a word. He wouldn't have to worry about that this time, now Moira and Bill were an item.

He just had to work out how to dance with one arm. William glanced down at his folded-up sleeve. His mother had taken such care to get the safety pin straight, wanting her boy to look neat and tidy in his uniform. Beneath the layers of his clothing, his stump was still tender while the scars slowly healed. He wasn't ready to bare it, he couldn't be certain people wouldn't be disgusted by the reddened, taut skin, or worse still, show pity for his loss.

"Is everyone coming along to the dance?" Bill asked. "Support the good cause."

The lads who were keen for everything replied in unison. "We'll be there with bells on."

A deep laugh echoed around the hall. "It'll be past your lads' bedtime."

"They're raising funds for the Home Guard so we can get the equipment we need." Bill ignored the taunting.

"More guns so we don't have to use sticks." Fred laughed.

William sighed. There was no point in getting guns for everyone if they didn't have the stamina for a prolonged battle.

"Right, drink up everyone," he said. "We'd better get back into it."

"Are we going to learn semaphore?" Fred grinned from ear to ear.

"What the hell is semaphore?" asked an older man whose patience for the young lads appeared to be wearing thin.

"It's a coding system, with flags," William explained. "And no, we haven't got any flags either, so we'll have to leave that for another day. I think we'll fit in a run before lunch, up the road to the racecourse, around the track and back again."

The oldest of the group sighed loudly. "That's a long way after all the marching we've already done. Is it necessary?"

"If the worst comes to the worst," William replied. "You'll likely be running further than that. Fitness will be key."

It was a straggly bunch that eventually made it back to the hall, mostly red-faced and sweating profusely. Some lay cast on the grass, others bent at ninety degrees bracing their hands on their thighs while they attempted to slow their pulse rates and calm their breathing. It was the first time the teenagers had been quiet all morning.

"We've got a bit of work to do," William observed.

He included himself in that comment as he wiped perspiration from beneath his eyepatch and gasped for air. It seemed he'd lost the peak fitness he'd enjoyed in training camp and abroad when he lost the end of his arm. His stump throbbed as if the blood was desperate to reach his non-existent hand. He raised his arm, held it above his heart while he imagined a cool beer soothing his throat. His declaration to never drink alcohol again was wavering. He'd stayed strong since the accident but that was easy when he had no way to get to the pub. Today, Bill was driving, and all William had to do was convince him he needed a beer too.

Meanwhile, William needed to find ways to increase the men's fitness. He remembered the games of rugby, the boxing matches, and the swimming the soldiers did to keep fit but couldn't envisage any of these men wanting to participate in those activities except for the lads and it wasn't their fitness that was the problem.

"Are we stopping for lunch now?" Fred asked.

Bill looked at his watch. "We can head back into the hall. Did everyone bring something to eat?"

"No, I wasn't expecting to be here this long. I'll have to go home for lunch."

"Me too."

"And me."

"I think I've wrenched my ankle," said the last of the men who'd limped back. "I'd better go home and put it up or I'll be no good for work tomorrow."

The men gathered their things and began heading for the gate. William could only shrug his shoulders when Bill looked to him for ideas to keep the group from disbanding.

"We'll meet again on Wednesday night then," Bill said. "Seven o'clock to go through the semaphore signals."

His suggestion with unenthusiastic grunts and groans.

"Well, I guess that's it then," Bill said. "We'd better head home."

"We could head into the pub," William suggested. "I think we deserve a beer after that."

Bill rubbed his chin. "I don't know. I've got farm work to do."

"Haven't you got Moira to do that?"

"Well, yes, but—"

William didn't give Bill the opportunity to provide another excuse. "The boys, Tom, Reggie, Bob, and the others, they'll all be there. You could try recruit some of them for the Home Guard. We certainly need all the help we can get."

He'd hit the jackpot. Bill's face lit up at the prospect of more recruits.

"We'd better get going then." Bill glanced at his watch again. "Just a couple of beers and maybe a pie."

As the saying goes, William's first beer barely touched the sides as he gulped it down. If it had been a sculling race, he would have won. He raised his empty glass above his head and called out to the barman.

"Any chance of a refill, Jim?"

The barman obliged but the drink he delivered came with a warning.

"You'd better make this one last a bit longer," he said. "You remember what happened last time you had too much to drink."

William had been trying to forget. He wanted to put the accident, and the war, behind him. Hell, that's what they were all doing, drinking to forget the past. Those who hadn't been away fighting would never understand.

"Any of you blokes keen to join the Home Guard?" William changed the subject and ran his tongue over his lips, licking up the remaining bubbly head of the beer. "Bill here is recruiting?"

"We need men with experience." Bill looked up from his half-eaten mince pie.

"And guns," William added.

"And probably two legs." Tom's gaze dropped to the folded up trouser leg that used to cover his limb. "So that counts me out, but I am off to Christchurch this week for an appointment with the prosthetist, so I may be back on two feet before you know it."

"Well, I've got both." Bob's mouth curved into a smile, as much as the scarred skin on his face would allow. "Experience and a gun, I mean, not two feet. Sorry, Tom. I'd be keen if I can work it around my new job."

"That's right," William remembered Bob's job at the cinema. "Any good movies playing?"

"Are you planning to take one of them land girls?" Tom wolf-whistled as if the women were in the pub.

William hadn't been thinking about Betsy, but he did now. "Not likely, Betsy's barely talking to me at the moment," he let slip.

"Ah, Betsy, is it?" Tom continued to tease. "What's she like Bill? Is she a looker?"

"Bill's got a land girl too." Annoyed by the heat that flared in his cheeks, William attempted to deflect the attention away. "A redhead and all."

"Ahem." Whether Bill was clearing a pastry flake from his throat or didn't appreciate the conversation was unclear, but the effect was the same. "That's great you want to join the Home Guard, Bob. We're meeting on Wednesday nights and Saturdays at the moment. At the Orari hall."

"Well, I won't be able to make Wednesday, but I'll be there on Saturday."

"Great. Thank you," Bill said. "Any other takers? German and Japanese submarines have been in New Zealand waters. It's important we protect our families and properties."

There were a couple of other men who said they could help so while it was beer making William feel better, it was the new recruits who cheered Bill.

"So, what is on at the movies?" William asked Bob. Perhaps he could take Betsy as a way of getting back into her good books.

Bob chuckled again. "A good one if you're trying to get a woman into your arms. *One Body too Many* it's called. Death threats, haunted mansion, everything you need to scare your lady."

"Mmm, not quite what I had in mind." William shook his head.

"There's a new one coming soon, it'll be perfect for you." Bob doubled over with laughter.

"What's so funny? Is it a comedy?" William asked. "Heaven knows, we need a good laugh."

"*The Lost Weekend,*" Bob managed to get out. "It's about a chronic alcoholic on a four-day drinking binge."

"Haha, very funny, Bob." Sarcasm peppered William's reply. He swallowed another mouthful of beer, along with the truth he didn't want to admit out loud.

CHAPTER

22

As the men had arranged, Moira arrived on Monday morning in Bill's truck.

"Are you ready to take the milk to the factory?" she asked Betsy as Duncan rolled the cans onto the tray and secured them behind the cab.

Betsy waited for Duncan to finish and caught his eye. "Is it alright if I go for a drive?"

"You'd better," Duncan replied. "Someone has to make sure the milk makes it to the factory safely but don't be too long, we need to be sorting the calves for the A & P show or we'll never have them ready in time."

Happy memories of attending the Christchurch Agricultural and Pastoral show with her parents, made Betsy smile. She and her sister had been more interested in the sideshows and carousel rides than the livestock judging and parades. She guessed she was now going to get to experience the show from a different perspective.

Inside the cab, Moira huffed. "I see nothing's changed around here. He still thinks women are useless."

"It's not so bad. Once he knows you're proficient, he leaves you to it. He trusts me to train the new land girls how to milk. You're lucky Bill is different."

"He's different alright."

The tone of Moira's voice hinted that Bill's differences weren't entirely good. Betsy hesitated before deciding to question further.

"Is your placement not working out how you thought it would?" she asked.

Moira huffed again. "That's just it, it feels like a placement. I'm no more than a land girl getting worked from dawn to dusk."

"I thought you two were getting along fine." Betsy wasn't bold enough to question Moira directly about her sex life but imagined she would understand it was implied.

"And now he's gone and volunteered to run the Home Guard I have to stay at home and do even more work," Moira complained.

"But … your relationship is more than just boss and worker, isn't it?"

"You think because we sleep in the same bed that makes up for everything?" Moira turned to face Betsy and the truck started to veer in the same direction.

"Keep your eyes on the road!" Betsy braced herself, one hand on the dashboard, the other gripping the door handle.

Moira adjusted the steering wheel and looked out the windscreen. "Sure, we have sex, but we don't have what you and William have."

Betsy coughed. "William and I don't have anything but friendship and even that is a little strained at the moment."

"Not according to Bill." Moira's smile indicated she knew something that Betsy needed to hear.

"Well, tell me, you're obviously dying to."

Moira concentrated on the road ahead as if talking and driving at the same time were no longer permissible.

"Moira!" Impatience sharpened Betsy's tone. "Tell me, now!"

"Oh, don't get your knickers in a knot," Moira retorted. "Bill said that William was asking Bob what was on at the movies."

"So, what's that got to do with me?" Betsy asked.

"William was going to ask you to the movies … on a date." Moira grinned like she always did when there was even the slightest hint of shenanigans.

"Why did you say *was*?" Betsy frowned. "Isn't he going to ask me now?"

"Well, I wouldn't be surprised if he didn't," Moira replied. "You're so grumpy, like some other dog has stolen your bone."

"Sorry. I'm just tired." Betsy slumped back in the seat. "William's not my bone though and he can't be while Roland is still alive."

"Aha!" Moira thumped her hand on the steering wheel. "Now we get to the truth of the matter. You want William and you're grumpy because you're frustrated by some silly notion of loyalty to a man, whose probably dead on the other side of the world, that prevents you from taking what you really desire."

The words hit Betsy like an arrow plunging into the bullseye. She sucked in a breath and digested the truth contained in Moira's perceptiveness.

"Well, am I right?" Moira wasn't going to let Betsy off the hook. "I am, aren't I, otherwise you'd be in full denial."

"We don't know that Roland is dead." Betsy's feeble attempt at refuting Moira's claim was barely audible.

She was saved by their arrival at the dairy factory where the sight of Jake on the platform distracted Moira.

"Look, there's Jake, all macho and muscle. It feels like old times," she purred.

"Well, look who we have here." Jake's grin showed he held no resentment for being cast aside by Moira at the last dance. "And just in time for me to ask you out to the dance."

"I'll be there."

If Betsy wasn't mistaken, Moira fluttered her eyelashes as she leaned on the side of the truck, lit a cigarette, and blew suggestive smoke signals toward Jake. Betsy itched to finish the sentence, to let Jake know Moira would be there with Bill, but she kept quiet. Unlike herself, Moira didn't appear to be loyal to anyone.

The full milk cans were unloaded and replaced with empty ones before Jake jumped down from the platform with the milk docket.

"Here you are, Moira." He placed the docket in her upturned palm and closed his fingers around hers, holding for longer than Betsy thought necessary.

"It's the milk from *Whipsnade Farm*," she snapped. "I need the milk docket for Duncan."

"Excuse Betsy," Moira said. "She's a bit grumpy today."

Betsy huffed, climbed into the cab of the truck, and yanked the door shut, avoiding eye contact with the pair but still glimpsing the kiss Jake planted on Moira's cheek.

"There was no need to embarrass me," Betsy growled at Moira when she finally climbed in the cab and shut the door.

"There's no need to be so grumpy." Moira turned the key and restarted the engine.

"You're supposed to be with Bill, not flirting with Jake."

"It was Jake flirting with me." Moira smiled out the back window as she drove off. "And any good- looking man who isn't embarrassed to do that in public is fine by me."

"But what about Bill?"

"Bill needs to decide where his loyalty lies," Moira replied. "The same as you do."

Neither of the women spoke on the drive back to *Whipsnade Farm* but their thoughts filled the cab with an energy that would have ignited if there had been a live flame. Betsy hated to admit Moira may be right, and she told herself the redhead didn't know anything about serious relationships, she'd never been engaged, and had claimed marriage wasn't for her. Betsy twisted the gold band that tied her to Roland, around and around on her finger. It was loose. All the hard physical work had thinned her fingers. The ring could easily be removed. Could the obligations and commitments that the band symbolised be cast aside by the simple act of removal? Betsy doubted so and something inside her, robbed her of the courage to try.

Duncan was in the calf paddock with Jean and Peggy, so Betsy joined them when the empty milk cans had been stowed in the milk room. Either curiosity or the association of humans with food, made the inquisitive group of calves come to sniff out the visitors

"Just in time," Duncan said. "We're about to select the calves for the show. Captain Boyle's cattle have been consistent prize winners and he insisted we continue the tradition while he's away."

One calf, more confident than the others, stood ahead of the group, like a natural leader. It stretched its neck and bellowed as if declaring itself the chief. Betsy liked the white diamond that adorned its forehead and decided if she had to have a calf, she'd pick that one, and call it *Diamond,* despite Duncan's abhorrence for the naming of animals.

"How can you tell they're going to be prize-winners?" Peggy asked.

It was a question Betsy wanted the answer to, but one she imagined Duncan would roll his eyes at

"You put yourself in the place of the judge." Duncan remained focused on the animals as he explained. "Look for the same criteria that they'd be searching for and then train and groom the animal to look its best on the day."

"How long have we got?" Peggy seemed enthusiastic.

"The show's at the *Winchester Domain* at the end of next month." Duncan leaned on a stock stick and eyed the animals.

"And what criteria do you judge them by?" Peggy continued.

"First, you've got to stand front-on to them." William approached the group and took over the explanation. "So, you can see whether they are knock-kneed or bowlegged."

Betsy's breath hitched in her throat, she hadn't anticipated William's presence and it threw her. Her knees followed his words, knocking together then bowing out, a pulse tracing a line up her inner thigh. She hoped the reaction was so subtle nobody noticed her body's betrayal. How could she stay angry at this man or was she angry at herself?

"William knows." Duncan beamed. "He had a prize-winning calf every year when he was at primary school."

Betsy hoped William heard the pride in Duncan's voice. It was a first since he'd been home and might be the start of the defrosting of their relationship.

"I thought men got bowlegged from riding too many horses," Jean said, a confused look on her face. "How do calves end up like that?"

"They're born that way, if the genetics aren't so good." William pointed at one of the calves. "Or they get scrunched up inside the womb. See this one. You should be able to draw a straight line from the shoulder to the hoof. This one, bows out. It'd be no good."

Betsy's knees snapped back together, she straightened her spine and squeezed her legs together, pushing all thoughts of William aside to focus on the calves.

"It looks like it's pigeon-toed." Peggy giggled and looked down at her own feet as she swung her gumboots in and out.

"They're no good splayfooted either," Duncan added.

"What's splayfooted?" This time, Peggy's question was met with a roll of Duncan's eyes.

"Pointing outward," William explained.

They eliminated two of the calves on that basis even though Betsy thought the defect wouldn't have been indiscernible to the untrained eye.

"Then you need to look at the hooves." William moved to stand side on to the calves. "Neither too straight nor too much angle."

Betsy hid her amusement behind her hand as Peggy's heel-toe-heel-toe movements caused a deep furrow in Duncan's brow.

"Which ones do you think we should keep based on this criterion?" Duncan tested the land girls.

"This calf looks like it's walking in stilettos," Peggy suggested.

Duncan cleared his throat. "More correctly, we'd say it was too straight in the pastern but yes, right outcome, it wouldn't be a prize-winning show animal."

"And this one's hooves lean too far the other way." Jean pointed at a jet-black calf.

Eventually they were left with four calves. *Diamond* was among them and now Betsy was on high alert to ensure this calf was hers.

"All that's left to do is pick the one you are going to show," Duncan said. "You need to build up a rapport with the animal, so on show day it responds to your commands and does what you want it to."

William sidled up beside Betsy. His warm breath brushed her neck as he whispered in her ear.

"Pick the one on the right. It's certain to be a winner."

Betsy's head jerked head. Was her reaction from guilt at the delight of William's breath or fear *Diamond* would become Peggy's or Jean's? She didn't wait to be told twice; *Diamond* was on the right. She walked up to the calf and offered her outstretched hand. "I'll take this one here."

Diamond sniffed, then extended a rough pink tongue to curl around Betsy's fingers as if they were a teat offering a tasty feed.

"Looks like he likes you." Peggy moved to the calf on the opposite side of the group, it was the offspring of the cow that had caught milk fever. "This one has panda eyes; I'll take this one."

"Jean," Duncan caught her attention. "You take the one at the back and that'll leave the last one for William."

William moved back, squared on to his father and shook his amputated limb. "What? What do you mean one for me? How am I going to lead a calf with this?"

Duncan wasn't to be deterred. "You only need one hand to brush, one hand to build up a rapport and if you do that properly, which you've already proven you can, then one hand to lead."

"That was before!" William's anger throbbed through the arteries that bulged either side of his neck.

"No time like the present though." Duncan ignored William's outburst. "Bring this lot over to the fence and we'll start with the halters. Get them used to having something on their heads."

He walked off and the land girls were left staring awkwardly at each other and William, whose head and mood remained downcast. The gaping silence urged Betsy to fix the situation, to do something instead of nothing. Rather than risk William's wrath she reached her fingers out to *Diamond*.

"Come on then," she said to the calf. "We'd better do as he says."

She glanced across at William, hoping he too would respond to the encouragement. He held the stub of his right arm in his left hand and rocked gently backwards and forwards on his heals. His eyes blinked, his lip quivered, and he sniffed. Whether in the moment he was a child trying to restrain a tantrum or a grown man mourning the loss of more than just a limb didn't matter, his emotions wrenched at Betsy's heart. She wanted to hurry to his side and enclose him in an embrace that conveyed her feelings for him and a hope everything would be alright, but uncertainty stole the courage to do so. How could she convince anyone life would continue as normal when she was unable to believe that herself?

"And remember." Duncan stood at the fence waiting and yelled. "The calf will sense your mood. The more wound up you are the more wound up it will be. You need to be calm and in control."

Peggy and Jean giggled nervously.

"Calm and in control." Peggy took a deep breath, relaxed her shoulders, and stepped towards her calf. "Come on, *Panda*, how about we head over to the fence?"

Panda stopped nibbling the grass, stood looking at Peggy for a second then bounded off in the opposite direction, flicking its hind legs up in the air before rejoining the rejected calves.

"Umm ..." Peggy glanced from the calf to Duncan and back again. "That didn't go so well. I don't think that's the sort of calm and in control Duncan was meaning."

Betsy laughed at Peggy's choice of names She wasn't going to reveal in front of Duncan, she'd picked the same name for the mother cow. She accepted her slimy saliva-covered fingers as the price to pay for *Diamond* not following *Panda*. She offered her other fingers to William's calf, silently repeating the 'calm and in control' mantra, to ease the cringe she felt as the calf's long tongue wrapped around her fingers. Certain they had latched on; she took a small step backwards. Slow progress was better than none as they edged their way towards Duncan.

The rope halters Duncan held out to each of the land girls when they finally reached the fence with their calves looked more like messy coils of knots and loops. He must have seen their blank looks so demonstrated with William's calf how to feed one rope loop over the nose and the other up behind the ears, with a gentle but firm pull on the lead before tying it to the fence post.

"It'll likely protest for a few minutes." Duncan grabbed a brush from a bucket at his feet and handed it to William. "But give them a brush and they'll soon calm down and associate the halter with something good."

The calf pulled back on its tether, stomped its front hoof in protest at the restriction, not dissimilar to William's reaction to the limitations that now bound him. William snatched the brush, glared defiantly at his father but stepped slowly up to the calf and ran the brush down its back.

Betsy glimpsed the smile that lit up Duncan's face. It wasn't a satisfied smirk, but a smile filled with gratitude for a small triumph, and she imagined, as much love as Duncan would publicly demonstrate for his son.

Duncan stood at the rear of each of the remaining calves while the land girls tried to fit them with halters. Peggy managed to get the nose loop over the ears, leaving the ear loop to hang loose under the chin.

"Here," Duncan stepped in and fitted it correctly. "We haven't got all day."

Eventually four calves were tethered to the fence, standing still while their coats were brushed.

"Brush them for another five minutes then remove the halters and let them go. We'll do that for a few days before you start leading them." Duncan went through the gate. "Right, I've got phone calls to make. William, make sure you explain the best way to groom them. We've got the prize-winning genetics; the rest is up to you."

Betsy hoped the responsibility Duncan placed on William's shoulders wasn't a load too heavy to bear.

CHAPTER

23

"That girl …" Nel tutted. "She needs cheering up."

From the dining table, William couldn't see who his mother was looking out the kitchen window at, but he imagined it would be Betsy returning from the letterbox.

"No letter again today?" he asked.

"Betsy's got something in her hand but she's not looking happy." Nel wiped her hands on her apron and turned away from the window to face William. "Why don't you ask her to the dance?"

Nel's directness caught William unaware. Although a question, her tone indicated William taking Betsy to the dance was a *fait accompli*. Just like his father assuming he could groom and lead a calf with one hand, now his mother presumed his dancing ability would be unaffected by his injuries. They might be able to carry on as if nothing had changed but for him everything was different.

Betsy pushed the kitchen door open, so any protest William wished to make was silenced. She tossed the newspaper onto the table and discarded the letters, none of which, must have been addressed to her.

"Hello, dear." Nel went to Betsy with open arms. "No news is good news."

William chomped noisily on his toast. He could be the one to comfort Betsy. He'd be her second choice, but he'd already acknowledged to himself he'd never be anyone's first choice. Not now. Who would want a one-eyed, one-handed ex-soldier? He wasn't ready to go to the dance, to peg himself against other young uninjured men in a battle he'd be certain to lose but sitting in the darkness, watching a movie, he could do that. If William made sure he sat to her right, they could even hold hands. He smiled, imagining the warmth that would pass between them.

"Morning, Betsy," he spoke up before he lost courage. "Sorry, the mailman hasn't brought you the news you want. Perhaps the movies, this Saturday, might cheer you up. I could take you, that is, if you want to go."

Betsy broke free from Nel's comforting hug and blinked her glassy eyes. She smiled at William, but he knew she was just being polite.

"What's playing?" she asked.

William swallowed, not just his mouthful of toast, but the confidence he'd mustered. Betsy was only interested in the movie, not in spending time with him. He remembered the titles Bob had told him. It was probably for the best Betsy refused his invite; she wouldn't enjoy a scary movie and she wouldn't want to be seen with him.

"Probably not your cup of tea," he replied, all enthusiasm gone. "*One Body Too Many*, about a haunted house."

Betsy clapped her hands together. "Oh, great, nothing like a scary movie to make you feel alive."

William shook his head and did a double take. "Really?"

"Yes." Betsy giggled. "I'd love to go to the movies this Saturday."

William took another bite of toast, chewing quietly to savour Betsy's response. Before he'd swallowed, her facial expression changed from delight to disappointment. He knew it was too good to be true.

"What's wrong?" He might as well hear her change of heart now than later.

"How are we going to get to Geraldine?" Betsy's eyes went wide. "Without the truck."

"Oh, bugger," William cursed. His own foolishness was coming back to haunt him.

"Perhaps you could take Captain Boyle's car," Nel suggested. "It hasn't been out since you took the land girls to the dance."

"Who's taking Captain Boyle's car and where to?" Duncan hung his hat on the hook in the washhouse and entered the conversation.

The look William received from his mother was one he'd seen on numerous occasions, a conspirator's glance that encouraged him to be quiet, acknowledging she knew how to deal with his father to get the desired result.

"There's still no news from abroad for Betsy," Nel said. "So, an outing to the movies is just what the doctor would prescribe, and they need the car to get into Geraldine."

Duncan rubbed his bristled chin between thumb and forefinger and his eyebrows merged into one as he looked from Betsy to William to Nel contemplating his reply. William wanted to fill the ensuing silence. He was a grown man and shouldn't still be answerable to his father, despite crashing the truck. They were only going to the movies, not the pub.

Duncan's mouth opened and he raised a finger as if ready to object but then lowered himself to his seat at the table.

"It would have been polite to ask before making arrangements," he replied.

"Well, it's only just happened, dear." Nel rested her hand on Duncan's shoulder. "And the car could do with another run. It's been a while since William drove it to the dance."

"Yes, yes." Duncan growled. "Where's a cuppa, Nel? A man shouldn't be dying of thirst in his own home."

Nel quickly placed Duncan's favourite cup and saucer in front of him and poured a steaming cup of tea from the pot that had been warming on the coal range.

"And you'll need to make sure all the jobs are done first. Those calves should be leading well by then too."

Defeat was conceded in the only way Duncan knew but William was grateful. He'd thank his mum later and hold onto hope Betsy wouldn't change her mind before Saturday.

Determined nothing would jeopardise Saturday's 'date', William was up at first light the next morning, grateful the nightmares that plagued his sleep had been absent for the first time since he'd been back home.

"I know I can't do everything I used to," he said to Betsy as they stepped out into the cool morning air. "But I need you to let me do the things I can."

Betsy nodded quietly. A verbal agreement would have been better, but William continued.

"I can get the cows in, and I can rinse their teats. I've—" William stopped himself before mentioning how he'd helped

Rosey. Betsy's reaction was never pleasant when Rosey's name came up in conversation. He hoped it was jealousy because that meant Betsy had feelings for him. "I can hand milk them to finish them off, I can lock the cows into the paddock, and I can hose down the yards."

"There won't be anything left for me to do."

For a few seconds, Betsy's face was devoid of any emotion that gave William comfort he hadn't mucked things up completely, then she broke into a smile and giggled.

"Don't look so worried, William," she teased. "I'm sure that will be fine. We've managed it before, or have you forgotten?"

"Yes … umm, I mean no," William stumbled over his words. "Of course, I haven't forgotten!"

Annoyed he'd got so flustered, William kept quiet until they reached the horse paddock. "I'll take Jess and bring the cows to the yards."

Away from Betsy he was able to regather his thoughts. He closed his eye and inhaled, fresh country air tinged with the familiar and comforting earthy aroma of the horse. Jess's steady clip clop was a reassuring rhythm William had enjoyed since childhood, sturdy and dependable, attributes he needed to find within himself. They were traits he had exhibited before but stolen from him in the desperation and futility of war, abandoned in the battlefields where survival became paramount, where the mentality was shoot or be shot. For a life back in New Zealand though, he was expected to be sturdy and dependable. His parents, Betsy, the other land girls, Bill, the Home Guard volunteers, they had no concept of the knife's edge on which soldiers lived. How did he temper the adrenaline that coursed through his body at any hint of danger or attack? He, like the other soldiers, had tried to do it with alcohol, savouring the numbness that came with each mouthful of beer, like a golden elixir. Crashing the truck had put paid to that. In the eyes of his father, it only served to make him look anything but dependable.

Perhaps Betsy was the solution. If she believed in him, it would be easier to believe in himself. But did she? William still had no answers by the time he reached the cow paddock.

"Come on, girls," he called out as he lent down and unhitched the gate.

The noise of the milking machines didn't allow for much conversation, but each time one cow finished milking, and another started, William and Betsy came face to face as they moved between the bales. When William's smile was returned by Betsy on the first swap, his boldness grew, and while he pulled on teats, his mind was busy thinking of new ways to engage with her. On the next swap he bowed and spoke like an English gentleman.

"Good morning, Miss."

Betsy responded with a pretend curtsy. On the third swap, he wrapped his fingers around hers and raised her hand as if to kiss it.

"Oh no, it's too dirty to do that." Betsy protested but let her hand linger before they broke apart to attend to the cows.

The herd didn't need the usual encouragement to enter the shed. It was as if the cattle wanted to see the show. The next time a cow was released from the bale, William again took Betsy's hand in his. This time he raised it above their heads and spun Betsy around like a ballerina. Her giggle echoed off the iron roof to spur William on, but he was running out of ideas. If only he had two hands, he could lift her by the waist and spin her around.

Cold water splashing his face as he rinsed the next cow's teats gave him another idea. Instead of being annoyed by the limitation of his eyepatch, he embraced it and scanned the walls of the cowshed for a steel hook his father always had for hanging slaughtered animals. He grabbed it and stuffed the blunt end up his sleeve.

"Aye, aye, me hearty," he said in his best pirate imitation. "Look what treasure there is to behold. Cap'n Hook is me name and what pray tell is yours, fair maiden?"

Betsy joined in the charade, brushed her fringe off her forehead with the back of her hand like a damsel in distress, and faked a swoon to lean on the wooden post between the bales.

"Oh, Captain Hook," she squealed. "You'll not find any treasure around these parts. Just a farm girl doing her chores."

"A beautiful farm girl who carries the treasure in her smile." William smiled as a blush coloured Betsy's cheeks. She smiled back, and her eyes smiled too. He should have stopped there but he didn't. "Aye, I should tie you to this post and claim you as my own."

Betsy's head dropped, her smile was gone and so was she, out amongst the remaining cows in the yard. Annoyed at himself, William wrenched the hook out from his sleeve and slammed it into the nearest timber post.

"Bugger," he swore. "Can't you get anything right?"

He waited until Betsy brought another cow into the bale.

"Sorry, Betsy. I got carried away. I didn't mean to upset you."

"You didn't," she replied, her head hung low, her fringe hiding the brown eyes William so wished to see.

"Umm …" William hesitated, not wanting to make matters worse but needing to understand. "It looks like I did. You're not smiling. You look sad."

"I am sad."

"Sorry," William repeated.

"William, you have nothing to be sorry for. It's not your fault."

William frowned. "I thought I'd just lost an eye and a hand, not half my brain but I can't work it out. Why are you saying it's not my fault, when I stupidly implied, I was going to take you against your wishes?"

"Because … because it wouldn't have been against my wishes."

Betsy's reply was barely audible, her face went scarlet, she leaned over and pecked William on the cheek before rushing away to attend to the cow. He was left open-mouthed, digesting the revelation, trying to convince himself he had heard correctly. He repeated the conversation over and over in his head, seeing if any misinterpretation was possible. The kiss was confirmation, it was only a peck on a pirate's cheek, but it was like an exclamation mark emphasising the desire Betsy felt for him, even with his eyepatch and ugly scar. He ran his fingers over his cheek, following the jagged scar up to his uncovered eye. His eyepatch was missing. He'd forgotten to wear the very thing that made him act like a pirate. Betsy had, yet again, seen him in all his ugliness and still she kissed him. Finally convinced Betsy wanted him, William did a little skip on the spot before returning to milk out the cow Betsy had removed the cups from. Determined not to jeopardise anything, he kept quiet for the rest of the milking, content to absorb the frisson in the air and the knowing looks that passed between them.

The hour before the afternoon milking became the time for preparing the calves for the A & P show. By the end of the week, they were becoming quite friendly, they came when called and no longer pulled on the rope when tethered to the fence. Aside from the childhood memories that the time evoked, William looked forward to it as another excuse to spend time with Betsy. She'd been a little quiet since the incident in the shed but didn't pull away when he stood close to her to help with her calf.

"*Diamond* is going to be a winner," he whispered to her as he demonstrated the direction in which to brush the calf to ensure its coat took on the smoothness and sheen of a silk tuxedo.

Betsy's hand was warm beneath his. He imagined their bodies intertwining the way their fingers were. It was a struggle to ensure Betsy was the only one aware of that desire, conveyed in the surreptitious looks that passed between them.

"They like us," Jean said brushing her calf's rump.

"I think they like the bucket of milk reward at the end," William replied. "We'll have a go at leading and you'll see how much they like you. When you're in the ring, you'll have to walk around some pegs so the judge can see the animal front, back and side on. Then you'll have to stop, stand still for a few seconds before moving on. We'll just start with straight up and back today."

They unhitched the calves from the fence.

"Stand by the calf's left shoulder so you have the lead in your right hand." William gave the instruction before he realised, he couldn't follow it himself. "Bugger," he cursed. "Why the hell my father thought I could do this, I'll never know."

"We'll just do the opposite of what you're doing," Betsy suggested.

William liked the idea and swapped sides, holding the lead in his left hand. The end of the rope hung listlessly at his feet. His immediate reaction was to simply bend and pick it up with his other hand. Moments ticked silently by before his brain registered this was an impossibility. Perhaps he should have a permanent pirate's hook.

William grunted. "I can't even demonstrate the next bit. You need two hands."

"Show me," Betsy said. "And the other girls can follow."

The excuse to get close to Betsy was all the encouragement needed to pull William out of his self-pity. She was like an anchor in a stormy sea. Whenever he could feel his anger and frustration mounting, Betsy smiled at him and offered a solution. He tied his calf to the fence again and moved to stand beside her. Their arms touched. William justified the closeness as necessary to show the correct technique. Unless he imagined it, Betsy leaned closer rather than backing away.

"Hold the lead about six inches from the calf." William's hand lingered over Betsy's longer than was necessary to demonstrate. "And the other end loosely in your left hand. Give a little tug on the lead in the direction you're heading. One that's imperceptible to the judge but lets the calf know where it needs to go. Pull to the left and we'll turn around and head up the paddock."

Diamond was a quick learner. William had to release his hold and let Betsy and her calf walk up the paddock.

Peggy's calf stomped a front hoof like a petulant toddler and remained standing by the fence.

"Come on, *Panda*." Peggy pleaded with the animal. She tugged the lead with a little more force. "That's a good calf."

Neither the encouragement nor the yank got the calf moving. Instead, it bellowed and shook its head.

"You might need to go the other way, Peggy," William suggested. "Use your body weight to push onto the calf's shoulder. Don't yank the lead too tight around its neck."

With the lead scrunched up in his hand, William stood to the side of his calf, and nudged its side with his thigh. The calf sensed who was in charge and moved off as directed. Betsy and Jean were halfway up the paddock, William was impatient to join them, but Peggy looked like she was about to cry.

"Hang on, Peggy. If you get all worked up the calf will too. Just wait and I'll take this one up to the others and go get a stick."

"Don't hit it," Peggy pleaded. "It's not the calf's fault I'm not good at this."

"I'm not going to hit it." William shook his head. "And it's nobody's fault. You're both just learning."

William heeded his own words as he walked off. There was no one he could blame for his injuries, and he just had to learn how to manage tasks that were no longer simple endeavours.

CHAPTER

24

Betsy hummed her way through the Saturday morning milking. William must have heard her as he accompanied her happy tune with a whistle. Anticipation for their night out had Betsy's mind racing, making lists of all the jobs she had to do before she could luxuriate in a bath and get herself freshened up for the movies. She welcomed the opportunity to wear a dress. Overalls were a necessity on the farm but there was nothing feminine to either their shape or colour. Perhaps she could leave her hair down too, without the risk of it dirtying with cow muck and mud.

She wanted to call their outing a date but that only served to remind her of Roland. He'd been the last man she'd dated, and he should still be the only man she was thinking of. Humming helped keep the guilt that threatened to ruin the moment at bay.

"Are you all right to hose down and clean up?" William asked as he lifted the lever to release the last cow from its bale. "I'll go and shut the cows in the paddock."

Of course, Betsy was fine to do the jobs she'd been doing for months, but it was nice to be asked.

"Yes, thanks." She smiled at William.

After completing their respective tasks, they arrived back at the house at the same time. A horn tooted, drawing their attention to the driveway. Betsy's heart skipped a beat. What if it was the mailman with news about Roland? Could she hold off opening it until tomorrow, so her day wouldn't be ruined? The sight of Bill's truck saved her from that decision. She exhaled the breath she didn't realise she'd been holding.

Bill pulled up beside them and leaned out the window, his Home Guard band on his sleeve.

"Are you ready to go, William?" Bill sounded impatient. "Home Guard training. Remember?"

"Oh, blast, I'd forgotten about that. I've been a bit distracted by other things." William turned away from Bill and winked at Betsy. "I'll just grab some breakfast and get some tea for later and be right with you."

"Hurry then. The gun supply came through." Bill grinned. "We can practice shooting for real now."

William was gone from Betsy's side so quickly it felt as if he'd never been there. By the time she'd washed up in the washhouse tub and headed into the kitchen, he was seated at the table with everyone else, squashing a fried egg between two pieces of toast. Nel filled an empty beer bottle from the teapot, added some milk and pushed a cork into the top before stuffing the bottle into an old sock to keep warm.

"There you are, son," she said as she tucked the bottle under his arm. "That'll keep warm for a while."

The men turned to leave but were met by the mailman in the washhouse. Betsy's heartbeat seesawed again. Mail was only delivered direct to the house when it was bad news. She sat down and clasped her hands together under the table.

"Have you heard?" the mailman asked, his voice raspy as if he'd been talking a lot.

"Heard what?" Nel wiped her hands on her apron. Betsy saw the worried look she sent her way. "Do you have news for Betsy?"

"What?" A confused look passed across the mailman's face as he placed the newspaper and some envelopes on the table. "No, nothing like that. News much closer to home."

"What is it? Quick." Bill fidgeted, glancing from the mailman to the back door. "We've got to go."

"Be careful out there," the mailman warned. "There's a killer on the loose."

A collective gasp filled the room.

"Have the enemy landed?" Duncan asked. "Japs or Huns? We're prepared. We've got our drums of supplies stashed. The women can go into hiding while we defend our property."

"Nothing like that," the mailman continued. "Yesterday, out at Graham Stanley's property. He was always a bit strange if you ask me."

"Graham Stanley's dead?" Duncan sought clarification.

"No, no, he's on the run, loaded up with arms and ammunition, after a big shootout."

"Why would he do that?" Duncan asked.

"Mustn't have liked Ridley turning up at the farm with the sergeant and two constables," the mailman said to his captive audience.

"Stanley's animals have never been in good condition," Bill added his opinion. "I heard the agricultural officer wasn't getting anywhere having him up about his animal welfare. Ridley must have felt threatened to take three policemen with him. Who got shot?"

"All four of them."

The room went silent. The shock of such a horrific tragedy in their community shook everyone.

"Four dead! That's terrible." Nel's voice quivered as if she was close to tears.

"Three coppers are dead," the mailman said. "Ridley's been taken to hospital with serious bullet wounds."

Betsy looked across at William. His face had gone white as if his memories had drained him. She wanted to catch his eye, but he stared into the distance. When he finally returned from wherever his mind had taken him, his face went red and there was anger in his voice.

"We'll catch the bastard," he spat out. "We'll make sure he gets his just desserts. Come on, Bill, we'd better get going. Teach the Home Guard recruits how to use those guns you've got them. We've got a manhunt to go on."

"No, William." Nel rung her hands in the folds of her apron. "That's not your responsibility. Leave it to the police."

Betsy's turned from William to Nel and back again. Silently, she willed William to heed his mother's advice, to stay out of danger; he'd already endured his fair share of that, but she sensed from the rigidity of his stance he was primed for a battle.

"Mother," William turned to face Nel. "In case you weren't listening, the policemen are dead."

"They've called in reinforcements," the mailman said. "The sooner they catch the bastard the better I say. I don't like being out there not knowing where the armed madman is lurking. The Geraldine Home Guard are joining in the manhunt."

"Safety in numbers." Duncan nodded as if that would ease Nel's concern.

"What about his poor wife?" Nel asked. "I hope he didn't harm her."

"Word has it, the ambulance officers found her cowering in the bedroom, no injuries, just shock."

"Thank goodness," Nel sighed with relief.

"Right, we'll be off then." William nudged Bill. "You ready?"

"You'd better take your coat, William." Nel retrieved her son's coat from the hook in the washhouse and draped it over his arm. "Those clouds look like they're primed for torrential rain."

William rolled his eyes but accepted the coat.

"We'd better call in on Moira on the way," Bill replied. "Just let her know to be on the alert, stay inside and lock the doors if she sees anything suspicious."

"Or perhaps she could come over here with us?" Betsy offered.

"I'll suggest that." Bill said as the pair dashed out the back door, closely followed by the mailman.

"Be careful," Nel cried out a final plea.

"Is there some more tea in the pot, Nel?" Duncan asked. "I need a cuppa after that news."

Nel went to the back door, closed it after the men and turned the key in the lock.

"What are you doing?" Duncan growled. "There's no need to lock the door in broad daylight."

"Those poor people were shot in the daytime," Nel defended her action. "We've got the land girls to protect too."

Duncan sighed, stood, and left the room. Betsy could hear him shuffling around in the couple's bedroom but never expected him to return to the kitchen with a shotgun. He checked it was loaded and leaned it against the wall beside his armchair, like a soldier standing on sentry duty.

There was silence among the women, as if all were too frightened to speak. Duncan unfolded the newspaper in front of him and began to read.

"Where's that cuppa, Nel? You know I always like a cuppa when I'm reading the newspaper."

Nel poured the cup of tea. "I think the land girls should have a day inside today. Just to be safe."

"Farm work doesn't stop just because some lunatic went on the rampage," Duncan growled. "Besides Stanley's not going to be around here. We don't have enough bush for him to hide in and I doubt he's stupid enough to attempt a river crossing."

Memories of Ben, the escaped soldier Grace helped conceal, flooded back. He'd managed to hide out on the farm, tucked away in the implement shed. He didn't need the cover of bush to elude the authorities.

"It's going to rain anyway," Nel persisted.

"We'll still have to get the cows in for milking," Duncan insisted. "And we need to get the bull in, the cows are starting to cycle again. We can't afford to miss the opportunity to get them in calf. Betsy, you can bring him into the yard this afternoon."

Duncan never looked out from behind the newspaper as he delivered the instruction, it was a barrier that indicated any protest would be futile.

"William will be back by then," Nel responded on Betsy's behalf. "He'll be able to go with you and keep you safe."

Betsy nodded. Her thoughts had moved beyond the afternoon milking to their date at the movies. Would the cinema still operate with all the drama going on? She'd be disappointed if it didn't.

"Look, there's mail." Nel picked up a bundle of envelopes from the table. "A letter for Peggy. A letter for Jean and look, a letter for Betsy. That'll give you all something to do. Read your mail and write a reply to catch them up on all the excitement."

Peggy didn't hesitate to rip into her envelope. "It's from Rosey." Delight curved her mouth into a smile as she quietly read the letter.

Betsy tried to swallow. Guilt sat like a heavy lump in her throat. She could have been nicer to Rosey, more tolerant and understanding. Would Rosey have complained to Peggy about Betsy's frostiness?

"What news does Rosey have to share?" Betsy fished for a clue as to the tone of the letter.

"She's working in the munitions factory in Christchurch," Peggy replied. "As far away from animals as she can. All steel and heavy lifting. Hard work, but a nice bunch of girls."

Betsy received the jab, whether intended or not. The land girls might have been a nice bunch as well, if only she hadn't been jealous of Rosey's flirtatious ways. There was nothing she could do about that now. Instead, she focused her attention on the envelope addressed to her. She recognised the handwriting and the pyramids on the postage stamp confirmed the letter was from Irene.

"News from abroad, Betsy?" Nel asked.

"Just my sister, probably more gossip about her adventures in Cairo." Betsy picked at the flap, hesitant to discover whether her sister had found out anything about Roland. Certain she didn't want to share the letter's contents; she stood and tried to sound cheerful as she headed for the passage. "I've got some mending to do. I'll be in my room until lunchtime unless Moira turns up or anyone needs me."

"All right, dear." Nel's look indicated she didn't believe Betsy was telling the truth. "I'll make us a fresh batch of scones for lunch."

In the quietness of her room, Betsy could hear her heartbeat thundering in her ears. Delaying wasn't going to change the outcome nor ease the unsettled squirm in her stomach.

"Now or never," she murmured to herself before yanking open the flap and pulling the letter from the envelope.

A photo fell from the folds of paper to land on her bedspread. It was a small black and white image of Irene and a man. In the background pyramids rose majestically in a cloudless sky, manmade mountains that had endured for centuries. The man's arm was casually draped over Irene's shoulder, and they wore happy smiles for the camera.

Dearest Betsy

I was saddened to hear that Roland may have been captured by the German forces. I haven't been able to confirm that for you, there was so many that went into the bag, as they call it over here. Peter says that those captured were first taken to transit camps, not very nice, more like holding pens, overcrowded and unsanitary with a lack of food and shelter.

Betsy's heart plummeted. Thanks Irene, for trying to cheer me up.

But Peter says the Germans signed up to the Geneva Convention, which means they must provide humane treatment and adequate sustenance. So once the POWs get to the permanent camp, Peter reckons they should be fine. They can put them to work but Peter's sure they wouldn't make Roland work if he was injured.

Assuming his injuries weren't so severe he never made it to a permanent camp. Betsy blinked away the tears that welled up.

She dropped the letter and picked up the photo. Who is this Peter that knows so much? He wore an officer's uniform and Betsy had to admit he was rather handsome. She could see why Irene would be attracted by his neat grooming, confident stance and the cheekiness Betsy perceived in the look he gave the photographer. It almost seemed like he was about to wink.

But was that a wedding ring on his finger? Betsy studied Peter's hands, confirmed that it was a ring, and it was on the ring finger of Peter's left hand. Oh, Irene, have you gone and done something stupid with a married man? She dropped the photo and retrieved the letter, hoping for her sister to confirm that Peter was merely a colleague.

As you can see in the photo we've been out to the pyramids. Oh Betsy, you stand in awe of these, imagining the effort involved in their construction, thousands of years ago. That's Peter and I. He's such a lovely gentleman and we're having a wonderful time. I can hear you and Mum telling me not to let my heart get away on me, but it may be too late. I wanted to share my news with you but please don't tell Mum and Dad. I'll do that when the time is right.

Oh, Irene, the time will never be right. He's a married man. Does he have no loyalty?

Peter's different and the times are different. When you live in the midst of a war, you get daily reminders that life is precious and can be gone in an instant. Even though you're on the other side of the world, I am hoping you will understand that and not judge me.

Betsy understood and Graham Stanley's actions had proven, even close to home, you needed to make the most of every moment as you never knew which would be your last. She also knew it was difficult to have control over affairs of the heart. She never intended to feel an attraction to William. She had no control over the way her body reacted when she was close to him. Was she the only one who remained stupidly loyal instead of seizing the moment? She couldn't judge Irene; she was too busy judging herself.

In the quietness of her room, something shifted, like a burden eased, a weight lifted from her shoulders, forgiveness for a sin, pardon from a crime. A lightness settled in Betsy's heart, and she knew then following that feeling, staying true to her desires, was the most loyal action she could take. And she could start today when William returned home. Her thoughts drifted, images of them holding hands in the cinema, resting her head on his shoulder, a goodnight kiss filled her with joy.

Betsy jumped up from the bed and spun around on the spot. She felt energised, like a child filled with anticipation for the wonders of the world. She folded Irene's letter back into the envelope, she'd write back and thank her but not now, she was too excited to put pen to paper.

She pulled her dress from the closet, draped it down her front and admired herself in the mirror. The self-criticism that would normally have filled her head with negativity remained at bay. There was a glow about her, and she was ready to let that radiate

CHAPTER

25

"Have you heard the news?"

"We need to join the manhunt now."

"That Stanley, he needs a bullet between the eyes."

"Now, now, settle down." William tried to calm the Home Guard volunteers gathered at the Orari Hall. "We'll join the manhunt if the police request it. It needs to be a co-ordinated search so there aren't any more casualties."

"Meanwhile our rifles have arrived, twenty Lee Enfields with plenty of 303 ammo," Bill added. "So, we can start with allocating those and learning how to maintain them."

"And shoot them." Fred shaped his fingers into pistols and shot into the air.

Bill shook his head as he handed the rifles out to the group. "We'll get to shooting them when William is satisfied you can do it safely."

"What about ammo?" Fred asked.

Bill glanced at William as if he wanted confirmation it was a good idea to issue ammunition to each of the men. William looked around the group, they were all off farms and weren't total novices around firearms.

"No point having a rifle if you haven't got ammunition," one of the men remarked.

The group nodded their heads in unison and agreement.

"Besides Stanley could be in the trees spying on us as we speak," added another volunteer.

Everyone turned, eyes peeled. The wind whistled in the row of macrocarpas lining the perimeter of the field but if Stanley was there, he was well concealed. A shiver ran down William's spine. He was back on the front, that unwanted feeling that danger was imminent sat heavy on his shoulders. He couldn't deny the Home Guard volunteers the very supplies they all needed.

"We need to be able to protect our families and our property, that's the whole point of the Home Guard."

An image of Betsy filled William's thoughts. He needed to protect her, his parents, and the other land girls. There were so many valid reasons that he quickly handed out a box of ammunition to each volunteer. The men were equipped but without the ability to hold a rifle William remained unarmed.

"I requested this for you." Bill handed over a leather belt with holster. A Colt 45 revolver was clipped securely into the holster. "And here's a box of ammo."

"Thanks, Bill." William needed Bill's help to wrap the belt around his waist and do up the buckle but once in place he felt reassured by their weighty presence.

By mid-morning the rifles had been loaded and unloaded, disassembled, and reassembled so many times the volunteers could have done it with their eyes closed. William had only been able to issue the instructions, not demonstrate himself but he felt like his commander from training camp as he paced up and down the line of volunteers, his good arm behind his back. He watched them follow his orders, pointing out their errors and gained a sense of satisfaction from their mastery of the task.

"Job well done, men." William had respect for the commanders that showed appreciation for his efforts, so he tried to emulate their actions. "We'll do some marching drills with the magazines loaded but bolt unlocked before moving onto target practice."

They marched the length of the field, everyone except William, with the rifle butt cupped in their left hand, and the barrel resting against their left shoulder. Although the line of marching men remained straight and in time, their eyes darted around the field perimeter. William too, was alert to any movement in his periphery. Was Stanley watching them? Was Stanley about to shoot at them? Was William the right man to lead these volunteers and keep them safe in an attack? Did he have a choice?

He had no time to find the answers. As his commands halted and about turned the group for the march back to the hall, a black car pulled into the gateway. Its red rooftop siren wasn't flashing but it was instantly recognisable as was the policeman that climbed from the vehicle and donned his helmet.

"Morning men," the policeman greeted the group when they stopped in front of him. "We need to enlist your services in searching for a fugitive at large."

"Yes! Some real action." Fred couldn't contain his teenage excitement, not even when William cast him a look that suggested he be quiet. "Wanted! Dead or alive!"

"Nothing vigilante required," the policeman continued in a serious tone. "An organised but calm search of the area. The suspect is believed to have a cache of weapons and ammunition and is considered dangerous."

"As you can see, officer," Bill said. "We are all armed."

"Is it Graham Stanley you're talking about?" William wanted confirmation.

"Yes," the policeman replied. "We're working on getting photo identification but assume most of you will have knowledge of the man in question."

"We sure do," one of the older Home Guard volunteers answered. "He's an experienced bushman, I would have thought he'd disappear into the forest behind his place, not come out this way."

"The wanted man was seen in the vicinity of the Winchester Hall during the night." The policeman retrieved a map from his car, laid it out on the bonnet and pointed to the hall's location. "Locals have also reported sightings at the hotel and an attempted break-in to the Catholic Church."

"He must be needing to confess his sins," one of the men joked.

The policeman's face gave no indication he appreciated the humour. "More likely seeking shelter. The weather forecast isn't good, there's a storm on its way."

"What would you like us to do, Sergeant?" William asked.

"We need your assistance in apprehending the suspect," the policeman replied. "More shots were fired overnight."

"No further fatalities I hope." William secured one corner of the map with his hand.

"No. No injuries to our men either but traces of blood have been discovered in an area southeast of here. It is currently unconfirmed that the blood is from the suspect, but he may be injured and seeking shelter and supplies."

"He'll be easier to capture if he's wounded." William was transported back to the battlefield where injured soldiers became prisoners of the enemy if the allied forces were outmanoeuvred.

"He might try and sneak back home," a volunteer suggested. "Get his wife to patch him up."

"She's been evacuated. The house has been secured, trip wires, flood lights. We'll get him if he goes there."

On the map the distance between Stanley's house and the Orari Hall was barely more than a thumbprint. The fugitive could be literally on their back doorstep.

"What about protecting our own folk?" Bill asked.

"We've got officers in the area, advising locals to stay indoors."

"We're farmers, you can't farm from inside," a volunteer groaned.

"Yes, we are aware of that, everyone is doing their best to apprehend the suspect as soon as possible." The policeman pointed to an area on the map. "We'd like your group to search this area, between the railway track and the river. Start here and move south. Leave a sentry at the hall as a reporting base for any sightings or evidence of his presence."

William nodded while silently formulating a plan. His feet itched to move, to get started on the chase. Adrenaline quickened his pulse, the anticipation of a manoeuvre, the element of risk, a heightened sense of danger, the prospect of success. He could bring this man in; he could prove himself useful. The war hadn't stolen everything from him, it had given him the tools to use to protect those he loved.

"We'd already planned to be here for the day," William said. "We can get started right away."

"How many of you are there?" The policeman looked around the group.

"Twenty," Bill replied.

"Right, I recommend you break-into two groups." The policeman folded the map, so the assigned area remained visible. "Twelve-hour shifts, around the clock, always reporting back to the hall. When not rostered on you can rest and attend to your farming duties."

"We can do that." William's automatic reaction was to salute but the impulse could only throb in the nerve endings of his stump. Instead, he took the map and turned to face Bill. "You want to head up one group and I'll lead the other?"

"Sure," Bill replied. "That way we'll always have someone around home."

"Good, I'll leave you to it then." The policeman removed his helmet to get into his car. "I'll check back in later today unless you phone in with a sighting."

"Fred," William waited until the police car left before he summoned the teenager. Fred's enthusiasm mirrored William's before the war. He was young and could still be shielded from the harsh reality of death. "I reckon you'd make a good sentry, in charge of headquarters here at the hall."

"Nah!" Fred protested. "I want to go on the chase. I can get the bastard."

It was the response William expected. Fred might be a loose cannon out on a search and having to report bad news to his parents was the last thing William wanted to do. He had to make the sentry job seem attractive.

"You might get him from here. He was seen at the Winchester Hall last night remember."

"Yeah … yeah, that's true."

William could almost hear the cogs whirring away in Fred's brain.

"You'd be responsible for communications too," William added. "It's an important position, keeping everyone informed."

"Yeah, you'd all have to check in with me." Fred's face lit up. "I could set up a bed here, bring my sleeping bag, be on the job twenty-four seven."

"That's not necessary," Bill said. "Your parents would want to see and know you were safe."

"Nah," Fred laughed. "Me Mum would be glad for the peace and quiet."

It was settled, Fred went home to gather his things and update his parents, the other men split into two groups, half headed home, the other half readied themselves for a search, guns loaded, hats on and coats buttoned up against the worsening weather.

William and his group of men set off from the hall towards the Orari River in a single line that spanned the road and then spread across the paddocks in the search for clues.

"Keep your eyes peeled, men," William warned as they approached a patch of scrub.

"Something's been in here." The volunteer raised his rifle to point out an area of trampled grass and a broken Manuka branch at the side of the scrub. "I'll go in and ferret him out."

"Wait!" William raised his hand and his voice. "Stanley! You in there? We've got you surrounded. There's no escape. Put your weapons down and come out. We don't want any more trouble."

The Home Guard stood still, rifles poised ready, ears peeled, waiting for a response. Silent seconds ticked by. The feeling of balancing on a tight rope, one wrong move and disaster would strike, had William's heartbeat thundering in his chest.

Something rustled among the bushes. Click! Click! Click! Bolt were cocked, and fingers hovered over triggers.

"Fire some shots!"

"Flush him out!"

"Get the bastard!"

"Get him before he gets us!"

The men were riled up. The fugitive didn't stand a chance. Only it wasn't Stanley who charged from the scrub but an equally agitated wild boar, head down, tusks ready to gouge the enemy. Its stench filled the air like a warning to stay away. Before its low-pitched grunts could be mistaken for friendliness, the boar issued a battle cry, a high-pitched squawk echoed across the paddock. William stood between the boar and freedom.

"Let him go," he yelled before opening a gap that the boar barrelled through.

"We should have shot it for the freezer."

"It was a boar," William replied. "The meat would have been tainted. You could smell it."

"Would have done for dog food."

"Yeah, but we're here to catch Stanley, not food for your animals. Uncock your rifles, men. We'll keep walking."

Several hours later the men arrived back at the hall with the collars of their coats turned up against the bitter southerly wind darkness had brought. They'd not detected any traces of Stanley's presence and despondency had edged in where energy levels had seeped away. The outdoor light provided the only illumination and the men, like the swarming moths, were drawn to its glow.

"We've covered a lot of ground." William struggled to sound positive. "You men head home for a hot meal and some well-deserved sleep, ready to search again tomorrow."

"I won't sleep knowing he's on the loose."

"Lock your doors," William called out to the men as they headed off. "Keep your rifle ready."

"How did you get on?" Bill asked.

"No luck. We've covered all this area though." William showed the map to Bill. "Where's Fred? I thought he was supposed to be here but there's no lights on."

"I am here," Fred called out.

It made no sense, but the voice had come from overhead. William and Bill both looked up. Fred waved to them from the roof.

"What are you doing up there?"

"I'm on sentry duty like you asked," Fred answered. "Bird's eye view from up here."

William shook his head. There was merit in the lad's way of thinking, but it must be freezing up on the roof.

"No point having the lights on," Fred continued. "Stanley's not going to come if he thinks somebody's here."

"The lad's got a point," Bill said.

"Just don't go catching hypothermia," William warned.

"Hypo… what?" Fred asked.

"Keep warm!" William laughed and shook his head. "I'll be back tomorrow."

Twenty-four hours passed, William and his men were back on the search after their break. Bill's group hadn't seen any trace of Stanley and now the weather was turning nasty. They checked in with Fred, who climbed down from the roof to stay out of the rain. He'd received an update from the police, there'd been another break-in, a house had been entered overnight.

"Whose house?"

"What'd the rat pinch?"

"Was anybody hurt?"

The men were on edge. It wasn't the sort of news that would keep them calm on their search.

Fred stood tall; his chest puffed out. "The Stewart place, off the end of Ohapi Settlement Road."

"That's a dead end, down by the river."

"Perhaps he's going to attempt a river crossing," a volunteer speculated.

"He'd be a fool to do that in this rain, the river will be in flood for sure."

"What else did the report say, Fred?" William tried to steer the conversation back.

"No injuries," Fred reported. "A tin of fruit, some biscuits, and a quantity of eggs were missing."

"Nothing substantial that's going to sustain him for long," William pulled the brim of his hat down and folded the collar of his coat up to protect himself from the driving rain. "Come on, men, we'd best be off. We'll head towards that area. He's probably sheltering in the bush that runs adjacent to the river."

No soldiering experience was required to know the bush would provide wood for a fire and cover from the elements. Any good boy scout camping outside would have taken matches and a billy to boil water from the river. The eggs and biscuits wouldn't provide an injured man with enough sustenance though, he'd be wearing down. William sensed the hunt would soon be over.

A short time later they reached the bush, a dense area of native forest that bordered the Orari River. The overhead branches of the Kanuka and Manuka meshed to form a canopy that allowed the Home Guard to take respite from the weather and regroup.

"It'll be like looking for a needle in a haystack in this."

"No," William said. "He'd have to hack his way through the undergrowth to be in here, which means it'll be easy to track him. We just have to follow the bush line and see where he's gone in."

The men set off again, single file, William at the head, tramping the line where the grass ended and the bush began, squeezing around the ends of fences that dissected the cleared land into paddocks. They hadn't gone more than ten minutes when William stopped suddenly, dropped to his knees, and waved his hand to indicate for the men to follow suit.

"What is it?" the man behind William murmured.

"There's something ahead on the ground, half out of the bush." William couldn't tell if it was man or beast, dead or alive but the adrenaline pulsing through his veins warned him to proceed with caution.

Instinct had his right arm reaching for his weapon. His stump stalled uselessly in mid-air.

"Bugger," he cursed before awkwardly grabbing his pistol from its holster. The seconds of delay were enough to allow doubt to creep in. How accurate would his left-handed shot be? If only he had sight in both eyes, he could confirm his target. Should he let one of the other men take the lead?

"What is it?" The volunteer's repeated question demanded an answer. "Is it Stanley? Let me get him."

The man didn't wait for a response, he charged out from behind William. Whether he was reckless, or brave didn't matter, it all happened in seconds, too quick for William's leadership to prevent.

With his rifle ready to fire, the man scanned the bush line, sighted the target, and edged his way towards it. William stood, at least ready to offer back up.

"It's just a dead animal."

Disappointment echoed down the line of men.

"Yes, but look," William crouched down beside the carcase. "It's a fresh kill."

"Another wild boar's attack."

"No, look, the meat has been cut out." A chunk of meat had been carved from the animal's rump. "The farmer would take all the meat. This will be Stanley. He must be close by."

The Home Guard were back on high alert, staring into the bush for any sign of the fugitive. Broken bracken a few feet from the carcase provided the trail to follow, a narrow track into the undergrowth.

"Stay alert, men. Stay alert." William buried any doubts that threatened to steal his courage and headed into the bush, determined to lead the men from the front.

CHAPTER 26

Betsy's dress remained on its hanger, as lifeless as she felt, when the afternoon disappeared into night and William still wasn't home. Every time she decided to let her barriers down to embrace life, some disappointment or another, robbed her of her courage.

As was his nightly habit, Duncan settled into his armchair to listen to the war report on the radiogram. Betsy imagined the weekly war news that would have screened at the cinema. The news and the movie would still be played but without her and William in the audience. There would be no holding his hand, no resting her head on his shoulder. She silently prayed that was only for tonight and not forever. Betsy couldn't bear to hear more bad news, she said goodnight and escaped to her bedroom.

Restless hours later, Betsy was still awake when she heard hushed voices in the passage. She scrambled from her bed, grabbed her dressing gown, and went to investigate.

"Did you find him, son?" Nel asked.

"No." William put a reassuring hand on his mother's shoulder. "But we will, don't worry."

"Are you hungry? I can cook scrambled eggs on toast."

"Thanks, Mum, but I'm more tired than hungry. I'd better get some rest. We're on twelve-hour shifts."

When William turned to go into his bedroom, Betsy moved out of the shadows of her doorway and caught his eye.

"Sorry," William apologised. "Sorry I missed our night at the movies."

"It's alright." It wasn't but Betsy couldn't add guilt for her disappointment to William's burden when he already looked exhausted. "There will be another night."

"I sure hope so." William yawned and leaned against the door frame. "Sorry, I've got to sleep."

"Good night, William." Betsy returned to her room.

She heard the click of his door; the rusty squeak of the wire woven bed as he lay down and moments later a quiet rumble. William's snoring was a calming rhythm and knowing he was safe next door meant sleep wrapped Betsy in its comforting cloak with ease.

Another forty-eight hours and life still hadn't returned to normal; Betsy's restorative sleep was a distant memory. Updates from William in the brief times he was home, and awake, revealed further break-ins, theft, and injuries but Duncan insisted they were in no danger at the farm and work was to continue as normal. Betsy had the task of rounding up the bull by herself and bringing it to the yards to join the cows but that was the least of a long list of concerns. Following Irene's letter, she hadn't been able to get an image of Roland lying on the ground, injured, trampled by other prisoners, trapped behind barbed wire, gaunt and deprived of water and medical attention. That picture then morphed into a madman with a cache of weapons aiming a shotgun at William who with his injuries was unable to see the murderer off to his right nor was he able to hold a shotgun to defend himself.

Chin up girl, she murmured to herself; the mantra that in moments like these was all that kept her going. Trudging up the race, placing one heavy foot in front of the other until she reached the paddock and unhitched the gate. The bull hadn't looked so intimidating when there had been a barbed wire fence between her and the beast but now there was only ten feet of paddock or more correctly brown trampled earth where the bull had, and continued to stomp its hoof, like a tribal warrior preparing for battle.

Betsy gulped. Roland and William would have to look after themselves. She needed her wits about her to deal with the bull. The beast towered over Betsy and its charcoal-coloured head rose from muscled shoulders that were so broad there was no room nor need for a neck. Betsy would never know whether the short tuft of black hair atop its head was soft to touch, she would need a milking stool to reach it, but had no intention of getting that close. They were like duelling foes standing at ten paces assessing one another. Despite the ring in the bull's nose, it snorted, raised its head skywards and bellowed a challenge.

The black eyes that stared at Betsy, were as scary as the dark of night and her leg muscles tightened. Her heart pounded in her chest and adrenaline had her ready to run. She hoped it wouldn't be necessary. She contemplated taking a tough stance with the bull, using her voice to show who was in charge but a nervous giggle was all that escaped when she realised the futility of that approach.

"Come on, Mr Bull," Betsy adopted a friendly tone. "There are lots of Mrs Cows that would like to meet you."

Betsy stepped aside and waved her hands to usher the bull forward through the gate. The animal tilted its head as if to acknowledge the words but otherwise remained still, without so much as a blink.

"It'd be really nice if we could work together here, you know, help each other out."

Nothing.

"Don't tell me you're like Duncan and think all women are useless farmers."

Still no response.

"Well, I give the cows a whack on the rump when they won't move." Betsy stood legs astride, hands on hips trying to appear staunch while making her idle threat. "Perhaps you need that as well."

The bull's black eyelashes swept briefly over the animal's eyes. A reaction, but not accompanied by any progress toward the gate.

"Stupid animal. You're too ugly to flutter your eyelashes anyway. As if you're going to win me over. Duncan says you've got to come to the shed, so you've got no choice."

Betsy wouldn't be beaten but she was running out of options. It was only out of necessity she'd come to the back of the farm alone; knowing there was a fugitive still at large. She walked in a wide circle around to the bull's back end. She'd never be brave enough to get anywhere near the hind legs that could kick out viciously without warning, so chose to wave her arms furiously and yell in the deepest voice she could.

"Raar raar!"

The bull gave a defiant flick of its tail and took one step towards the gate.

"Raar raar!" Betsy imagined she looked ridiculous and sounded even worse, but the bull was moving, so she kept it up until the bull reached a steady pace heading down the race, the muscles on its rump rocking from side-to-side and its tail flicking to dislodge any insects that attempted to hitch a ride.

The bull raised its head as they neared the yards and sniffed the air. He must have recognised the distinctive pheromones of a cow in season and quickened his pace. Betsy almost had to jog to reach the yard gate before the bull.

"Now you hurry up." She opened the gate to let the bull into the yard. "You'd have been here a lot sooner if you'd listened to me."

Jean already had the first of the cows in the bale, cups attached and was moving to round up another. Betsy saved her the job, ushering a cow into the empty stall and attaching the rope behind her. She straightened and turned to come head-to-head with the bull. She squealed with fright and jumped out of the way.

"Now you want to be friends." Her rhetorical question was asked in a tone she hoped sounded braver than she felt. "Too late, I've got work to do."

She sat on the stool to wash the cow's teats while the bull moved closer to sniff the cow's rear. Betsy hadn't paid much attention to the anatomy of cattle before now but if it wasn't her imagination, the cow's vulva appeared red and swollen. She remembered back to a biology class in school, human anatomy couldn't be that different from cattle and recalled her own limited sexual experiences. She blushed when she finally realised what the bull was doing.

"Don't you get up to any funny business in here," she warned.

The bull's nostrils flared, and its top lip curled up. Normally, Betsy would interpret that as distaste, but the bull lingered and continued to sniff.

"Just wait till you get back to the paddock, will you!"

Jean released her cow and chuckled at Betsy through the railings.

"Sounds like you're jealous," she teased before laying a hand on the bull's shoulder. "Come on, big fella, there are plenty more cows in the yard for you to check out."

Was there more truth in Jean's teasing than Betsy wanted to admit to? Memories of the forty-eight hours she'd spent with a man spread a warmth throughout her body and beneath her overalls she felt her nipples harden. No time for that now, she growled silently.

The rest of the milking proceeded without a hitch. The bull continued with its mission out in the yards, sniffing and riding those cows that would stand and Betsy focused on milking the cow in front of her, banishing all other thoughts from her head.

Too much planning and organisation had gone into the A & P Show for it to be derailed by the pursuit of Stanley. The authorities were confident everything would be under control by then and the show would be an opportunity for the community to gather, connect and regroup following the tragedy.

That meant Betsy, Jean and Peggy still had to groom and lead their calves daily. William's absence left them to their own devices; they had no idea if they were doing things correctly, but *Diamond* seemed to be a natural. The calf was happy to do everything Betsy asked of it. There were no tugs-of-war like Peggy had to contend with, nor a runaway calf that had Jean chasing down the paddock. *Diamond* walked, head held high, stopped, and started in response to Betsy's subtle tugs on the lead; turned left or right according to the nudge or pull.

"Looks like you might have a winner there, Betsy," Duncan commented one afternoon. "Captain Boyle will appreciate some more silverware being added to his trophy cabinet in his absence."

Betsy smiled. She wasn't doing this for the captain she'd never met; she was doing it to prove she could. Who would have thought a typist could win a trophy at an A & P Show? Who would have thought she would become a land girl, milk cows, drench animals, make hay or any of the multitude of tasks she'd undertaken since arriving at *Whipsnade*? Certainly not herself. Betsy was grateful for Grace's insistence it was what she needed. Sometimes her friend knew her better than she knew herself.

When the rain pelted down, they tethered the calves in the shed and brushed their coats until they shone. With an arched back, *Diamond* absorbed the repetitive strokes of the brush Betsy ran from the tip of the animal's head to the top of its tail. She swapped the brush for a comb to ensure the tuft of white hair at the end of its tail was free of knots.

The raindrops on the iron roof left no room for audible conversation between the women but Betsy didn't mind, she was content with her own thoughts, imagining a time when the Stanley saga was finally resolved, and life returned to normal.

William's return that night turned life upside down again. He was earlier, perhaps because of the weather or perhaps because of the news he brought with him. Betsy had just hung her rain drenched coat on a hook in the washhouse when the back door opened again to let William escape the storm. Drips ran off the brim of his hat and the hem of his coat, splattering on the floor.

"You're soaked." Betsy reached out to William. "Here let me help you."

"I'll do it!" He turned away from her.

Betsy flinched and took a step backward. William was just tired she thought; he never liked to show weakness and she'd been too pushy in offering to help. She stood, patient and quiet, waiting for him to calm. He struggled to remove his coat but eventually it hung on the hook beside hers and William turned to face her. She saw his pained stare, the quivering of his lips, the trembling of his fingers and worst of all the blood staining his shirt front.

"William," she gasped. "You're bleeding. What happened?"

He looked down at his shirt. "It's not mine. I'm alright."

"Whose is it? Did you capture Stanley? Did someone else get hurt?"

William walked past Betsy into the kitchen. "I need to sit down."

"Of course, you do, sorry," Betsy apologized. "I'll make you a cuppa."

"Something stronger would be good but I'll settle for a cuppa."

Betsy was all fingers and thumbs as she spooned the tea leaves into the pot. Her relief that William was uninjured was countered by anxiety to get the answers to her questions. The cups and saucers threatened to topple as she hurried them to the table. She turned the teapot three times so fast the tea leaves would have become dizzy if they'd been human. As soon as she'd poured William's cup, she sat opposite him, her hands clasped together on the table. Waiting only long enough for him to swallow his first mouthful, she repeated her question.

"Whose blood is it, William?"

William looked down at his shirt and sighed. "Stanley must have killed a beast to get some meat to eat. It was such a waste to leave it there, we cut it up for the Home Guard volunteers to take for their families."

Betsy nodded. There was something William wasn't telling her. The death of an animal wouldn't cause him to look so forlorn.

"Did you capture Stanley?"

William leaned across the table, a determined look on his face. "Not yet, but I will. I must. The bastard shot Bill."

Betsy's head jerked back as if she too had been shot. "Bill … Moira's Bill … is he … is he dead?"

"No." William shook his head. "They've taken him to hospital with gunshot wounds. We're waiting for an update."

"Does Moira know?"

"Yeah, I stopped in there on the way home."

"She'll be all alone. I should go and be with her."

"No point. She dropped me off here and was heading straight to the hospital." William downed the last of his tea. "I've got to get forty winks, then get back on the hunt. We can't let Stanley hurt anyone else."

Betsy remained at the table long after William left the room. She felt numb, as if her limbs had been drained of blood. How could tragedy happen so close to home? What if William was injured too? It didn't bear thinking about.

"Have you got any jobs to do in town, Betsy?" Duncan asked. "The truck's finally been repaired. Just in time with the A & P Show this weekend. I thought we were going to have to walk the calves. Moira's off to visit Bill again so I'm going to catch a lift with her into Geraldine to pick it up. Nel's got a list of supplies, you could get from the general store while I get the truck."

She hadn't seen Moira since the shooting and wanted to see if she was doing alright. Betsy had managed over the past few nights to pen a reply to Irene too. She'd written and screwed up several sheets of paper, eventually deciding it was not her place to chastise her sister for her relationship with Peter, opting instead to avoid the topic altogether and relay news of life at *Whipsnade*.

"Yes, that would be good," she replied. "I've got a letter to post too."

A few minutes later the truck horn tooted outside, urging Duncan and Betsy to hurry into their coats, out the door and into the vehicle. Being wedged into the front seat, Duncan's broad shoulders on one side and Moira on the other, reminded Betsy of Alice and she wondered how her pregnancy was progressing. Imagining Alice cradling a baby in her arms stirred Betsy's maternal instincts. She shook her head, there was no need to be getting ahead of herself.

"How's Bill doing? Do you know when he's going to be home?"

"It's so frustrating." Moira slapped her palm onto the steering wheel. "I'm not officially Bill's next of kin, so the doctors won't tell me anything. I have to eavesdrop from behind the curtains."

"Have you explained that you live with him?" Betsy tried to gauge Duncan's reaction, but he gazed out the side window seemingly oblivious or choosing to ignore their conversation.

"Bill would have kittens if I announced that to all and sundry." Moira sighed.

"But you need to know so you can manage the farm."

"Apparently, I'm not good enough to do that either." Moira's grip on the steering wheel tightened and her knuckles went white. "Bill's sister, Ann, and his brother-in-law, John, are arriving. To take care of things they say."

"They're probably just worried about Bill." Betsy tried to placate Moira.

"So am I." Moira was adamant. "And I can take care of things too."

"Well, hopefully Bill will be back on his feet before you know it, and the pair of you can go back to normal." Betsy hid her despair there never would be a normal. "What did you manage to glean from your eavesdropping?"

"It's not good, Betsy, it's not good." Moira shook her head and sniffed. The quiver in her voice urged Betsy to change the subject.

"Are you going to come to the A & P Show?" she asked. "All of us *Whipsnade* land girls are leading calves. You'd enjoy the outing. It'd help keep your mind off things."

"Mmm, I'll see." Moira's tone sounded as non-committal as her words.

CHAPTER

27

"Thanks for the update, Fred. We'll head out that direction now." Fred's mother wouldn't appreciate the black shadows darkening her son's eyes. William gave him an encouraging pat on the shoulder. "Get some rest while we're away. Come on, men; we've got a villain to capture."

"I reckon we should shoot first and ask questions later."

"Yeah, Stanley doesn't deserve to live, not after what he's done."

"Three dead and two hanging in the balance, a life sentence will never compensate for that."

Inside William's head he agreed with everything the Home Guard volunteers were saying, but the police had requested Stanley be taken alive … if possible. It would be the right thing to do in the eyes of the law, but William wasn't convinced. His holstered revolver rubbed on the stub of his amputated arm; both felt like an annoying rash he needed to itch. He could feel the familiar thirst for retribution festering inside him. It was like being back on the front, witnessing the fall of one of your own, and needing to take revenge. This time Bill had fallen, and Stanley was the enemy.

William felt certain today was the day. He'd brought Patch along; confident the dog would sniff out the fugitive. The police dropped off an old jacket belonging to Stanley, retrieved from his house. Patch sniffed the jacket and now, as the group reached the last search area, was head down onto the trail. The dog strained on the leash as they approached a thicket of bush. William weighed up hanging onto Patch or arming himself; with only one hand he couldn't do both. He passed the leash over to the man beside him, hoping his dog would be kept safe, and retrieved and cocked the revolver, knowing that was the only chance he'd have to keep himself safe.

Beneath the Ponga fronds, something rustled in the bush. William's heartbeat thundered in his ears. He took a step closer, peering into the undergrowth, silently cursing the Kawakawa leaves that moved in the breeze. Was it Stanley, an animal, a bird, or just his imagination? Patch barked and yanked on the lead. William wasn't hearing things. The Home Guard formed a semi-circle, the barrels of their rifles all aimed at the bush.

Seconds ticked by like the countdown on a time bomb. Another rustling in the bush foreshadowed the blast of a shot, so close to William, he sensed it flying by. It was aimed low, not high enough to kill a man. He sucked in a breath, paused ready to fire a shot, his arm extended at shoulder height. His bullet would get a man in the chest.

It was a cock pheasant that staggered from the undergrowth to take its final breath, its white collar and auburn chest stained with blood from a gaping wound. William's shoulders slumped. He was disappointed the pheasant had become another victim but even more so that it wasn't Stanley lying in front of them.

"That'll go good in the pot." The man who'd fired the shot stepped forward to claim his bounty, plucking a tail feather for his hat before he bound the bird's feet with string and hitched it to his belt, unperturbed by the blood dripping to the ground.

The snapping of a branch silenced everyone and refocused their attention. Another pheasant's squawk echoed a warning. Was Stanley here or were they wasting their time? Had the killing of the pheasant allowed him to elude capture again? William scanned the area, straining to see into the shadows of the trees; he wanted to rip his eyepatch off, but knew it was futile. He had to rely on the body he'd been left with to prove he was still whole.

A movement caught his eye, he blinked to clear his sight and his imagination. He needed to be certain what he saw was a man; not lichen and silvery bark painting pictures on the trunk of an ancient Kahikatea tree. A smear of red offered confirmation. It was too high on the trunk to be from an animal, covered too great an area to be a bunch of tiny berries. It must be blood. Stanley was here and he was injured.

"I'm going in," William murmured to the men. "I'll flush him out. You pin him down. If you must shoot, make sure you identify your target before you fire."

William was gone before the men could respond. He edged his way into the undergrowth, carefully placing each foot, holding his revolver ready, keeping his eye out for Stanley. A Piwakawaka flittered about in front of him, he silently prayed the mythological messenger of death was for Stanley, not him.

He'd never been trained for battle in this environment. The trees closed in around him. Where was the open sky of the desert to give him the light he needed to trace his enemy, to chase away the shadows? He focused on the bloodied tree, like a bullseye on a dart board and moved stealthily towards it.

The grass around the tree had been trampled, by boots and not animal hooves. William brushed the back of his hand across the reddened trunk and raised it to his face. It was blood and it was fresh. He peered around the tree, his heart pounding. Stanley was close. Like Patch, William had the fugitive's scent, he wasn't going to let him get away.

A broken fern frond hung down, its pointed leaves signalled the way and William inched forward, one careful step at a time. More blood on the flaky bark of a Manuka tree confirmed he was headed in the right direction. It was further away from the men; from the support he hoped he wouldn't need. Doubt threatened. Should he call them in? The volunteers were inexperienced, and naïve about the impact of shooting another man. If William could save them from that burden, he would.

High up in the branches of a Kanuka, a startled Kereru, furiously flapped its wings. William caught sight of its clean white breast moments before he saw the whites of Stanley's eyes. They were the eyes of a crazed man, the dilated pupils stared at William atop the line of a barrel pointed in his direction.

Whether Stanley winked at William or merely lined up his prey before he shot, William didn't have time to consider as the fired bullet ricocheted off a branch inches from his head. Army training and self- preservation set in motion a response William was powerless to prevent. His finger pulled the trigger. His revolver fired a shot. He knew they weren't accurate at a distance, but he hoped the twenty feet, between him and Stanley was close enough. He saw the moment of impact like a slow-motion movie. Stanley's shoulder was wrenched back as the bullet dug in. Instinct told William it wouldn't be fatal. As a lad he'd watched his father many a time shoot the wild boars the dogs had cornered. A bullet between the eyes was needed to stop them snatching the newborn lambs.

William's wrist strained with the weight of the revolver as he raised it slightly, positioning his eye behind the sight and Stanley's forehead in front. He pulled the trigger, again and again in quick succession. He couldn't give Stanley the chance to return fire when his only protection were the spindly branches of a Manuka. He had to take advantage of the seconds gained as Stanley reacted to his injury. William's revolver only had six shots, one of them had to work.

He darted forward and took cover behind a Kahikatea, its ancient trunk rising through the heads of the pungas, its roots burrowing deep into the earth. William drew on its strength, the wisdom of a long life and peered around the trunk at Stanley. One of the bullets had penetrated his forehead, another his chest, the third was lost. Stanley slumped against a tree; blood oozed from his wounds, but William saw rage in his face, not defeat. The man's anger gave him strength to raise his rifle again, to point the barrel at William and pull the trigger. Stanley's anguished howl rang out through the bush as the rifle's butt rebounded off his injured shoulder and he fell backwards to the ground.

William pulled back behind the Kahikatea until he was certain Stanley's shot had gone askew. In the moments of silence before he knew he was safe, William swore if he survived, he would never live a half-life again, he may be permanently maimed but he was still whole.

From the safety of the tree, William's heightened sense of hearing listened for Stanley's next move. Overhead the wind rustled the Ponga fronds, beside him a Piwakawaka pecked at the bugs in the earth he'd disturbed, inside his heartbeat slowed but from Stanley's direction there was only a disquieting silence. Had William been successful? Had he put a stop to the tragedy of Graham Stanley? It was too soon to allow jubilation to flow through his veins.

The Home Guard pierced the silence, yelling as they stampeded, thrashing through the bush, like a pack of wild animals.

"Where is he?"

"We heard shots."

"Are you alright?"

"He's injured. He's gone down but be careful, he still managed to get off another round." William pointed to where Stanley had fallen and lowered his voice. "We'll split in two, circle the area. You go that way; we'll go this way."

The group did as William suggested. They surrounded the tree where William had last seen Stanley, rifles ready, eyes and ears alert. When there was no evidence to suggest he'd escaped they closed in, drawing the circle tighter until Stanley lay at their feet. He no longer held a rifle, but it was within reach, so William snatched it away.

"Looks dead to me," one of the men prodded Stanley with the barrel of his rifle.

William had seen too many dead men but few of his doing. He looked at Stanley, the whites of the madman's eyes staring into eternity, and swallowed the guilt that tightened his chest. The rage had gone from Stanley's face, he almost looked at peace. Perhaps William had done him a favour, rescued him from a life not worth living.

One of the men knelt beside the body, and held his fingers to Stanley's neck, searching for a pulse.

"Nothing there. He's dead."

"Well done, William." A volunteer gave him a congratulatory slap on the back.

"Three cheers for William," yelled another. "Hooray! Hooray! Hooray!"

William wasn't convinced the celebrations were warranted; after all the orders had been to bring the fugitive in.

"He deserved to die."

"We're safe now. Our families can rest easy at night again."

"Life can return to normal."

The Home Guard men must have shared William's need for justification for the death. He nodded, everything they said was true and William allowed thoughts of his new normal to fill his heart. An image of Betsy was foremost, her smile, the warmth of her laughter, the curves of her body but mostly her ability to see the good in everyone and everything. He knew she wouldn't judge him for what he'd done, and he needed that.

"Right, we'd better get back to base." William, keen to get home, clean up and begin the rest of his life, holstered his revolver, and picked up Stanley's rifle and unloaded it. "Report in and deliver the body."

The men took turns to carry Stanley's dead weight, one holding his feet, one hitching his hands under Stanley's armpits. They cleared the bush under the darting eyes of a flock of Piwakawaka, whose fanned tails appeared to wave in farewell. The trek across the paddock seemed endless. William's emotions seesawed between jubilation and trepidation, exhilaration, and exhaustion. He wanted to celebrate his success but worried about the consequences.

Several vehicles pulled up at the roadside, in front was the police car, its siren flashing.

"We received reports of gunfire," the policeman said as they approached. "We came immediately."

The men lowered Stanley's torso to the ground and released his limbs which landed with a thud.

The policeman knelt and checked for a pulse. "But I see we're too late."

William swallowed as the policeman examined the wounds. Three bullet holes was probably two too many in the eyes of the law.

"William's the hero," one of the Home Guard proclaimed.

"It was in self-defence; Stanley fired the first shots," added another.

"Nevertheless, I will need you to come into the station and give a statement." The policeman looked directly at William, his face giving nothing away.

William decided silence was best in this instance and nodded, a feeling of dread settled in the pit of his stomach. His new normal wasn't going to start yet.

"Thank you for your efforts, men," the policeman continued. "If you please carry the body back to the vehicles, we'll get it covered and back into town."

Dinner was on the table when a police officer finally dropped William at home. His statement had been corroborated by the other members of the Home Guard; self-defence was accepted, and no charges would be laid. William reached the dining room, grinning from ear to ear, eager to share his good news but a solemn silence filled the room and Betsy's seat was empty.

"You all look as if someone's died," he joked. "Has the grapevine fed you the news already?"

"What news is that son?" Duncan asked.

William allowed pride to straighten his stance. "I shot Stanley. He's dead."

"Oh, that's wonderful, William." Nel smiled briefly. "No, we hadn't heard that."

"What's got you all looking so glum then?" It dawned on William their long faces may have something to do with Betsy's absence from the table. "And where's Betsy?"

"She's in her room," Jean replied.

William sucked in a breath. "Is she alright? Shall I go and see her?"

"She wanted to be left alone," Peggy replied. "She's had some news."

Exasperated, William squeezed his eye shut, all he wanted was answers. Just when he was ready to embrace life, it seemed another hurdle was put in his way.

"What news?" he asked, impatience peppering his voice.

Nel placed a calming hand on William's wrist. "She received a letter from Roland's parents. They've been notified that he passed away in the P.O.W. camp."

"Damn!" William thumped his fist on the table, angry the war had claimed another innocent man, frustrated he couldn't protect Betsy from the harsh realities of battle.

"She'll be alright," Duncan said. "We've got the A & P Show tomorrow. We'll keep her busy, her mind occupied by other things, and she'll be right as rain in no time. You'll see."

William suppressed the scoff that formed at his father's solution to everything. Keep busy, pretend it never happened. He vowed in that moment to support Betsy, console her, give her time to grieve as she had given him space to deal with his injuries, not pressure her to pretend everything was alright.

"Here, son." Nel passed William a generous serving of beef stew. "You must be hungry."

He'd been running on adrenaline all day. As he sat down at the table fatigue took its place. William knew he'd be no use to Betsy unless he took care of himself first.

"Thanks, Mum."

Tender chunks of meat in rich gravy, melted in his mouth. The stew was as nurturing for his stomach as it was for his soul, like the comforting arms of his mother's embrace.

"Tell us how you got him, William," Duncan said.

In between mouthfuls of stew, William relayed the events of the day. Having already repeated the details several times at the police station, he had a sanitised version that removed all the emotions he'd felt at the time.

"Just like shooting those wild boars," Duncan concluded.

"We'll be safe now." Nel smiled at her son. "Thank you, William."

There was apple crumble for dessert and Nel ensured William's piece was larger than everyone else's.

"Would you like seconds?" Nel offered as soon as William lay his spoon in his empty plate.

"No, thanks, Mum." He patted his stomach. "I'm as full as a bull. I just need a good sleep now."

He stood from the table, said goodnight, and left the room. In the darkness of the passage, a sliver of light shone beneath Betsy's bedroom door. William hesitated, he wanted to go to her, to offer comfort but was unsure if his intrusion would be welcome. He cleared his throat, there was no room for doubt, if he hadn't fired at Stanley, he'd be the one lying in a makeshift coffin in the mortuary. There was no need to concern his parents though, William pulled his bedroom door shut, hoping his mother wouldn't check on him like she often did when he was younger. He tapped quietly on Betsy's door before edging it open.

"Betsy," he whispered. "Can I come in?"

"William, you're back."

The relief William heard in Betsy's voice was all the encouragement he needed. She was curled up on her bed and in the light of her bedside lamp, William took in her red-rimmed eyes, sniffly nose and tear-stained pillowcase. He knew then he wanted to spend the rest of his life with her. He chose not to speak, not to ruin the moment with the wrong words and walked around the end of the bed to lay down. He cocooned Betsy's body with his, laying his head behind hers where his warm breath gently brushed her neck. William draped his arm over Betsy and when he felt the rigidity in her spine settle and the raggedness of her breath dissipate, he enclosed her hand in his. Their fingers entwined, like a weaving together of threads, a comforting shawl in which they found solace and sleep.

CHAPTER

28

Wakefulness came to Betsy gradually like a butterfly emerging from the safety of its chrysalis. A sense of *deja vu* took her back to a time when she'd woken next to a man. It had only ever happened on two occasions. There had only ever been two men. And now, as the reality of yesterday's news permeated every cell in her body, she knew one of them was dead. She felt the weight of the other behind her, not as a burden but as a support, a haven where she could find comfort.

The rumblings of a stirring household brought another realisation. Betsy and William had shared her bed, his parents were along the passage, this was their house, and they would be horrified. Any defence of comfort and not intimacy would be invalid.

"William," Betsy whispered, she nudged him and rolled over, reluctantly lifting his arm away from her body. "William, your parents are awake."

"Mmm." A slow smile formed on William's face as he wriggled closer to Betsy.

They couldn't be found together. They were unmarried. She should be mourning the loss of Roland. Betsy inhaled deeply, now was not the time to panic, to make rash decisions and draw attention. She needed to move calmly and quietly, maintain a level of composure that would give no indication of how she had spent the night. They were both fully clothed, nothing had happened, but she felt the strength of her desire, surely others would see it too.

She cast a final glance at William's sleeping face and saw strength not ugliness in the jagged scar that ran through his eye socket. Like a bolt of lightning flashing across a stormy sky, it had a beginning and an end. It was the evidence of a moment in time that shaped William but didn't conquer him. It was proof he could suffer and still be there for her.

Betsy lifted the blankets away and climbed out of bed. The rush of cold air stirred William.

"What? What happened?"

Betsy raised a finger to her lips to hush any more questions.

"It's time to get up," she murmured. "Your parents are up and about. We must get you out of here without them knowing."

William looked wide-eyed around the room, he eyed Betsy up and down and mouthed an obscenity when the meaning of her warning finally registered. He edged his way off the bed, smoothed down his clothing and tiptoed across the room to the door.

"Careful," Betsy warned as he inched the door open.

The whistle of the kettle on the coal range and the clatter of plates and cutlery indicated Duncan and Nel were already in the kitchen. William turned back to peck Betsy on the cheek.

"I'll see you in the kitchen." William's thumbs-up was echoed in a smile that said everything would be alright. "The A & P Show is today."

Yesterday's news and last night's events all blended into a confused melee that Betsy knew she would have to put aside. The A & P Show was today and wouldn't leave any room for wandering thoughts, what ifs nor maybes.

If anyone sensed the change between William and Betsy, they didn't bother to voice it aloud. She wondered if that was merely because there was so much to do, or they were keeping their opinions to themselves.

After milking, they downed a quick breakfast before loading the animals onto the truck. With only room for three in the cab, Captain Boyle's car, driven by William was used to transport the large picnic basket Nel had prepared and the land girls.

"Oh, this is grand," Peggy gushed. "I want to sit in the front seat with our hero."

The remark caught Betsy unawares; firstly, she remembered the last time she'd climbed into the back seat of Captain Boyle's car. It was after the dance when William had disappeared with the more-than-tipsy Moira. She could admit now that she'd misjudged him, her anger muting any claims of innocence he'd uttered. Secondly, because Peggy had referred to William as a 'hero'. His presence last night, cocooning Betsy's body, had certainly been her saviour in a time of sadness but why was he Peggy's hero? Had he done the same for her? Was he not Betsy's alone? He'd never said so, had she made assumptions, in her own desire for love and happiness? She squeezed her eyes shut, hoping everything would be resolved when she reopened them.

"Didn't you hear the news?" Jean must have seen the confused look on Betsy's face. "William was the one who downed Stanley yesterday. Killed him dead. Rescued Orari from the madman on the loose."

Relief brought a slow smile to Betsy's face. She looked at William and the grin he sent her way, reflected in the rear vision mirror, dispelled any lingering doubts.

It was a short drive to Winchester, the venue for the A & P Show. Outside the car, the countryside passed in a blur of greens and browns; inside the car Betsy kept her eyes on William, admiring the broadness of his shoulders, the way he held his head with pride. She noticed the newfound confidence with which he drove. Seemingly unhindered by the patch over his eye, his left arm managed the heavy steering wheel with ease. His stump found its purpose, braced to hold the wheel steady, when a change of gears was required. Killing Stanley hadn't just saved Orari, it had saved William as well.

The showground was already a hive of activity by the time the group from *Whipsnade Farm* arrived. Duncan was able to park the truck with the other exhibitors, but William was directed to the paddock set aside for carparking.

"This is so exciting." Peggy bounced from foot to foot, barely able to contain herself. "I can't wait to look around."

"We'll have to get the calves groomed and ready first," William said.

Peggy groaned like a petulant child. "I haven't got any chance of winning. *Panda's* just a big fat lump of lard."

"Well, we're here now. Might as well give it a go after all our hard work," Jean said.

Betsy kept her thoughts to herself. Duncan and William had both said *Diamond* was a winner, good both in nature and structure but she'd never led an animal at a show before, she was a town girl and like Peggy would have gravitated more to the side shows than the show ring if she had a choice. She drew on some of William's confidence, if he could do this, she could.

They unloaded the calves, tethered them in their allotted pens and began the final grooming, brushing their coats to a sheen. Duncan stood behind the pens, pointing out marks on hooves that needed buffing, errant hairs that needed smoothing, and ordering the land girls to check in nostrils and ears and under tails.

"Morning, Mr Buchanan." Duncan's formal greeting was addressed to a man who looked equally as formal, attired in a dark grey suit, a clipboard in his hand. "You're judging today, I presume."

"Yes." The men shook hands. "Nice to see you again, Duncan. You haven't brought last year's champion back? I do hope nothing untoward has happened to her."

"No, no, she's still our top producing cow," Duncan replied. "With petrol rationing, we couldn't afford to make two trips with the truck, and it was too far to walk her, so we've just entered calves today."

"Yes, I see." Mr Buchanan glanced around the shed. "There aren't as many entries as normal, farmers away fighting or petrol rationing, as you say, all having an impact in these tough times. It's a shame but still a high quality in those present." Mr Buchanan cast his judge's eye over the

Whipsnade calves. "The test will be in the leading. Who do you have for that today?"

"Our land girls, Betsy, Jean and Peggy," Duncan said. "And of course, you know William."

"Yes, William, I hear congratulations are in order for you, young man." The judge reached out to shake William's hand. "Well done in putting an end to the Stanley fiasco."

The moment of hesitation when William had to put down his brush and return the shake with his left hand passed with ease as if it now came naturally.

"Thank you, sir. It was a team of volunteers from the Orari Home Guard. We all played our part."

"The program says the Home Guard are going to lead the grand parade," Mr Buchanan said. "I'm sure the crowd will justifiably applaud your efforts then."

William smiled and nodded, and if Betsy wasn't mistaken, swelled with pride and stood another inch taller.

The centre of the racetrack was a criss-cross of posts and rails for the showjumping circuit. Behind the grandstand, next to the stables, smaller temporary rings had been roped off, one for the judging of cattle and one for sheep. There was a shed for the poultry, another for the pigs full of pens spread with hay, dust motes dancing to the cacophony. The sideshows were, as expected, out to the side where a row of tents, each with bright and alluring signage hosted a variety of shows, acrobatic acts, fortune tellers, magicians, and knife throwers. The carousel was already cranking out its merry tune, ornately decorated horses rose and fell as they circled under sparkling lights. Another ride offered the more daring a seat suspended by chain from a giant rotary washing line.

A deep voice boomed from speakers mounted on poles around the venue, requesting all calves and leaders present themselves at the cattle show ring. Duncan inspected the animals one last time and satisfied they were as good as could be, ushered the land girls over to the ring.

"Now, remember, dip your head but keep your eye on the judge, no yanking on the lead, smile but don't lose your concentration," Duncan rattled off his final words of advice.

"Duncan," Nel growled. "Let them be for goodness' sake."

"I'm just looking out for Captain Boyle's interests, Nel. It's what he would expect."

The land girls and the other contestants, a dozen in total, some barely taller than their calves, stood in a line down one side of the ring. Mr Buchanan walked firstly behind them and then down the row out in front. Every now and again he stopped, 'ummed' and 'ahhed' to himself, and jotted something down on his clipboard before moving on. Out of the corner of her eye, Betsy tried fruitlessly to decipher his actions, but it was like a secret code she couldn't solve.

When Mr Buchanan had finished his inspection, he ordered the first of the handlers to lead their calf. It was a smaller jersey calf and about the same height as the primary-school-aged child leading it. Animal and leader had obviously spent a lot of time together, their rapport was evident in the easy way they completed their circuit around the yard.

"We'd be as good as that, if we didn't have to work as well," Peggy moaned.

Jean was next. Her calf hesitated at the makeshift gate and tried to pull away when made to stand still. She didn't look at all happy when she completed her round and returned to the line-up.

Peggy was nearly pulled to the other end of the ring when it came to her turn.

"There's no food over there, fatty," she growled as she yanked on the lead before realising everyone could hear her, dashing any hopes of a placing.

Then when Peggy wanted her calf to move, it decided it was time to empty its bowels, spreading its hind legs, arching its back, and lifting its tail. She had no option but to wait, her mortification reflected in her scarlet cheeks.

The other more experienced handlers showed their skills, their calves followed obediently and stopped when reined in. Both animals and handlers adopted stances that said, 'look at me, I know what I'm doing.' This did nothing to ease the nerves churning Betsy's stomach. She cleared her throat and rubbed her sweaty palms down the legs of her overalls before the attention of the judge and the burgeoning crowd was focused on her and *Diamond*. She doubted she'd be able to better the high standard of the other entrants despite the secret stash of meal hidden in her overalls pocket. It was a trick William had taught her. *Diamond* knew it was a reward to be earned for good behaviour.

"You've got this, Betsy." She heard William's encouraging whisper as she stepped out with *Diamond*.

They walked the circuit without incident, stopped and started with ease, and turned where they were supposed to. It was almost an anti-climax; Betsy had got herself wound up about nothing. It didn't matter if they didn't win, she knew she'd done her best.

William was next. He glanced at Betsy before heading off. Having been out with the Home Guard, he hadn't bonded with the calf the way he should have. It was evident when the calf went to go in the opposite direction. There was a battle of wills, marked by a stamping hoof and tug from both sides. With two hands, it would have been easy for William to overpower the calf but with only his weaker left hand, he lost grip of the lead and it fell to the ground. Sniffing out the longer grass at the edge of the ring, the calf dragged the lead away.

Betsy itched to help but resisted. She knew going to William would embarrass him. He'd saved the people of Orari from a fugitive. He could deal with a weaner calf by himself. And he did it with dignity, retrieving the lead from the ground and nudging the calf away from the grass with his leg. They completed their circuit without further incident and the gathered crowd applauded his effort.

There were two more calves after William and then everyone had to wait patiently while Mr Buchanan referred to his notes and decided the placings.

"Thank you, everyone, for your patience." The judge stood in front of the line up, the association secretary to his side holding a selection of rosettes to be presented to the winners. "There are two parts to this competition; some animals will rank high in the breeding scores, exhibiting good muscling and bone structure and others will score high in the leading, demonstrating your ability to build a rapport between man and beast. The combination of these two factors gives a ranking on which today's rosettes are awarded. Without further ado, I'll ask the winning handlers and calves to step forward when I announce your names."

"Are you ready, Betsy?" William whispered.

Betsy giggled, thinking he was merely teasing. "It won't be us. You're the one who got applauded."

"That's just because they felt sorry for me, the one-armed calf handler. You're the one in winning form."

A sudden rush of heat had Betsy itching to undo the button at her neck. It would be nice if William was right. Was she in winning form? Or was he simply trying to make her feel better, to help her forget about yesterday's news? She fidgeted, as if movement would make things go faster. More likely it would make the judge reverse any good thoughts he may have had about her.

"In third place, Sally Jefferies," Mr Buchanan announced.

Sally was the young girl who'd gone first. Her parents cheered and clapped, and Sally blushed a deep red as a yellow rosette was attached to her calf's halter.

"In second place, John Taylor." An older gentleman who'd clearly been showing animals for years stepped forward to receive a red rosette, shake hands with the judge and bask in the crowd's applause.

"And in first place, in what has been a tough competition, making this award all the more deserved for a novice entrant." Mr Buchanan scanned the line of animals and handlers, giving nothing away. "Worthy of a drum roll, I award this first place rosette to … Betsy Nolan. Congratulations on carrying on the fine presentation of cattle from *Whipsnade Farm*."

Betsy jiggled on the spot and emitted a little squeal of delight. She smiled at William before stepping forward to receive the winning blue rosette, hoping her grin would convey her thanks for his faith in her. She'd find another way to thank him properly later.

When the calves had been taken back to their pens, fed and watered, everyone was free to enjoy the rest of the A & P Show.

"Would you like a cup of tea and a scone first?" Nel asked.

"No thanks, Nel." Betsy was still too excited to eat. "I've got a teddy bear to win."

"I'll have a cuppa with you, dear," Duncan sat down on a hay bale. "We'll let the young ones go and have some fun. Just remember to be back in time for the grand parade."

William and the land girls headed off to the side shows and were soon lost amongst the crowd where laughing children ran merrily about, holding toffee apples and candyfloss, calling to their friends over the noise of the fair. Outside each tent, smartly-dressed entertainers recited their spiels, attempting to lure people inside to see daring acrobatic acts, a magic show, or the house of horrors. The carousel's jolly organ music rang out above it all.

They walked past the shooting range where a line of teddy bears was hoisted above the rows of ducks sliding along as if swimming on a pond.

"The teddy bear is all yours, miss." The sideshow worker reloaded a gun. "It's easy, miss, all you have to do is shoot a duck. No problem for a young lady with a good eye and a steady hand like you. Five pellets for five pence."

"Go on, Betsy," Jean suggested. "You're on a winning streak today."

Betsy glanced across at William. She couldn't read his face. Did he think it should be him shooting? She felt lucky and decided to give it a go. She handed over her coin, picked a gun and eyed up the ducks like she was a professional shooter.

"Looks like we should have you in the Home Guard with us, Betsy," William teased.

She ignored his jesting and pulled the trigger. The bullet went astray, and the ducks kept gliding by. Betsy reloaded and refocused, a determined look on her face. The second bullet went astray.

"Third time lucky," the sideshow worker encouraged her.

She glanced up at the teddy bears and then back at the ducks, before lining them up. This time she moved as they moved and this time her shot went ping as it struck metal and the duck fell backwards.

"Well done, Miss, see I said you could do it." He handed over a small brown teddy bear.

Betsy cuddled the teddy into her shoulder and decided then and there to call it Rolly. It felt like Roland's spirit had been with her all day and would be forever.

CHAPTER

29

Every seat in the grandstand was taken, with spectators all vying for a good view of the grand parade. The Drum Major, in a red tartan kilt, emerged from the gates at the far corner of the racecourse. His ornate baton signalled the pipers and drummers that followed, as they launched into a Scottish tune with familiar chanting notes.

The Home Guard followed, William at the head, the other volunteers marching as William had trained them, all eyes forward. He swelled with pride as their line remained straight. William's only regret was that Bill wasn't with them. He was still in hospital with an infection in the gunshot wound inflicted by Stanley and it wasn't looking good. But that was tomorrow's worry, William planned to enjoy today and being able to walk in front of the crowd with his head held high was part of that.

Applause rang out from the crowd, accompanied by loud cheering as the parade reached the grandstand. The Drum Major raised his baton and brought the pipe band to a halt. The Home Guard drew up adjacent to the stand and turned to face the spectators. Everyone in the stand stood as a collective show of respect. William caught sight of his parents, his mother bobbing up and down excitedly, waving her scarf. His father was, as expected more controlled, but William could still see his grin and mirrored it.

Following the Home Guard were the winning livestock and their handlers, each category with blue, red, and yellow ribbon holders in order, starting with the champion of champions and then each breed: Jersey, Friesian, and Brown Swiss. There were bulls, towering over their handlers, muscle, and bulk swaying from side to side with each deliberate step. Then came cows waddling around the udders that made them champion producers of milk and progeny. The calves were next, and Betsy and *Diamond* were the first of the Friesians into the arena.

William turned back to face the Home Guard volunteers. "At ease, men."

He relaxed himself and took the opportunity to watch Betsy. She was easy on the eye as the boys would say but she was more than that to William. The attraction wasn't just physical, although he liked the way her curves melded into his when he'd got close enough, he relished her openness, her determination, and the kindness she showed to others. Mostly he appreciated the way she hadn't changed, she treated him the same now as she did before the war. He wasn't an invalid in her eyes, and she wouldn't tolerate any self-pity. She saw beyond his injuries and in doing so, enabled him to.

The cattle and their handlers peeled off single file into the centre of the arena. By the time the horses followed, the grassed area resembled the ever-decreasing spirals of a conch shell. Betsy and *Diamond* were caught up near the middle;

too far away from William to give her the hug he wanted to. A half-hearted laugh escaped as he realised the insignificance of his concerns; thirty feet was all that separated them, it was nothing. It could have been the other side of the world if he'd still been a soldier; only connected by treasured memories and sporadically delivered letters. It could have been for all eternity if William had suffered the same fate as Roland.

The smartly dressed president of the A & P association, took his place at a rostrum positioned front and centre of the grandstand. He called for a moment's silence to honour those who had made the ultimate sacrifice in support of King and Country. William looked skyward, he needed to thank Roland for freeing the way and to assure him he'd take good care of Betsy.

The president's speech continued, congratulating the placegetters, commending the competitors, and thanking the judges in each of the categories. When the formalities wound up and the crowd's applause abated, the parade began in reverse with horses, cattle, William, the Home Guard and finally the pipe band's exit signalling the end of the A & P Show for another year.

While the townsfolk enjoyed the thrills of the side shows, there was still an afternoon milking to be done at *Whipsnade*. It took an hour before all the animals and equipment were loaded back onto the truck and Duncan and William were ready to join the queue of farmers leaving.

"Champion in the front seat." William opened the passenger door of the car and ushered Betsy in before Peggy could claim the spot. He planned to take every opportunity to be close to the woman he was certain he wanted to spend the rest of his life with.

Betsy blushed and smiled coyly, her hand brushed surreptitiously across William's as she climbed into the vehicle, and he knew she felt the same way.

"There's room for three." Peggy pushed past William and nudged Betsy over into the middle of the Plymouth's bench seat.

"But …" William's protest fell on deaf ears as Peggy pulled the car door shut.

His disappointment turned to bliss when he climbed into the driver's seat, grateful Captain Boyle had insisted on a right-hand drive vehicle. The left side of his body married with Betsy's right; a heat radiated between them; a frisson of excitement sent his blood pulsing. There was a moment of regret; if only he was still right-handed, he could have rested his left hand on Betsy's thigh, but it was required to manoeuvre the heavy steering wheel and his brain needed to focus on the road. He welcomed each change of gears though. Betsy's legs sat either side of the floor shift and his arm brushed across her thigh each time.

A line of vehicles headed slowly away from Winchester. It reminded William of the cortege he'd travelled in after each of his grand parents' funerals, a final farewell except on this occasion the car was filled with happiness and frivolity as the land girls reflected on the day. Although the world was still at war, a war edging its way closer to New Zealand, William silently said goodbye to soldiering, he cast off any lingering need to prove himself and vowed to only focus on the future.

Vehicles peeled off at intersections along the way until only the farm truck and the Plymouth were left to turn into the *Whipsnade Farm* gate.

"Oh, stop," Peggy called out. "Look there's something in the letterbox."

William felt Betsy flinch as if the letterbox could deliver more bad news. He glanced at her, hoping his smile offered reassurance everything would be alright. He stopped the vehicle on the driveway and leaned across Betsy to pull on the handbrake while Peggy went for the mail.

"We'll be alright," he whispered to Betsy.

Peggy was back in the car in an instant, the newspaper, and a single letter in her hand.

"It's addressed to you, Betsy." Peggy handed the letter over and shut the door.

William watched as Betsy didn't just flinch, she froze, and her face went a deadly pale.

"You look like you've seen a ghost," Jean remarked from the back seat.

Betsy looked wide-eyed at William; her mouth moved but no audible words were uttered.

"What is it, Betsy?' he asked. "Who's it from? What's wrong?"

"R-R-R-Roland." A single tear tipped from each of Betsy's glassy eyes and ran down her cheeks.

The letter shook in her hands, at first a tiny quiver which grew in intensity until William could feel the tremble rumble throughout her body. The letter was a ghost, a message from the dead.

"I'll get you home." William released the handbrake and shoved the vehicle into gear. The tyres skidded in the gravel as he floored the accelerator for the short distance up the drive.

"Come on, Peggy, we'll get started on the chores," Jean said when William pulled the Plymouth up outside the house. "Leave Betsy to read her letter in private."

A blast of cold air filled the car as the land girls exited.

"Would you like to go inside?" William asked as he turned the ignition off.

Betsy's head moved slowly from side to side, her eyes fixed on the envelope.

"I'll leave you alone then." It was the last thing William wanted to do but perhaps the trip home really had been a cortege and Betsy needed to say her final farewell to Roland. "Let you read the letter in private."

There was a desperation in the shake of Betsy's head. "No, don't go," she pleaded.

She turned; her glassy eyes stared blankly at William as she thrust the letter his way.

"You read it."

William couldn't deny her emotion-choked plea but neither could he one-handed open the envelope to ensure its contents weren't torn apart. His only hope was that Roland's words wouldn't tear his hopes of a future with Betsy apart.

"Please." Betsy interpreted his hesitation as refusal.

"I can't open it, Betsy." William raised his stump.

"Oh … oh, sorry." Betsy struggled with the envelope, edged her fingernail along under the flap and carefully lifted the letter out. She closed her eyes, raised the single page to her nose and inhaled long and deep before passing it over to William.

Curiosity urged him to repeat Betsy's action but that stepped over an invisible boundary he couldn't cross. He had no right to know what scented memories the paper carried; it was almost too much that he had to read the words aloud. He unfolded the page and looked at Betsy, seeing in her nod the confirmation it was the right thing to do.

Dearest Betsy,

I write to you knowing that this may be the last time. My injuries look set to claim me, to take me from this earth. I wish I could have stayed longer but it is not to be.

William paused to stifle the emotions threatening to strangle the words in his throat. He looked at the roof of the Plymouth and blinked before continuing.

Know that I leave with my heart full of memories of our time together, from our very first meeting in the school playground to the precious moments we shared before I shipped out. I know that you gave me the ultimate gift and the desire to hold you in my arms again has carried me through the darkest of moments in this godforsaken hellhole.

William glimpsed the blush that coloured Betsy's cheeks. He felt like he had invaded a very private moment and hurried on.

You have so much life before you. My wish is that you live it to the fullest, embrace every opportunity, think of me in those tiny moments but don't let my memory hold you back. You deserve to find love and not stay loyal to the ghost of me.

If it is destined, we will meet again in another time and another place.

Until then, all my love, Roland x

PS Chin up, girl.

William folded the page, dropped it onto Betsy's lap and then drew her into his arms. It was an embrace that said, I am here for you, I love you. William wanted to give voice to the words, but he held back. He knew he was following Roland, but he needed to be sure it wasn't as a consolation prize. He needed Betsy to select him as the rightful winner of the blue rosette.

He felt the rigidity slowly ebb from her body, the trembling ease until the only movement was the rise and fall of her breasts against his chest. He kissed her forehead. He held no expectation his kiss be returned, only a desperate hope it wasn't rejected. He tensed momentarily when she raised her face to his, fearing chastisement but all he saw in her eyes was love. Her lips sought his. Their first kiss was tentative, a taste to check the fruit was no longer forbidden.

The inside of the Plymouth became their haven. While the world carried on its faraway war and the farm carried on its seasonal routine, William and Betsy were cocooned against any more sadness. They held each other, their kisses dispelled any need for words, conveyed unspoken promises and honoured all of those who had brought them to where they were.

Author's Note

The men who were fortunate to return from war had to forge ahead and rebuild their lives. The women who had stepped into roles traditionally reserved for men had to deal with their return. This third book in my Kiwi Land Girl series seeks to recreate a relationship that came with a happy ending or the chance for a new beginning. Not all of them did.

Again, I pay homage to *Diane Bardsley,* whose interviews with land girls were the basis for her book *Land Girls, In a Man's World 1939- 1946* and a source of inspiration for my Kiwi Land Girl series. Insight into the world of a soldier has also been gleaned from *1941 A Kiwi O.E.* published by Opaoa Publishing in May 2022 where letters, diaries, and photographs from a New Zealand soldier's time during World War II.

And yet again, I have tweaked history to suit my story. The fugitive Graham Stanley was based on a real-life villain called Stanley Graham. His tragic shooting spree took place at Koiterangi (near Hokitika) on the west coast of the South Island (Orari is on the east coast). The Home Guardsmen were involved in the hunt in which four policeman and two home guardsmen lost their lives. And there will be other, more subtle changes I have made that I hope you forgive me for.

Inspiration for storylines and characters arrives from many sources. In *Battle of Hearts* special mention must go out to my mentor, Joan Rosier-Jones, whose father, Sidney was a steward on the Rangatira during World War II.

My heartfelt thanks go out to all the people who have contributed to bringing Battle of Hearts to you. The same team has been behind every book in the Kiwi Girl Series. Kura Carpenter from www.thebookcarpenter.co.nz has brought my four land girls to life in her beautiful cover design. Annie Seaton, award winning Australian author www.annieseaton.net has helped me craft my drafts into a finished manuscript. Dixie Carlton www.dixiecarlton.com has shared her marketing wisdom. These are the people that make a living from sharing their expertise but without you the reader there would be no story to be told, no history to be gifted a voice. Thank you to each and every one of you. Beta readers, fellow critique writers, family, friends and complete strangers who enjoy reading about a slice of New Zealand history.

Thank you also to my wonderful partner in life. Although not a reader, he made the effort to read my manuscript and correct the technical jargon about vehicles, guns, and farming.

If you would like to read more about the Kiwi Land Girls you can subscribe to my monthly newsletter through my author website to get updates, excerpts, and bonus epilogues.

www.taniarobertsauthor.co.nz

Facebook: Tania Roberts Author

Dance of Soldiers

"Hello love." Bill greeted Moira with a peck on the cheek. "Let me take your bag."

She still wasn't used to his gentlemanly ways. Very few of the men previously in her life had shown such consideration. Neither had they called her love. She soaked up the term of endearment, holding tight to whatever promises it held.

Moira smiled as Bill put her bag on the tray of his truck and hurried around to open the passenger door for her. Although it was only a short drive from Whipsnade Farm to Bill's property, merely swapping one farming property for another at the end of her training, Moira wanted to make an occasion of it and discarded her land girl's uniform. Swapping, biscuit-brown, baggy overalls for a cinnamon hued dress that hugged her curves, accentuating her hourglass figure. Her freshly washed hair, now more strawberry blonde than red after three months in the outdoors, sat in soft curls on her shoulders. Careful to avoid snagging her last pair of rationed silk stockings, Moira edged one leg up into the truck. Her dress's rear split parted temptingly as she paused to glance back at Bill. Was that anticipation she saw in his smile as he watched the split rise, revealing her shapely leg?

"I'm so glad you applied for me to be your land girl." she chortled. Moira planned to be much more than that.

Bill shifted awkwardly, cleared his throat, and rushed around to the driver's side of the vehicle. If Moira wasn't mistaken, his clean-shaven face, coloured as bright as the Besame Victory Red lipstick she wore.

The truck's cab filled with the aroma of tobacco and aftershave. Moira inhaled deeply, reassured that she made the right decision. There would be no more scowls from Duncan, the *Whipsnade Farm* manager, every time she wanted a cigarette; Bill was a smoker too. Memories of the dance they'd attended at the Orari Hall, were as vivid as Bill's Old Spice scent. He certainly had the moves and she always maintained that if a man had rhythm on the dance floor it would follow him into the bedroom.

Bill's farm was one over on the opposite side of the road. This would be the third time Moira had been in his house but only the second Bill knew about. On her first visit she'd found no one at home except the ethereal presence of Bill's late wife. Her photos, happy images of momentous occasions and loving poses with her husband, were neatly assembled on the sideboard. Moira had felt threatened by the portraits, imagined that there would be no possibility of a relationship between her and Bill with this woman's influence so real and potent but when she had returned to the house, at Bill's request, all but one of the photographs had been removed. She could live with a sole photograph. The six by four inch, black and white image of a woman was just that, a record of someone passed. Moira was real, she was here in the present and she would make sure that Bill knew it.

"Here we are then," Bill announced as he parked the truck by the back door. "Welcome to your new home. Come on in." He grabbed Moira's bag off the back of the truck and strode ahead to open the door for her.

Moira stopped momentarily, hopeful that Bill might do something romantic and carry her over the threshold. She looked at him, saw no sign in his tanned and weathered face of a romantic notion and laughed at her foolishness. She wasn't usually taken to whimsical fantasies, whatever was she doing now?

"The bathroom is in here." Bill opened the first of several doors off the living room. "We passed the toilet, out the back, off the porch. Sorry about that, not quite the luxury of Captain Boyle's."

"That's fine." Moira glanced around the living room. It was just as she remembered it; newspapers neatly stacked in the corner, firewood piled ready on the hearth and only the one portrait still on the sideboard.

"I'll put your bag in here." Bill had moved onto the next door and stood to the side so Moira could enter.

Sunlight filled the room. It was warm and welcoming but obviously not Bill's room. A single bed with a floral bedspread sat centre stage, its mahogany bed head matched the bedside tables and dresser. All very nice but single. Sleeping alone was not what Moira had planned.

Her imagination had pictured a double bed, with Bill in it.

She coughed, almost choked on the reply forming in her throat. At least the cough stopped her from blurting out her frustration and disappointment. This was only the first day after all. Having to start in a single bed in a separate bedroom didn't mean she had to stay there. Moira had been able to tempt Bill before and she could easily do so again.

"It's lovely," she said. "Thank you."

She turned to face Bill, stepped forward and kissed him. Her lips lingered longer than was necessary for a simple thank you and it had the desired effect. Bill dropped her bag to land with a thud on the wooden floorboards and wrapped his arms around her. She felt every inch of his body against hers, and every ounce of lust that surged in his loins.

When they finally broke apart, Bill cleared his throat.

"Sorry about that, totally ungentlemanly of me." He fidgeted uncomfortably, his face was flushed, and he moved awkwardly on the spot as if he needed to escape. "I'll leave you to settle in, unpack your bags. I'll go make certain the truck is ready for you to drive the others."

Before Moira could say thank you again Bill had gone. She smiled to herself, a satisfied grin, secure in the knowledge that no, she wouldn't be in the single bed for long.

***

When Moira had returned to the farm after dropping the other land girls, Grace and Alice off at their next assignments, Bill had a cup of tea waiting and they sat quietly at the table like an old married couple.

"Right, there's a fence at the back of the farm that needs fixing," Bill said after downing the last mouthful of his drink and standing ready to go. "You'd best get your overalls and boots on."

If Moira had been hoping for an easier assignment, she was wrong. Bill's farm was a smaller version of Captain Boyle's with a small flock of sheep, a dozen milking cows, several beef cattle for fattening and some pigs. Although the numbers were less, that didn't reduce the workload.

Moira placed her empty cup and saucer on the bench and looked down at her red toe peepers as she walked to the bedroom. Her shoulders slumped; she sat on the single bed to remove her shoes. So far, this wasn't going according to plan. She'd assumed Bill asking for her to be assigned as his land girl was just a ruse; a cover up so that they could be together without the judgement or condemnation of others but, putting her into a separate bedroom with a single bed and now, after a mere half hour, expecting her to change and go fencing; it appeared Moira had misjudged the situation. She put the toe peepers in the bottom of the wardrobe and silently promised them it wouldn't be for long.

***

"Can I drive?" Moira asked as they left the house. The use of Bill's truck was another advantage of being at his farm that she wanted to retain. There would be milk to take to the factory and Moira hadn't entirely forgotten that was where Jake worked. No harm in keeping him in the background in case things with Bill didn't progress the way she hoped.

"Sure. We'll just grab the posts, wire, and some tools first."

Moira stood to the side and lit a cigarette while Bill loaded the truck. Mid-morning, the temperature was steadily rising, and he stopped to roll his shirt sleeves up. Blowing her cigarette smoke skywards, Moira smiled. Bill's tanned and muscled forearms were one of many reasons, she had to make this work.

The pigs, two sows and a boar were in the paddock next to the cowshed. Even with rings in their snouts they'd managed to create mudholes. The sows' bellies sagged low to the ground; two rows of teats swollen as if they were feeding. Moira couldn't see any piglets and hoped there were none. She'd ended up in a mudhole at *Whipsnade* trying to catch them.

"Have you sold the piglets already?" she asked.

"The sows haven't farrowed yet," Bill replied. "I try to time it with calving so that I've got the whey to feed the weaners."

Moira stifled the swear word that formed with that news by dragging on her cigarette. Milking and feeding pigs would start again soon. More physical work. There didn't seem to be any escaping it. She knew she was supposed to be grateful, getting the opportunity to do her bit for the war effort but working in a shoe shop was certainly easier.

The track out to the back of the farm needed grading and Moira seemed to find every hump and hollow possible. The worn springs of the truck seat poked and prodded and made conversation difficult. They passed the cow paddock where, all but one of the herd, sat lazily chewing their cud. The remaining animal appeared agitated, pacing backwards and forwards down the fence line as if it wanted to escape.

"They're close to calving," Bill said. "I'll come back and check on that girl later."

Moira felt for the beast, giving birth certainly wasn't on her agenda any time soon, if at all.

"Pull up here." Bill pointed to the broken strainer post they'd come to fix. "Sorry about that," he apologised when they finally stopped. "I haven't been able to back blade it since they requisitioned the tractor for the war effort."

"Can't be helped then," Moira conceded. She turned off the key and waited for Bill to be the gentleman and come around and open the door for her.

Another disappointment: he grabbed the shovel off the back of the truck and went to study the fence line without appearing to give a second thought to her.

Reluctantly, she joined him by the sagging wires. At *Whipsnade Farm*, Duncan had insisted she dig a hole for a strainer post; the memory of the aches in her arms and shoulders from doing so, was still raw. She didn't fancy having to do it again.

"Too hard to get the broken post out. I'll just have to dig another hole to the side," Bill said as he began scraping the grass and topsoil aside.

Moira breathed a sigh of relief. "I'll undo the staples on the broken post," she offered.

"Thanks, that would be helpful."

The mound of fresh earth grew as the hole got deeper. Bill stopped often, to catch his breath and wipe away the sweat beading his brow with the back of his hand.

"How did the others like their posting?" he asked, removing his shirt, and tossing it toward the truck.

Moira gulped. She wished she could look as relaxed as Bill's shirt hanging casually from the side mirror, but answering his question would either involve lying or revealing Grace and Alice's secret. She returned the pliers and bent staples to the truck while she pondered her answer. Moira considered Grace and Alice her friends, but their swapping places was going to be discovered sooner or later, it was just a matter of time.

"Unlike me, they've both gone to places where they know no-one," she replied, neither lying nor revealing.

"I hear Miss McPherson is like a mother to the women who work under her."

"Miss McPherson?" Moira feigned a lack of knowledge.

"At the linen flax mill. She's been there forever."

"I don't know her." That was the truth, Moira had heard the factory manager speak about Miss McPherson, but she hadn't met the woman. She momentarily considered offering to dig the hole to distract Bill from the conversation but the effort to keep a secret that wasn't hers, was too much.

"I'm certain she will look after Alice," Bill continued.

"Yes … umm … possibly," Moira stumbled over her words.

"What do you mean 'possibly'? Her reputation as a good boss is well known throughout the community."

"I've no doubt about Miss McPherson. It's just that … umm … Alice isn't at the flax mill."

"Pardon, I thought you said Alice was assigned to the flax mill. Did I hear wrong?"

"No, you heard right."

"Well, I'm sorry, Moira. I'm a simple man, not a simpleton but you are confusing me." Bill stood, his hands resting on the top of the shovel handle, a frown creasing his forehead.

"Grace swapped places with Alice," Moira blurted. "Alice is at Orari Estate and Grace is at the flax mill."

"Why ever would they do that?"

"It was Grace's idea." Moira hoped Bill wouldn't let the secret go further. "Alice didn't have a clue until it happened, but she sure appeared grateful."

Bill shook his head in disbelief and resumed digging. "Well, I never," he murmured into the depths of the hole.

***

The following day dawned bright and sunny, but it didn't reflect on Moira's mood. She'd spent a restless night tossing and turning in her single bed. After the double bed at Captain Boyle's, it was hard to get used to the narrow space, where stretching out a limb left it exposed to the cool night air. The thought that Bill was asleep through the wall was even more frustrating. He'd excused himself shortly after dinner, claiming the fencing had done him in. The kiss he'd bestowed on Moira's forehead was the extent of his affections. Moira had lifted her face, paused in anticipation that Bill's next kiss would be on her lips but when she reopened her eyes it was to see him turning away from her towards his bedroom. She was still contemplating how to remedy the situation when she heard a steady rumble from behind the bedroom door. There was no point disturbing the snoring man.

"Good morning my dear," Bill announced cheerfully when she emerged from the bedroom. "I've made porridge. Did you sleep alright? I hope so, we got another big day ahead."

Moira turned away from Bill and sighed, the exhalation left her lungs as deflated as the rest of her felt but she didn't want him to see it.

"What are we going to do today?" she asked, deflecting his question while serving herself a big bowl of steaming porridge.

"There's an area down by the creek I want to get fenced off. When the winter floods come, as they always do around here, I need to be able to keep the animals safe. I've lost a few sheep over the years, been carried away in the rushing waters. I can't afford to lose any more."

The thought of more fencing, or more importantly, the outcome of more fencing leaving Bill too tired for anything else didn't sit well with Moira. She pondered various solutions as she stirred some cream through her porridge. There was no other choice. Moira was going to have to do as much fencing as Bill, to get in and get her hands dirty, not sit back and look pretty. The latter hadn't worked, hopefully the former would. Glancing down at her fingernails, Moira silently apologised to them as if they were a precious friend that she would never see again.

***

"Park up over here," Bill suggested when they arrived at the creek. "Not too close, the weight of the truck might cause more subsidence."

Moira could see where the paddock dropped away, an existing fence suspended in mid-air between two posts sagged ineffectively, flood waters having gouged out its footing. She parked the truck several feet away, pulling the hand brake on hard to ensure the vehicle didn't become one of the river's victims.

"Aargh!" Moira groaned as soon as she opened the truck door. "What's that stink?"

"Bugger," Bill muttered under his breath. "That's the odour of a decaying carcass, another one dead."

He grabbed a shovel off the back of the truck, although it was unlikely, judging by the stench, that there would be anything much left to bury.

Moira had already reached the embankment before Bill had time to warn her. The sight of the semi-decayed carcass, an eyeball staring blindly, and entails picked over by a scavenging magpie had Moira doubled over, regurgitated porridge spilling from her mouth. The vomit was indistinguishable from the dirty woollen sheep's flesh being slowly devoured by a wriggling mass of maggots.

"Come away, love." Bill dropped his shovel, put his arms around Moira's shoulder and led her away from the river edge, rubbing her back in calming circles.

Moira heard the term of endearment; she almost burst into laughter that it took a dead sheep to get Bill to comfort her. She wiped a dribble from her chin, feeling not the least bit beautiful, now was not the time to take that comforting further. Moira grabbed her smokes from her overall pockets. She needed to draw on the nicotine, to calm her nerves and overpower the lingering smell of dead sheep and vomit.

"I'll get used to it," she said, hoping to convince both herself and Bill. "I'll have to if I'm going to be a farmer."

■■